MW00775150

SALEM VI

SALEM

SALEM

REBECCA'S RISING

JACK HEATH
&
JOHN THOMPSON

PRESSQUE
PUBLISHING

Published by Pressque Publishing, Charleston, SC

This is a work of fiction. Names, characters, places, and incidents are the product of the author's imagination or have been used to create this work of art. Any similarities to actual persons, living or dead, events, etc. is completely coincidental.

ISBN eBook: ISBN-10: 0985793708
                      ISBN-13: 978-0-9857937-0-8

ISBN Hardcover: ISBN-10: 0985793716
                      ISBN-13: 978-0-9857937-1-5

ISBN Paperback: ISBN-10: 0985793775
                      ISBN-13: 978-0-9857937-7-7

Typography by Torborg Davern

TO MY WIFE PATTY FOR ALWAYS SUPPORTING *and believing in me. To my sister, Marjory Wentworth, a great poet laureate and writer whose steady encouragement helped inspire me to write and finish this book. Also, to Rebecca Nurse whose strong spirit impressed me from an early age. Rebecca's courage against her accusers and her faith served as a compass for me to follow and create this story. Finally, to my late father and his family who taught me the importance of Salem's incredible history and gave me a love to write and report on the things around me, both past and present. . .*

— JACK HEATH

PROLOGUE

Burlington, Vermont, October 17, 1978

THE MAN STOOD IN THE SHADOWS, SHIVERING, rocking from foot to foot to keep his toes from freezing and watched his breath whiten in the cold air. It was only mid-October, but up here in Vermont the unseasonably frigid night felt like January. Across the street the lights of Davis Hall burned through the clear air and reflected a dull glow off the frost-rimmed grass.

The man checked his watch. Nearly four a.m. Most of the college kids seemed to have turned in for the night because the vast majority of the room lights were off. The man didn't *care* about most of the kids at all. He cared about one single kid, in room 321, and he didn't care about him in the way a parent might. He cared about him the way a risk management specialist cares about looming liability. The kid wasn't a problem yet, but the man knew he had the potential to become a big problem. Nobody knew exactly when it might happen, but according to people who knew more about this than he, the kid had begun to glow with *awareness* in the past couple days. It was way too early. It was pure luck that somebody with the ability to see such things had spotted him and gotten word back to Salem. *Awareness* didn't normally develop, if it ever did, until much later in life, but if people said it was happening now, the man wasn't going to argue. As a self-defined *risk management* specialist, his job was to nip problems like this in the bud.

He looked again at the window of room 321. It had been dark for two hours, and he knew the room's three occupants were totally dead to the world. He'd made sure of that because earlier that afternoon, dressed as a University of Vermont janitor, he had picked the lock on their room and injected their pony keg with a little mixture of his own, a concentrate of dissolved sleeping pills that would put them down deeper than the alcohol ever could. The whole point was to make sure they were sufficiently unconscious so the smoke and heat could do their job.

And now as he watched the window, he saw the first wisp of smoke escape. It was very subtle. If he hadn't been staring at the window he never would have seen it. It meant that the very small incendiary device he had planted in one of the room's electrical outlets had ignited and was starting to feed on the old dormitory's walls. The device would never be detectable, not after the tinderbox dorm had fully caught fire. And it would *definitely* catch fire. He knew this because earlier that evening he had also disabled the dorm's sprinkler system. The three boys in the room would be dead within fifteen minutes. No doubt some other kids would die, too, but that couldn't be helped. It would be collateral damage, just like what the papers used to call it a few years earlier when the Air Force accidentally napalmed a village in Vietnam.

John Andrews tossed his head from side to side on his pillow and wondered for the hundredth time if he was going to hurl. Maybe two hours earlier when he'd gone to bed he'd suffered through the exact same thing, and now here it was back, the room spinning like a top. He cursed himself for sucking down so much of the pony keg he and his suitemates had tapped. Stupid, really stupid, he told himself.

But then he corrected himself, he really *hadn't* swilled that much beer. He'd drunk more lots of other nights and not felt half as smashed. Same with his suitemates. Both guys could usually hold their beer, but they'd both been slurring their words, and when they first went to bed he was pretty sure he'd heard one of them barfing out the living room window.

Now, strangely, he was awake again, and it was still the middle of the night, and he had the bed spins for the second time in a couple hours. How was this possible? Usually when he went to sleep with a load on, he slept like the dead until sometime around noon the next day. Only something had disturbed him. He struggled to remember. Had it been a shout? If that was it then he'd heard it in a dream because it had been an old lady's voice, but a harsh and forceful voice and incredibly loud, and there weren't any old ladies in Davis Hall.

In spite of having a terrible case of the spins he was keeping his eyes closed and starting to sink back into sleep. He was so totally out of it he didn't even care if he blew lunch all over his bed. But then he heard the voice again. *"Get up!"* The voice slammed him, as impossible to ignore as a dental drill in his ear. Actually it was even worse than that because it was coming from inside his head, like some strange old lady was locked in there wanting to get out.

He struggled to open his eyes, working hard against the heaviness of alcohol, feeling like a diver trying to swim to the surface in a pool filled with Jell-O. Had it been beer or tequila shots he'd been drinking? He really *hadn't* had that much to drink. How could he feel this hammered? He heard the voice a third time, a female drill sergeant shouting, *"Get up!"* and this time it slices through his drunkenness like a sharp knife cutting through rope. Knowing he had to stand if only to stop the painful caterwauling in his brain, he slid one foot out of bed and put it flat on the floor.

Weird. Davis Hall had a lousy heating system so the floor should have been cold, but it was hot. In fact it was *really hot*. He pushed himself up on one elbow, took a deep breath through his mouth, and right away started to cough.

Boy, am I a mess, he thought as he continued to hack. He tried to suck down another breath, but it caught in his lungs like a jagged piece of chicken bone. He sat up reflexively, and that was when he began to realize that, between the hot floor and the air, he had a much bigger problem.

He was still coughing, nearly retching, as he reached over and fumbled for his bedside lamp. When it came on a surge of panic helped sober him because he saw that the room was full of thick gray smoke, so much that he couldn't even make out the door about ten feet away.

He lurched out of bed, stumbled to the window, and threw it open. He shoved his head into the cold air and took deep breaths until he stopped coughing. Slowly, as his brain started to work he looked down three stories to the frozen ground, and then his eyes went across the street to where a man was standing in the shadows. The man was nearly invisible, just a shadow slightly darker than the night, but John hesitated because he thought the man was staring up at him.

"Help," he called, his voice hoarse from coughing and barely more than a whisper. "Fire."

Strangely, the man did not move. John blinked. Was he imagining this? Smoke was pouring out the window all around him, but the guy wasn't budging? The smoke had to be easily visible from across the street, and yet the man continued to stare up at the dorm like he was waiting for something to happen, or maybe like he was looking directly at John. What was wrong with this jerk?

"*Move!*" Another shout pierced his brain, the feeling like somebody was stabbing the inside of his skull with an ice-pick. It made him forget about the guy and think about his roommates and all the other people on the floor. Where had the fire started? Did they know about it? Were they already evacuating? Why weren't the alarms going off? Weren't there supposed to be sprinklers?

Feeling a surge of panic he left the window open, got down on his hands and knees where the smoke was much thinner, and crawled toward his door. On the way he pulled on the jeans he had thrown off when he got into bed and pulled on his boots. He didn't bother to lace them. The bedroom door was hot, but no hotter than the floor. He opened it and looked out. More smoke, but thankfully no sign of flames.

He crawled into the living room, found a pitcher of beer that was still three-quarters full then grabbed a crumpled sweatshirt off the floor nearby, soaked it with the beer, and held it against his face like a filter. Then he crawled to the door that led to his roommates' bedroom. When he turned on the wall light he could barely make out two lumpy forms under the blankets on the two beds.

"Fire! Get up!" he croaked.

Neither one moved. John crawled to the window, stood up, and heaved it open to let in some fresh air. He stuck his head out and took a quick breath so his lungs could work. "Get up! Get up!" he shouted. At that, Steve, one of the suitemates, made a groaning sound and started to cough. John crawled over and jerked him out of bed and onto the floor.

"Wha're you doin', man?" he mumbled, barely coherent. He seemed terribly out of it, much drunker than he should have been given how much beer they'd consumed.

"The dorm's on fire." John slapped him hard across the face. "Wake up!"

Steve barely seemed to register the slap. John dragged him to the window, pulled him up, and hung him out. "Breathe!"

He left Steve and crawled over to Mike's bed. Like he had with Steve, he grabbed Mike by the arm and jerked him to the floor.

"Lemme 'lone," Mike slurred.

John slapped him just the way he had Steve, alarmed at how little Mike responded. He dragged him over to the window and pulled him to his feet beside Steve, and a second later both suitemates were hanging out the window coughing.

"Stay here," John said. "Don't leave the window unless you can get out on your own. I'm gonna go pull the alarm and knock on the other doors on the hall. I'll be back in a minute."

John crawled toward the door that led into the hallway, felt it, and realized it was hotter than the other doors had been but still not in flames. He cracked the door, half afraid a wall of fire would come shooting inside. He was relieved to see only thick walls of smoke in both directions. He tried to recall where the smoke alarm was located. They had showed him during freshman orientation, but of course he hadn't paid attention.

To the left was a double with two girls, one from Massachusetts, the other from Virginia. He had fantasized about getting the blond from Virginia into bed, but now he only thought about keeping her alive. He tried the door handle, but it was locked. He banged on the door, then swiveled around, sat on his butt, and hammered the door with both feet. The third time the lock gave and the door swung inward.

"Get up!" he shouted.

Fortunately the girls had gone to bed reasonably sober. They were coughing, but they woke up and got their window open.

"Get out as quick as you can, okay?" he said

As soon as they said they would, he crawled out and since the girls' room was the end of the corridor, he went in the other direction. He kicked in three more doors and got the occupants out of bed before he managed to spot the fire alarm in the near darkness. He stood up, broke the glass, and pulled the switch. Suddenly the loud smoke alarm filled the hallways with noise.

With the alarm blaring, he continued on. That's when he saw the flames glowing lurid and yellow through the smoke. He also saw the bathroom door. Knowing what he had to do next, he crawled into the shower, turned it on, and soaked himself from head to toe, then tore the shower curtain from the rod and soaked it as well. Crawling back into the hallway, he took the biggest breath he could, stood, and wrapped the dripping shower curtain around his head and torso and ran toward the flames at the farthest end of the hallway.

His lungs were burning before he'd gotten halfway, but there was nothing he could do. The wall just past the last room door was totally in flames. He grabbed the door handle and jerked his hand away because the metal was so hot it blistered his skin. He took the shower curtain, put a thick wad of it against the handle, and tried again. The door was unlocked, and he stumbled inside, went straight to the window, and jerked it up.

He sucked down a couple quick gulps of air then went to the single bed in the room. He tried to wake the sleeper, but she did not open her eyes. John could hear voices in the hallway now as other students from other floors responded to the alarm and began to knock on other doors, making sure everyone was out.

"Two guys in three-twenty-one!" he shouted into the smoke. "Get them out."

He went back to the window, took one more breath, returned to the bed, and heaved the girl over his shoulder. She was deadweight, nearly impossible to carry in his current condition. John stumbled to the door, which was now on fire. He shouldered it open, felt a lick of flame on his exposed ear and neck and kept moving, passing open doorways as headed toward the stairway at the far end of the hall. As he was going down the stairs he met two campus security officers coming up. They took the comatose student from his shoulders.

"Any others up there?"

John nodded as he bent over coughing. "Gotta check on my suitemates," he managed after a few seconds. "Three-twenty-one."

"We got 'em both a minute ago," one of the officers said. They carried the unconscious student out and helped make sure John got down the stairs. When he stumbled into the freezing Vermont night, he realized he wasn't wearing a shirt. At the same time the cold air lit up the burned skin on his hand and his ear and neck. The pain nearly took him to his knees, but he didn't think about that. He was thinking about the guy who had stood and watched the smoke roil out around him when he opened the window and who hadn't done a damn thing to help.

John pushed past the security officer who was trying to get him over to an ambulance where EMTs were treating students for burns or smoke inhalation and headed across the street to where the man had been standing. He wanted to find the jerk and drive his fist right into his nose, and he looked around, trying to recall exactly what the guy had looked like. He could only remember a dark silhouette. The guy hadn't been too short or tall and hadn't been particularly fat or skinny. He'd probably been wearing a down parka and stocking cap like everyone else in Vermont in late October.

The only feature that had been distinctive had been the guy's eyes. Even from across the street John had felt the . . . what . . . the hatred that had seemed to make them burn brighter than the night. Well, if he found the guy, John was going to make him understand what hatred really felt like.

Late the next day, wearing thick bandages on his neck, ear, and right hand and still loopy from the prescription painkillers he'd been given, John accompanied his suitemates when they got permission to go back into what had been their college freshman room. A fireman led them up the stairs and down the corridor where water still dripped from the ceiling. What was left of the blackened carpet squished under their feet, and the reek of smoke came from every surface. The pony keg they had tapped was now a puddle of melted aluminum. John went into his old bedroom and saw that nearly all his clothing, bedding, books, shoes, ski and hockey gear, and UVM knapsack had been burned or badly charred. The few items hanging in his closet that hadn't been burned were soaked with soot-colored water that had dripped from above and heavy with the permanent stench of smoke.

He turned a slow circle, studied the devastation, remembering how little beer he'd actually drunk but how smashed he'd felt when he went to bed. It was a miracle he was still alive because he knew how soundly he slept when he'd had a few. What had woken him? Had it really been a dream? He remembered the shouting old woman. How could he forget her? He'd never heard a voice with so much power.

He was about to walk out of the room when he glanced once more at what was left of his desk and the skeletons of burned books atop it. As he scowled at the destruction, he noticed something white on the floor. Out of curiosity he went over to see what had managed to keep its color amid all the char. On the far side of his desk where it had apparently fallen to the floor in all the confusion, he could see what looked like one of his papers.

He bent over and picked it up, feeling the wetness of the pages that had somehow survived. He let out a sarcastic laugh because except for some black singe at the bottom of the cover sheet, they looked almost perfect. The paper's title, "Rebecca Nurse: A Wrongful Death in Salem's Witch

Trials," was still crisply legible.

"Dude, what's funny about this?" his roommate Steve asked from the doorway.

"This." John held up the paper. "I just finished typing it yesterday. Somehow it survived. I can still hand it in. Go figure."

He looked again at the paper and below it his name and the date, Sunday, October 17, 1978. Rebecca Nurse, his distant ancestor, he thought, recalling the family portrait of the woman that hung in his great aunt's house. She had been a grim-faced Puritan with a face like a Rottweiler, but it was weird because it had almost seemed like he had felt her presence looking down on him when he wrote the paper. It was probably her he had conjured up in his dream to make himself wake up. He snorted another laugh as he tucked the paper under his arm and headed out of the room. He was thinking Rebecca Nurse was so ugly she could probably wake the dead, so it was nothing for her to wake up a drunk college student.

CHAPTER ONE

Salem, Massachusetts, October 17, 2012

JOHN ANDREWS PULLED THE COVERS BACK FROM his face, slowly opened his eyes, and croaked out a curse. The early dawn light that managed to make its way through his curtains hurt like a stab wound.

"Crap," he said as he elbowed himself into a sitting position, put his feet on the cold floor, and started to bat his hands in the direction of the alarm. Some idiot announcer was saying it was unseasonably cold for late October. Like he needed to be reminded since he could nearly see his breath in the cold bedroom. He stood, shivered, padded into the bathroom to pee, then slipped on his terrycloth robe and slippers and headed downstairs to make coffee. At the bottom of the stairs he flipped the thermostat from 50° up to 70°. What had he been thinking last night?—well, the point was he *hadn't* been thinking—then pulled open the front door and snatched the three plastic bags containing *The New York Times, The Wall Street Journal*, and *The Boston Herald.*

In the kitchen, he tossed the papers on the counter, hit the switch to start the coffeemaker then started dumping the papers from their bags. On their one or two bounce trip from the delivery guy, across the sidewalk to his doorstep, each bag managed to pick up some street crap, which always dropped onto his counter. It made a mess, and the mess reminded him of Julie. She'd been a cleanaholic, always after him to sponge off the counters and put things away.

He missed being told to clean up. He missed the noise of another person. That wasn't even the start of it. He missed too many things.

He put the papers in a pile, wiped his hand across the granite counter, and swept the crumbs of street dirt into the sink. He glanced at the plate on the counter beside him and the dirty glass and empty bottle. Pizza crust on the plate, a bare drop of scotch left in the glass and none in the bottle. How many straight nights of pizza, he wondered. Maybe four, maybe five. How many straight nights of scotch? He chuckled a humorless laugh. Way too many to count. More to the point, how many nights had that dead fifth lasted? Two? Two and a half? Something like that.

If Julie was here she would have a fit, disgusted at his diet and his drinking. "It's your fault," he said to the empty kitchen.

He got his coffee, but before he started skimming the papers he looked at his reflection in the kitchen window. He

14

still looked okay on the outside, he thought, giving himself a frank appraisal. Mostly full head of brown hair with just a tinge of gray over the ears. Trim physique, flat stomach, much flatter than he deserved. Good genes helping to cover for bad behavior, he thought. The face was still there, too, good cheekbones, strong chin, reasonably tight skin, amazing lack of bags under the eyes considering how much single malt went down his throat every night. It was a face that still could be on national network news every night if that was what he wanted, but he didn't. He just wanted his quiet life and his quiet little newspaper. He was done with the big leagues and the stress. He was done with love. He was holding it together, he told himself. Just barely.

II

A MINUTE LATER HE TOSSED THE STACK OF newspapers on the bathroom sink and skimmed them as he brushed his teeth and shaved. Quick perusal of *The Wall Street Journal* and *The New York Times* showed that the economy still sucked, unemployment remained high, the Israelis were threatening to bomb Iran's nuke facilities, interest rates were supposed to remain low, and the stock market was "ahead of itself." *The Boston Herald* said the Red Sox would be better next year, the 5-1 Patriots were Super Bowl contenders again, and there was talk of floating a bond issue to fund terminal and runway expansion at Logan Airport. Another chunk had fallen out of the ceiling on the Big Dig, and one of the contractors was facing fraud charges for using substandard concrete. Blah, blah, blah, he thought, his eyes running down the columns of print at the speed of light.

But he slowed down when he saw that another teenage girl had been reported missing. There had been a long list over the past few years. He knew many of them had been runaways, but he suspected the possibility of something worse. The police and politicians denied that a serial killer was working the Boston area. They held up the fact that since none of the bodies had ever been found, there was no way to establish foul play. Besides, it wasn't like somebody was preying on young girls. The missing people had been sons and daughters and a few wives, even a husband or two. John shook his head, admitting to himself that the police might not be wrong. The idea of families aching with grief because of missing people and tragic death made him wince these days because of his own loss. *Takes one to know one*, he told himself.

He took a quick shower, dressed, and grabbed his keys and wallet off the dresser. As he went downstairs he glanced in the living room and came to a sudden stop. The antique map of the Massachusetts seacoast that always sat over the mantle was missing. In its place was a portrait that he hung around the corner so he didn't have to lay eyes on it often. It was the dour seventeenth century painting of a middle-aged woman with a face like a junkyard dog, sewing in a rocking chair. She was wearing an incredibly uncomfortable looking black dress that seemed testimony to the extreme religiosity of the early pilgrims.

He panicked for a second because he loved the map. He also wondered what was going on, because as ugly as the portrait was, it was valuable as hell, and it also involved a strange promise his aunt had extracted from him on her deathbed. She was leaving him the house, free and clear, she'd said, and her sole condition was that the portrait of Rebecca Nurse continue to hang in the house for as long as he lived there. Also, whenever he conveyed the house, presumably to his daughter, Sarah, or to another member of the Andrews clan, he would have the next owner make the same promise.

At the time, John had thought little about the promise. Thomas Wilder had painted the portrait in the early 1800s, probably over a hundred years after Rebecca Nurse had died, and based on the last appraisal it was worth at least a quarter of a mil. Now, worried far more about his precious map than about the portrait, he hurried into the living room, looked around the corner, found the missing map hanging where the portrait usually hung, and let out a sigh of relief.

He stood there for a few seconds and struggled to recall when he had moved the pictures. It must have been last night when he had a belly full of Glenmorangie, but what had he been thinking? He looked at the picture of Rebecca Nurse and winced. It wasn't just that the portrait was ugly. Rebecca Nurse disturbed him. It was crazy to admit it, but she got under his skin for reasons he couldn't explain, and she always had, ever since he'd done that paper on her in his freshman year at UVM. She was his ancestor and had been one of the women hanged as a witch during the Salem witch trials, but surely that wasn't what bothered him. John shook his head. He thought it was because he hated religious extremism in any form and hated even more to think that his own family had been caught up in such insanity. He glanced again at the picture. Rebecca Nurse a witch? No way. A bitch? That was more likely. It looked like the woman's face would have cracked if she'd ever tried to smile.

Still, moving pictures late at night when he was

three-quarters in the bag? He'd drunk even more than usual last night, and he knew why. The anniversary of Julie's death. It would be four years tonight. Maybe it was understandable, but he had to knock off the scotch. Julie wouldn't have respected it one bit.

III

THIRTY MINUTES LATER HE ENTERED THE FRONT doors of the *Salem News* and headed through the newsroom to his office against the back wall. He walked with his head down, trying to give the impression that he was a man with an important purpose. He was not to be disturbed by unnecessary greetings or people wanting to chat. He almost made it.

"John," Amy Johnson called out, clearly wanting to talk

"Morning," he mumbled as he hurried past.

He saw her out of the corner of his eye as she stood and started to follow, but he didn't slow down. Amy, bright, perpetually cheerful, and energetic, had a face and figure that could stop traffic and the startling blue eyes of a cover girl, but underneath all of that she had the work ethic of a German slave driver. She got in early and stayed late in spite of the lousy wages, and more than a few times in the past couple years she had covered for him when the emotional stuff just got too tough.

"I wanted to go over a couple things with you before we got too busy," she said, holding a steno pad and pen in front of her as if she was a secretary rather than the paper's associate editor. She was trying to be all business, but she knew as well as he did what day it was.

"Okay," John relented as he went around the desk and collapsed into his chair. He felt a burst of gratitude that she was pretending not to notice he was hanging on by a thread. She was trying to help him get his mind into the paper and away from Julie and death. "What have we got?"

"First off, we've got the annual 5k run for the hospital. You want us to do a couple interviews with different runners to find out why they're running, get the human interest stuff?"

"Yes."

"Who do you want to have do it?"

She took a pen and moved a lock of black hair out of her eyes. John watched her then forced himself to look down at his briefcase and make a show of unlocking it. "You figure it out. Anybody."

"Okay," she said, glancing at her list. "Um, that girl that went missing—"

He looked up again. "The one in *The Herald* from Beverly?"

Amy nodded. "We should interview her family, right?"

"Yes."

"You or me?"

"You do it."

"Gotcha." She made a note on her list.

He picked up a pen and tapped it against his blotter. "Have you thought any more about that series of articles?"

She looked up. "On the runaways and disappearances?"

He nodded. "I think it could put us on the map. I'm surprised *The Herald* hasn't done it already."

Amy nodded uneasily. "I'm still not sure what conclusions we can draw."

"We don't need to draw any," John insisted. Unaccountably, over the past few days this idea had become like a beacon to him. His mind could focus on it when he couldn't seem to concentrate on anything else. "Statistically we're in a league by ourselves in terms of people disappearing, and the incredible thing is it's been happening for years. Is it some kind of New England malaise? Is it the cold and the dark winters? Is it the Red Sox consistent failure to live up to everyone's hopes? Do these people run away or are they murdered?"

Amy shook her head. "There's no evidence to support murder. And if they were killings, it would have to be a generational thing. The disappearances have been going on for too long for it to be one person."

"Or even two people, or three. I understand that, but we've had too many people vanish. They never turn up living under a different name in a different state."

"Well, that's not *exactly* true."

He held up a hand in surrender. "Okay, you're right. Some people turn up, but our numbers are still out of line."

Amy looked at him, her face pinched. He could tell she wanted to find a way to agree with him. "I'm sorry. I don't mean to be negative, but we've got such a small staff. I just think before we make a big commitment to this story we need to find a better angle or get more details."

He gave her a grudging smile and wondered again why the idea of this story had gotten under his skin so badly. Amy was absolutely right about the staffing issues. They had barely enough people as it was to put out their small daily. This story was going to take months to research and compile and probably require two full time staffers, a commitment they couldn't afford, and he as executive editor should have known that better than anyone else. "Thank you for keeping me on the straight and narrow."

"It's a brilliant idea. We *should* do it. I'm just saying that before we assign people we need to think it out a bit more and know exactly where we're going with it."

"Agreed."

She nodded. She turned as if she was finished, then turned back. "You got anything special planned at lunchtime? A group of us are going to go out and have a little fun. We wondered if you might like to join us."

He looked at her, and his eyes narrowed. She knew *exactly* what day it was. He tried to swallow the anger that bubbled up inside and shook his head. "That's very thoughtful, but I don't . . . I've got too much on my plate, but thanks."

"You sure?"

He took a deep breath and let it out slowly. "You're wondering why I hang around here today, why I don't go someplace exotic to distract myself?"

She hesitated, then nodded.

He looked at the wall, unable to meet her eyes. There were moments when he knew he could talk to her in ways he couldn't to anyone else. The feeling frightened him. "This thing chases me around like a ghost that won't let me go."

"You think Julie would have wanted that?"

His head snapped around. When he spoke his voice was raw with emotion. "That's close enough," he rasped. "Close the door on your way out."

IV

AN HOUR LATER HE WAS FINISHING UP WORK ON an upcoming editorial on the need to increase the number of guards at Salem's school crossings when his phone rang. He glanced at the incoming number, made a wry face but picked up.

"Hi, Dad."

Out of long habit he swiveled his chair around so he could look at one of the pictures he kept of Sarah on his credenza. His eyes settled on the one taken when she was thirteen at a family picnic. In it she was awkward and coltish but already the spitting image of her mother. *You can't go back*, he thought, and it hit him almost like a stab wound in the heart.

"Morning, Sarah," he said. "Everything okay? I usually don't hear from you until later in the day."

"Everything's great. Just thought I'd check in," she said, trying but not quite succeeding in keeping her voice light. He *hated* being nursed, and she knew he hated it. They both knew the real reason for her call was to make sure everything was okay for him on the day of the terrible anniversary.

"Nice to hear from you," he said, the words coming out with a bit more distance than he intended.

"So, what are you working on?"

"Another of my scintillating editorials. It will probably be picked up by *The New York Times* and reprinted all over the world."

"What's it about?"

"Salem hiring more school crossing guards."

"That will rivet readers from London to Tokyo."

"Yes, thank you. I thought so, too."

There was a pause, and he knew Sarah was trying to think of what to say next. His gaze moved sideways to his favorite picture, one of Julie holding Sarah when she was just an infant. Julie's long blond hair was falling to one side of her face, and her bare shoulder was exposed to the camera. John grimaced, but he was powerless to keep from reaching out to the picture, putting his fingertips on top of the smudges that were already there. He closed his eyes and could almost remember how her skin felt. If he could just bury his face into that place where her hair swirled around her neck, just once more. *Suck it up.*

"So, I'm sure a big time TV news reporter has a lot more to do than talk to small town newspaper editors," he said, breaking the silence.

"No, so far things are quiet around here this morning."

"Liar. Thanks for the call, but I'm fine."

"I just feel bad I can't be with you. I wanted to come up so we could go to the cemetery together, but I've got a meeting I can't—"

"I understand. I've ordered some white roses. I'm going to

stop by a little later and put them on her grave. It's no problem. I got it under control. Okay? I gotta go—"

"Dad," she said quickly before he could hang up, "don't
be alone tonight."

"I won't."

"You have plans?"

"Sure."

"Really?"

"Yeah, I'm having dinner with some people," he said,
thinking maybe he'd call back one of the three people who
had already invited him over for dinner that night. Or maybe
not.

"Love you, Dad."

"Love you too, kiddo."

He hung up the phone, turned away from his memories
and put his elbows on the desk. *When does it get any easier?*
He shook his head and pasted a humorless smile on his face.

When he looked up he saw her. She was sitting in the
old Hitchcock chair over in the corner, the one with a broken spindle. Her hair was gray and in a tight bun, and she
was sewing or maybe embroidering on some cloth that was
stretched in a small circular frame. He recognized the dress
because it was the same ugly one from the portrait. The problem was, he knew exactly who she was, and he knew she
wasn't real.

He put his head down into his hand and rubbed his eyes
hard until they hurt. He'd thought he'd seen her several times
in the past couple days, but each time it had been a fleeting

vision, something in the corner of his eye, never distinct, gone almost before he'd realized it was there. But never like this, never sitting in plain sight in a chair.

When he opened his eyes again, she was still there.

"Crap," he whispered.

The image was foggy and bright, sort of like the retinal imprint of an old-fashioned flashbulb, so that when you closed your eyes you still saw the bulb. Only now his eyes were open. He rubbed them again, but it did no good. He could see right through her to the spokes of the chair, but she raised her head and looked right at him. For the first time he wondered if he was a man in serious need of help.

His mind was rejecting the terms "ghost" or "spirit" but the vision made his blood pressure spike in spite of his attempts at rationalization. Just beyond the glass wall of his office people were typing on keyboards, talking on phones, or moving around the newsroom floor, yet he had the feeling he was completely separated from them. A voice in his head told him to get up, walk out the door of the office, immerse himself in the companionship of the other reporters, but he didn't move. It was as if the "thing" had anchored him to his chair. When his phone rang his hand shot out as if he was reaching for a lifeline.

"*Yes!*" he said, his voice loud, tinged with hysteria.

"John, is everything all right?" The voice on the other end was crisp as a fall morning even if a little rough with age. It belonged to Jessica Lodge, the owner of the *Salem News*, also an eighty-year-old matriarch and Boston Brahmin of the highest order. She had inherited the paper from her father, along with a portfolio of much larger and more profitable companies, but much like a mother with a special needs child, she sheltered the paper and treated it as her pet project. Like a proud parent, she observed the daily goings-on in the news-room with diligence, but punctiliously avoided meddling in editorial decisions.

"Everything's fine, Jessica," he said with false cheer. "How about with you?"

She chortled. "I'm as good as an eighty-year-old can be."

"What can I help you with?"

"Well, dear boy, I'm not calling on anything about the paper. You run things much, much better than I ever could. I'm calling because, well, I know what day it is, and I wanted you to know that I'm sorry I'm out of the country but I'm thinking of you."

"Thank you," John said.

"Every year when I pass the anniversary of Thomas's death, even though it's been ten years now, I feel a heavy load of sadness. I just want you to know that I know what you're going through, and my thoughts are with you."

"Thank you, Jessica. That means a lot."

"Take care now."

As John put down the phone he couldn't help smiling. Jessica Lodge was one hell of a class act. Who else was lucky enough to have a boss like that? Nobody he could think of.

He was momentarily so distracted thinking about Jessica he nearly forgot about the figure in the corner. He glanced over and saw the woman still sitting there, only she was no longer working on her embroidery but looking at him as if she didn't like him talking on the phone. He shook his head and stood up. He was going to walk around the newsroom and possibly around the block, maybe even get an early scotch to help drive this craziness from his head.

He started to walk out and got as far as the door to his office when his phone rang again, and the caller ID showed a familiar number. "Dude," a familiar voice said when he picked up. "Everything okay? I catch you in the middle of something?"

"No, hey, Rich," he forced a laugh, knowing it was his best friend, Richard Harvey. "I was just heading out, but I ran back in. I didn't want to miss the call."

"You thought it was Jessica Alba."

John felt his heart rate begin to slow, and perspiration that had popped along his hairline start to cool. "Yeah, well, she keeps calling. I feel bad. She wants to get me in the sack so bad it's pathetic. You know how it is."

"Yeah, I keep beating my coeds off with a stick."

John let himself glance over at the corner chair and saw that it was now empty. He let out a relieved laugh. "I think at your age, they know you're harmless."

"Well, I'm *delighted* to hear you sounding so good. How about lunch? I've got an easy day, no classes until three. I can even let myself have a glass or two of wine because I'll have time to sleep it off before I have to lecture. You can have an easy day because Jessica Lodge is in Cornwall for a few days so there's nobody to look over your shoulder."

"Nobody ever looks over my shoulder," John said.

"Whatever."

"I knew she was in England. How did you know she's in Cornwall? She never tells any of us where she's headed."

"Don't you read your own paper? I'm sure it made Salem's Society Page? What does it matter, anyway? You're hungry, and I'm thirsty."

John knew exactly why Rich was calling. Sarah had probably put him up to it. That reason alone would have made him say no, but that . . . thing he'd seen sitting in his chair made him jump at the chance for companionship.

"I'm pretty thirsty too. A glass of wine sounds like an excellent idea."

Rich named the restaurant. They agreed to meet at noon. As soon as John hung up he stood and hurried out of his office, wanting to get out into the newsroom before the vision reappeared.

V

EVEN BEFORE MELISSA BLAKE OPENED HER EYES she knew what she would see. Nothing. Except for the single bar of light at the bottom of the door. It made the blackness she inhabited even worse because that tiny sliver of illumination reminded her that just beyond the door of her prison a real world existed. Someplace out there was her family, her school, her friends, her bedroom with posters of Justin Timberlake and Taylor Swift. Someplace out there people were laughing and texting and girls were flirting with boys. Someplace out there her parents were worried sick. They *had* to be.

Melissa wished so much she hadn't done it, hadn't pulled her stupid stunt. She'd wanted so badly to get stuff for Halloween, but she'd been grounded for staying out past curfew and hadn't been allowed to go shopping with her friends when they all went to Salem to get tricked out for the big costume party. It had seemed like no big deal. Actually, she had thought it was really a clever idea: just take a bag of clothes and leave them at the end of the street and on her walk to school, change out of her school uniform into some old sneakers, tattered jeans, and a scruffy hoodie. She'd keep her head down, and nobody would recognize her when she caught the train to Salem to head into Wicca Wonders to get her Halloween kit.

She'd been trying to look like a street kid so she wouldn't be bothered on the train. It was a stretch for her because even when she wasn't in school she always dressed in preppy clothes. Her parents pretty much insisted. They wanted her to look like "a nice young lady from a good family." *Gimme a break,* she used to tell herself, but now she wished she had it to do all over again. She would have listened. She would have done exactly what they wanted her to do. She would never have cut school to sneak out and go shopping. And even if she *had* cut school, if she'd just dressed like her usual self, it seemed likely they *never* would have touched her.

Whoever *they* were. They had kidnapped her right after she left the store. She had been walking back toward the train station when the woman had pulled up next to her and told her that the store clerk had given her the wrong bag by mistake. Melissa had glanced into her bag and sure enough, it wasn't the wig and fangs she had bought but rather some stupid child's costume. The woman told Melissa to hop in and she'd drive her back to make the exchange at the store. Then she'd bring her back so she didn't miss her train.

Melissa hadn't been paying attention, or it might have seemed strange to her that the woman knew she was walking to the station. She was heading in that direction, sure, but the stop had been a quarter mile ahead, and there were lots of other businesses on the street. Did that mean they had been watching her the whole time? She never had a chance to figure that out because she'd gotten into the car and as soon as it had started up, a hand came out of the backseat and put something wet over her mouth and nose, and that was all she remembered.

She'd woken up here, sitting on the cold stone floor in this dark place. At first she had panicked, and she had pounded on the door and screamed and cried for hours, begging for someone to come and let her out. Eventually, her fists sore from pounding, exhausted from the emotional effort, and lulled by the darkness, she had fallen asleep. She woke when someone opened the door of her prison.

Melissa had squinted at the brightness. The person in the doorway had been only a black silhouette surrounded by blinding light, but even so she had been able to tell it was a woman. The woman used her foot to shove a pail into the room. "Water and food," she said. "Then use it for a toilet when you've eaten."

"Who are you? Why are you doing this to me?" Melissa cried out.

"You are one of those who no one wants, yet we want you."

"That's not true!" Melissa shouted. "My family has to be going crazy. If you want money, they'll pay. They have plenty."

For reasons that Melissa could not explain at the time and still could not explain even though she had spent hours wondering, the woman had cocked her head sideways, the kind of gesture a person made when the information they were getting wasn't what they expected to hear.

"They really do," Melissa went on. "Just make a phone call or write them a note. Tell them I'm okay so they won't worry as much. Please."

Instead of saying anything further, the woman stepped back and pushed the door closed. Melissa heard a bar slide into place on the far side.

VI

HE HUNG OUT IN THE NEWSROOM BOTHERING his reporters and finding excuses not to go back in his office until it was time to leave for lunch. When he saw it was eleven-thirty, he grabbed his coat and left, deciding to take a walk before he met Rich at the restaurant.

Outside the cold fall air hit his nostrils and brought him partway out of his funk. The sky was clear with the hard blue color that only seemed to come in the fall and winter, and elms were tipped with red and fiery gold. The only thing that detracted were the droves of costumed idiots who flocked to Salem and packed its sidewalks in the weeks ahead of Halloween.

John shook his head in frustration as he elbowed past knots of green-faced witches, caped warlocks, or somebody's version of Dracula. Most of them walked at a snail's pace, busy showing their friends their new plastic fangs or their painted on scars, or the clever makeup that turned their flesh the color of vomit. Everywhere he looked he saw tourists carrying bags filled with healing crystals, candles, or herbs and with pentagrams or other pagan symbols dangling from their necks. John thought it was tacky that Salem seemed to become the Halloween center of the freaking universe every single October, but there was no way he was going to risk the community's wrath by writing an editorial complaining about it. That was especially true after one of his business reporters had just written a story that calculated the total economic impact from witch-related tourism at something north of $200 million annually.

He had to admit his strong feelings probably related to his current mental state, as well as to the fact that both sides of his family descended from women who had been deeply involved in the Salem witch trials. Rebecca Nurse had been a respected great grandmother who at age seventy-one had been charged with the crime of witchcraft. She was arrested, tried, and hanged as a witch on Gallows Hill. On the other side he was related to Ann Putnam, one of the young woman who accused Rebecca Nurse. The whole story had been immortalized in Arthur Miller's play *The Crucible*, and it was twisted into his family's history in ways he wished he could forget.

He finally managed to find a clear stretch of sidewalk and quickened his pace. He was walking fast, his head swimming with jumbled thoughts of annoying tourists and Sarah's call and the bizarre figure that had appeared in his office, when the voice seemed to cry out from inside his head.

"Watch out!"

He snapped his head around, looking in panic in front, behind, even above, expecting to see an out of control car careening toward him or even something falling from a building. There was nothing. The voice had come from so close he had expected to find the person standing right behind him, but no one was there. He was alone.

"The baby!" the voice said again. It was a woman's voice, rough and throaty with age.

He looked around again, feeling like an idiot. The only person nearby was a young woman who had been pushing her child in a stroller and was now unlocking her car, loading in some bags, and getting ready to put the child in its car seat.

Only then he saw it. The stroller was on a slanted section of sidewalk, and it was starting to move, picking up speed even as he watched. "Your baby!" he called out, but the woman had her head in her car and apparently couldn't hear him. The stroller was turning to follow the slope of the sidewalk, heading straight for the curb. Once it went off, it would roll into traffic.

A glance up the road showed a rusted panel van, its bumper half hanging off, its driver in a major rush, his broken muffler roaring as he shot up the street. The mother still hadn't reacted, and his words stuck in his throat as he dashed forward. John saw it like a terrible movie where the bloodiest scene plays out in slow motion, the van thundering down the street, thumping hard through potholes, the stroller just starting to tip off the curb, about to pick up serious speed.

John dove off the curb, feeling a sharp pain as his knee hit the pavement but catching the stroller's footrest just as the handles were starting to stick out past the mother's parked car. The stroller jerked to a halt as van shot past, and the baby inside started to cry, startled by the abrupt stop.

The mother pulled her head out of the car, panicked to find her stroller gone from sight. She let out a cry and raced around the back of the car to see John standing up, holding the stroller's handle in one hand and looking down at his torn pants and bloody knee.

"Oh my God," the woman said in a choked voice. "You saved my baby's life." She crumpled against the car for half a second before she rushed forward, snatched her baby from the stroller, and hugged it to her chest with convulsive sobs.

When she finally regained control, the woman looked at John and down at his pants. "I don't know how to thank you. I . . . how did you . . .?"

"I tried to call out to you, but you couldn't hear me."

"But you saw it? You noticed? Oh my God, if you hadn't . . ."

John tried to mask the confusion he felt by making certain the woman had calmed down enough to drive. He refused her offer of money to buy a new pair of pants and sent her on her way. As he watched her drive off, he wondered for the second time that day what the hell was happening to him. He had heard that voice, so close that it was almost inside his head. Otherwise he'd never have noticed the stroller beginning to move. The old woman's voice had told him of the danger.

He took a step, wincing as he flexed his injured knee. Fortunately he was only a block or two from the restaurant, and he started limping toward it.

VII

"SO, YOU KNOW WHAT THE BEST THING IS ABOUT being a college professor?" Rich asked.

"No," John said. They'd had martinis to start and then switched to wine. They were on their third glass when they finally put in their orders for food. He was feeling a delightful warmth spread through his body and knew that if there was nothing to stop him he could probably stay here for the afternoon and polish off an entire bottle. Thankfully Rich had to teach in a couple hours. "What is it?"

Rich smiled and raised his glass in a toast. "Being surrounded by young pussy." He laughed, gave his head a rueful shake. "Know what the worst thing is?"

"Being surrounded by young pussy," John said. He'd heard the joke about fifty times before.

Rich laughed again and ran his hands down across his Salem State University sweatshirt, making the bulge of his growing stomach unmistakable. "At our age, the only way one of these girls would want to get in bed with this walrus body would be if I stuck thousand dollar bills all over it. And if Lisa caught me, I wouldn't have enough money left to make a fig leaf out of one-dollar bills."

"Don't think you'd need many."

Rich raised his eyebrows in feigned offense. "What's that supposed to mean?"

"Doesn't Lisa refer to you as 'Two Buck Chuck'? I always thought she meant that two dollar bills would be enough to cover . . ."

"You heard wrong. It's Two Foot Chuck."

"In your dreams." John smiled. His friend was working hard to make sure the day passed with as many distractions as possible. He'd had enough wine to take the edge off his usual resentment, so he was actually able to feel grateful.

"Let me ask you a question," he said when Rich stopped chortling at his own joke.

"Shoot."

"You ever, um, see anything that's not there?"

"I've seen lust in women's eyes that I've come to realize wasn't there."

"We've all seen that. I mean have you ever seen, like, somebody who you knew wasn't real."

Rich's face grew sober, and his eyes narrowed. "Are we talking about Julie?" he asked, his voice going very soft. Rich was a theology professor, but John always thought he could easily have chosen to be a shrink instead. He indulged his dirtbag, dirty old man side with his friend, but at the drop of a hat he could be kind and compassionate and insightful in a way that few people could. John knew Rich spent as much time counseling students as he did teaching them, and it made him one of the most popular professors on campus.

"No," John shook his head. "Just this old woman who's in a painting I own."

"The old bag in your living room?"

"Yeah."

"I just . . . I think I'm having a mid-life crisis. Only instead of finding a twenty-three-year-old grad student, I'm day-dreaming about an old Puritan woman. Scary."

Rich folded his hands and pushed away his wine glass. "You know Lisa and I love you, man. We also worry about you."

John held up a hand to ward off whatever was coming.

"No, listen to me for once. You've been licking your wounds for four years. That's a mourning period that out-strips anything in modern times. The only other thing you could have done would have been to throw yourself on the funeral pyre."

"We didn't have one."

"Yeah, I know. Otherwise, you would have had to been restrained."

"What's your point?"

"Time to come out of your cave. Get a date. Show up at parties when you're invited. Let your friends fix you up."

John was already shaking his head. "I will when I'm ready."

"Then you need to give serious thought to the priesthood. The Church needs good men who aren't child molesters. They'd take you in a heartbeat."

"Even though I barely believe?"

"Probably especially because of that. They're trying to be diverse like everybody else."

VIII

JOHN HAD A PLEASANT BUZZ ON WHEN HE FINALLY said goodbye to Rich and left the restaurant. He needed another walk, partly to keep his knee from stiffening up, partly to sober up and prepare for his upcoming visit to Julie's grave. He knew after all this time, fourteen hundred and sixty days to be exact, that he ought to feel a greater sense of distance. He also knew that Rich was right and that he should try and get himself out more, let friends fix him up with divorcees or widows, and at the very least stop being such a hermit and accept invitations to dinner parties.

The problem was everything about Julie was still so damn fresh. Every single day things happened that made him think of her smell, her voice, her touch, her laughter. Every single day he would *feel* her presence in his life, as if she was in the next room, as if she was about to call him on the phone, as if she was looking at him from behind a nearby tree or from a restaurant table across the room. And every single day, things made him remember that indescribably horrific moment when he learned she was dead. Over the past four years he'd often wondered if there was something wrong with him that kept him from moving on. And then this morning when he'd found that painting moved and seen the vision or whatever in his office, and again when he'd heard the old lady's voice in his ear just before the baby got hit, he'd started to fear that he was getting worse rather than better.

He shook his head, hunched his shoulders, and picked up his pace. He walked several blocks at decent speed, feeling the bite in his knee every time he stretched the broken skin, but then he was forced to slow down again as he came up to the crowd of tourists standing outside a shop called Wicca Wonders. He rolled his eyes in frustration and tried to move through the mass of people, saying, "Excuse me," repeatedly, and finally giving up and stepping into the street.

A woman named Abigail Putnam owned the store. Like John, she was descended from the original Puritan Putnams. However, unlike her humorless forbearers who would have frowned on any public display, Abigail Putnam had built a thriving retail business by foisting herself off on the public as a direct descendant of the Salem witch trial witches and a practicing witch herself. In spite of being in her mid-fifties, she wore her hair long, decorated herself with ostentatious occult jewelry, and dressed in long robes with astral symbols woven into the cloth. John thought she regularly made an ass of herself, but he had to give her a bit of grudging respect in one thing at least. The woman knew how to make money and had built a mini-empire of occult and witchcraft themed stores. According to scuttlebutt around town, Abigail Putnam had made millions and millions of dollars shilling all kinds of pentagrams and crystals and other occult crap to gullible tourists. What had caused John to step off the sidewalk was the crowd of at least seventy-five people waiting their turn to get into Wicca Wonders. The store actually employed security personnel just to make sure their customers didn't break fire codes for overcrowding.

As he began to come even with the front doors of the store, John hunched his head reflexively and put his hands over his ears. He looked around in stunned surprise as a horrible noise assaulted him. It sent chills down his back, and he looked around in disbelief at all the smiling faces in the crowd because he was hearing the shrill bedlam of human beings wailing in unspeakable agony. He took another step, and the screaming grew a little louder. He seemed like it had to be coming from inside the store, but there was nothing fun or cool about it. It sounded like people being burned alive. How were all these idiots just standing around talking and laughing among themselves when those blood curdling screams should have emptied the store and driven every last one of them away?

John stepped back onto the sidewalk and into the crowd, gritting his teeth against the horrible keening. He tapped one of the waiting people on the shoulder. "Can't you hear that noise coming from the store?" he demanded, his voice loud to get above the screams.

The young man turned around and gave him a squirrelly look, then he cocked his head for a second as if listening hard. "I'm sorry. What noise? I don't hear anything."

John looked at the guy's face, trying to figure out if he was joking. He decided he wasn't. John nodded, embarrassed. "Sorry," he said, pointing to his ears. "I'm just hearing things, I guess."

He stepped off the curb again and walked away from Wicca Wonders. The sound began to fade almost immediately. He got back on the sidewalk, turned, and looked back. Not a single person in the crowd waiting to get into the store seemed troubled by the shrieking. However, as he stood there John felt something else, a sudden sixth-sense prickle at the back of his neck as if someone was staring at him. He looked at the faces of the people waiting to get into the store, but no one appeared to be paying him the slightest attention. Yet, the prickle intensified. He glanced toward the store, its front windows nearly opaque with glare from the gray sky, but he saw her. A woman he could sense better than see was standing at the window, her form little more than a vague outline, but there was no mistaking the intensity of her gaze. He could feel her eyes burning into him, and there was also no mistaking the enmity he felt coming from them.

Wondering who seemed to harbor such strong dislike for him, he took a step back toward the store, intending to brave the horrible noise long enough to satisfy his curiosity. The moment he did, the woman moved away from the window and disappeared. John stopped and retreated to a point where the sound of screaming died away.

A second later he saw a couple young women come out of the store and turn in his direction. He waited, and when they came even with them, he asked, "Pardon me, did you happen to see a woman standing by the front window of the store a moment ago?"

The girls looked at each other, clearly confused by the strangeness of John's question. They both shook their heads. "Sorry," one said.

"Also, did either of you hear that screaming back there?" John blurted, knowing the question was a mistake even as he asked it.

The nearest girl stopped and looked at him. Her eyes went to his torn pants, and her expression became wary. "No." She reached for her friend's arm, and the two of them started moving away.

"It wasn't coming from inside the store?"

"There wasn't any screaming."

"Okay, sorry to bother you."

The girls hurried away whispering, and John knew right away they were talking about him. One of them looked back at him, smirked, and then burst out laughing.

Shaken that they had thought he was some crazy old man, John looked down at his pants and decided to make a detour to his house to change clothes and clean and bandage his cut. He turned at the next corner and headed for the Pickering Wharf section of town and his 150-year-old Victorian house. He knew he ought to call into the paper, but he also trusted Amy to handle everything with complete competence in his absence.

He walked the blocks to Pickering Wharf and went up to his front door. He unlocked it, picked the mail off the floor and put it on the side table. At the foot of the stairs he stopped and glanced into the living room where the portrait of Rebecca Nurse still hung above the mantle, its unsmiling face seeming to cast accusations at him down through the ages. Not for the first time he wondered how he had descended from such utterly grim people. How was it possible that they had crossed the Atlantic and come to cast their fate on the shores of a rocky wilderness just for the opportunity to follow such a bitter religion? The question probably should have made him laugh out loud, but his mood was so grim he could summon no trace of humor. Instead, he shuddered.

He headed upstairs, but when he reached the top step, instead of turning right toward his bedroom to change his pants, he went left and down the hall to his home office. The room had always been his sanctuary. Its well-worn leather chairs and the glow of burnished wood on his Federal period desk and the Hepplewhite mahogany table in the bay window overlooking Salem Harbor warmed him like the embers of a fire even on the coldest winter days.

He had inherited the house when his Aunt Eleanor died, and rather than clearing out the clutter of older generations, he had added a few things of his own. Now his grandfather's binoculars sat right next to his computer, and the old Chinese screen in one corner stood behind a table crowded with sailing and hockey trophies. The combination of the old and the new helped remind him of who he was.

On weekends one of his favorite things was to rise early

and sit in the old captain's chair with his morning coffee and watch the sun slowly rise on the choppy gray-green waters of the Atlantic. Using his grandfather's old binoculars, he would watch boats going in and out of the harbor. Now that Julie was gone, his blood links to the past had assumed a new importance. His ancestors had been a vital part of this city ever since its founding. When he closed his eyes he could imagine how the busy wharf below his window must have looked in the time of his great-great-great grandfather. There would have been fast clipper ships tied to the dock, their ropes creaking in the wind, docks bustling with longshoremen as they loaded and unloaded ships and bars crowded with sailors getting drunk one last time before shipping out.

John knew it must have been a loud, foul smelling place, full of rotting trash, beggars, whores, and stray dogs, but Salem had been the shipping capital of New England. His great-great-grandfather, John Bancroft Andrews, had been part of a line of adventurous sea captains who amassed fortunes from the East India trade in the late 1700s and 1800s. Even today John enjoyed a degree of generational wealth, thanks to their daring.

He stood in the doorway and looked around the room where so many of his ancestors had sat. Had any of them been as unable to cope with loss as he? He thought not. They had been hard men who had survived, even thrived on the cold Atlantic. He shook his head and forced a smile, thinking that those same hard men had also been descended from that prune faced old hag whose face had freaked him out so much when he came downstairs that morning. It seemed that Rebecca Nurse's toughness had, indeed, carried down through the ages, but he suspected that it had been exhausted by his generation. "Suck it up," he said out loud, speaking to the empty room, the comment pointed at himself.

He glanced at his watch, thinking it was time to head to the cemetery, girding himself in advance for the massive feeling of loss he was about to experience. As he turned away from the window, his breath caught and the color drained from his face. She was there in his office, seated in one of the leather chairs. She was indistinct and white as a cloud, but there was no mistaking what he knew was the harsh black dress from the portrait. She was working on her embroidery, but then she looked up at him.

"Jesus H. Christ," he said in a whisper, horrified at the way his brain was manufacturing these phantasms. "What the hell do you want?"

He closed his eyes and shook his head as if he could dislodge the image. He felt disgusted at himself for talking to some ghost. Maybe he should go to Abigail Putnam and buy one of her stupid pentagrams.

When he opened his eyes again she was still there. She seemed to be regarding him with a combination of pity and disappointment. For some reason he could not explain he found the idea that she might have judged him and found him wanting in some regard to be profoundly threatening. As she continued to look at him he felt anger rise up inside.

"What?" he demanded.

The woman just kept staring.

"This is my house now," he went on, refusing to be intimidated by the fact that she seemed to be looking right into his thoughts. "I live here. I gave up a much bigger career in television news to come back to Salem and run my small time paper. I did it because I felt some stupid link to my ancestors and because I wanted a good 'quality of life,' whatever the hell that is. And it didn't work out, which you probably already know. Julie got killed in a goddamned car accident, and now I'm alone. I drink too much. I'm supposed to be learning to cope with my loss, but I'm not doing a very good job. In fact, I seem to be getting a whole lot worse, because after all, right now I'm seeing a ghost and talking to her. That makes me freaking nuts, just like I always thought you and your whole pack of loony Puritans were nuts." He laughed. "They always said acorns don't fall far from the tree. Guess I prove the truth of that."

In spite of the fact the woman's presence chilled him almost into paralysis, he forced himself to stand. "Well, you sit here and haunt my office as long as you wish. I've got things to do," he said.

He walked quickly from the office toward his bedroom, unable to resist looking over his shoulder to see if the ghost was following. To his great relief, it was not.

He quickly stripped off his torn pants, went to the bathroom medicine chest, cleaned off the bloody scrape with hydrogen peroxide and then covered it with gauze and tape. He put on a fresh pair of trousers then started down the stairs. At the bottom he stopped and looked into the living room and stared at the portrait over his mantle. The portrait stared back, hard and remorseless. It almost made him feel better to trade glares with that ugly old woman.

To help add a bit more fortitude for what he was about to do and to try to convince himself he wasn't really as rattled as he knew he was, he strode into the living room and went to the butler's tray that stood in one corner and held several silver decanters filled with single barrel bourbon and single malt scotch. He poured several fingers of scotch into a glass, brought it back and stood in front of the portrait and raised the glass. "Here's looking at you," he said and emptied the glass into his mouth. He squeezed his eyes closed at the burn, realizing to drink like that was a waste of perfectly good, very expensive scotch. But right now he needed it.

The most unsettling thing about the ghost was that he had sensed something very different when she had been in the room. He had sensed compassion and pity and even what had seemed like a wordless apology for something he could not understand. Why would a ghost apologize? He opened the front door and stepped out into the bracing, bright afternoon. He forced his lips into a smile and tried to walk like a man who hadn't a care in the world. *What crap,* he thought. He had to get his flowers and get to Julie's grave. Emotionally he was a man about to endure a whipping.

In spite of all that, the thought kept intruding: *Why would a ghost apologize?*

IX

JOHN WALKED A BLOCK TO THE FLORIST TO pick up the bouquet of white roses he had ordered then headed to the garage to get his car. On the way he passed a small liquor store, and after the slightest hesitation, he stepped inside and bought a pint of Johnnie Walker Black and slipped it into his back pocket. The drive to his family's burial plot took about ten minutes. He felt a minor buzz from the scotch he'd drunk at home, but he was glad he'd bought the pint because he knew it wasn't enough to get him through. He parked the car and started toward the cemetery entrance with the heaviness of a gathering storm in his heart. He hated the feeling and looked forward to taking a good nip from the pint when he was out of sight of the street.

Harmony Grove Cemetery was located in a hilly section of central Salem and surrounded by a cluster of old leather tanneries, some abandoned and some converted to more modern uses, along with several newer apartment buildings. Inside the cemetery's iron gates, the crowding and bustle of the city ended abruptly. Narrow tree-lined lanes wound up and down the grassy slopes filled with well-kept family plots, many of which dated back centuries.

John knew that upon entering the cemetery most people would see a contemplative, park-like setting, a place where their loved ones could be laid to rest in tranquil peace and beauty. Not him. Where other people might have seen graceful trees whose overarching bows created pockets of dappled shade, he saw pools of darkness that stood like stagnant water amid the cold slabs of grave markers and dour granite mausoleums. Others might have seen an idyllic setting, but even on the brightest days John found the cemetery dank and foreboding, the trees themselves sagging under the weight of all the collective sadness they had witnessed. He often shivered uncontrollably here, as if he was lying on a block of cold marble, even on days when it was hot enough to make a normal person sweat.

He stopped just inside the gates, holding his white roses more tightly than necessary to try and still the shivers that always started here, as he reached for the pint, unscrewed the top and took a long swallow. *God, he hated this place.* Every time he came here his senses seemed to become hyper alert. The cemetery did nothing to alleviate his pain; instead it raised every single thing he didn't want to feel to an entirely new level. An unbearable level. He reminded himself of a child who lies in bed and hears sounds in the dark and imagines monsters in his closet or beneath his bed, and as the hours of sleeplessness go on and on, the terror becomes bigger and more terrible until finally it borders on true hysteria.

It started to happen as soon as he began walking. The memory came barreling into him, slamming him with the power of a fist to the guts. In his mind he heard the ringing of a phone, and he saw his hand going out to grasp the receiver and bring it to his ear. Not to have been able to undo that moment, not to have ignored the ringing phone, not to have prevented the words that were about to be spoken in the next few seconds, those had been his primary failures. He lived them over and over and over. If he hadn't heard the words maybe they wouldn't have been true.

"Mr. Andrews," the state trooper said after he introduced himself. "Is your wife, forty-eight-year-old Julie Andrews of Chestnut Street Salem?"

"Yes," Andrews heard himself say, wanting every single time to say "no, you have the wrong number, this is a mistake," but he never was able to change his memory.

"I am afraid I have very bad news, sir. Your wife was involved in a terrible accident on Route 128 near the Peabody Mall. She was driving in the right hand lane when another car lost control and forced her SUV into the concrete guardrail. Her vehicle flipped over. She was wearing her seatbelt, but she received massive head and neck injuries. She appears to have died instantly. She did not suffer, Mr. Andrews, I can assure you of that. I'm very sorry, sir, for your loss."

Andrews recalled exactly what happened next, the wrenching pain in his guts, the way his brain tried to reject the information but his body knew it was real. He remembered bending over in agony, barely listening as the state trooper asked him not to drive to the scene. Instead, he was told to meet the policeman at the Andover State Police

Barracks where he would collect Julie's personal belongings. The trooper told him the medical examiner had already removed Julie's body from the scene.

"Who was in the other car?" Andrews heard himself ask.

The trooper paused to check his notes. "A man named Richard Putnam of Peabody."

"Was he drunk?"

"No, sir. According to tests done at the scene he had no alcohol in his system. We have several eyewitness reports that Mr. Putnam wasn't speeding or driving recklessly. It was raining hard, and visibility was quite poor. Mr. Putnam's car appeared to have skidded on the wet pavement. It was simply a tragic accident."

John took several shaky steps over to a bench that sat just inside the cemetery gates. He sat, sucked in a couple deep breaths and took another hit on the scotch. It wasn't the first time he'd had to sit here. The memory hit him the same way each time he came.

He knew it would take two or three minutes for the worst of it to pass. As he waited he suddenly remembered something he had forgotten from the time just before Julie's accident. Today hadn't been the first time he'd seen Rebecca Nurse's spirit. He had seen it back then, as well, one or two times just before the accident, but after the accident the appearances had stopped. He had been a different man back then, much less unaware of his own vulnerability, of how love could be so easily destroyed. Seeing the ghost back then hadn't shaken him nearly as much as it had today. He hadn't even remembered that it had happened until this very moment.

He stood up and walked up one of the lanes, not toward Julie's grave but toward his parents' graves. It was sort of an intermediate step that he thought might prepare him for what was to come. The graves sat amid a grouping of headstones for the Andrews and Newhall families, many of them from the 1700s or 1800s, the oldest of them leaning white marble headstones whose letters had been nearly obliterated by age and weather, silent evidence of his family's long involvement in Salem. John laid a white rose on each of his parents' graves then saluted them with another long mouthful of scotch. He was getting quite drunk, but he craved the deadness alcohol could bring.

He stumbled along, choosing a path between the oldest of the headstones when he suddenly recalled that none existed for Rebecca Nurse. He wondered why he was suddenly fixated on her. What in his subconscious had caused his brain to start manufacturing images of the old woman? He didn't know the answer, but he remembered the reason there was no marker for Rebecca Nurse. The day she was hanged on Gallows Hill, two of her sons waited for darkness to come, then they snuck up the hill, dug her corpse from its shallow grave, placed it in a boat, and rowed her down the North River toward home where they buried her on the family farm. There was a family legend that said her corpse had been drained of its blood, but whether it was true or not John had no way of knowing.

Prodded by thoughts of Rebecca Nurse's hanging, John

turned to gaze across at neighboring Gallows Hill. As if the cemetery wasn't gloomy enough by itself, he imagined what it must have been like to have stood on that same spot back on July 19, 1692 and look across from the cemetery at the gallows that held the body of the seventy-one-year-old great grandmother who had been accused of practicing witch-craft. It was hard for him to imagine the hysteria that had gripped Salem back then. It had allowed the judges to hang a respected old woman who had lived in that small community for the previous fifty years.

Of course, to make matters even weirder, Ann Putnam, the teenage girl who accused Rebecca Nurse of being a witch, was also his blood relative. Odd to think that a member of the Putnam family had been responsible for Rebecca Nurse's death, and over three hundred years later, another member of the same family had been responsible for Julie's death. For a second, as he thought about it, even as he knew it was irra-tional he felt a burst of something very close to hatred against all the members of that family.

He turned from Gallows Hill and glared higher up the hill on which he was standing, at the section of the old cem-etery where the Putnam family had buried its people from the 1600s to modern times. As he stared, he could have sworn a soft voice said, *"Look carefully."*

He spun around, thinking for the second time that day that somebody had crept up on him without him hearing. He was alone. There was no one else in sight in that entire sec-tion of the cemetery. *"Look,"* the voice said again.

He staggered sideways and reached out to grasp one of the old marble headstones to keep from falling to his knees. *Where the hell was that voice coming from?* Even worse, it was the same voice he'd heard earlier when he had kept the baby carriage from rolling in front of the speeding van. It was the hoarse voice of an old woman. He suspected it belonged to the same old woman who seemed to be tearing his sanity apart.

He ran his hands over his face, rubbed his eyes, then grabbed the pint and took another slug. He suddenly feared he was cracking up in a serious way. John Andrews, who had always mocked the costumed imbeciles who packed the sidewalks of his city and squandered their money on occult gewgaws, was suddenly so weak in the head that he was being "haunted" by the ghost of an old ancestor. If it wasn't so pathetic, he might have laughed.

"*Look,*" the voice commanded for a third time.

Unable to resist, he finally did, and that was when he noticed the pattern.

It almost seemed that the ghost was affecting his vision because five of the Putnam graves were glowing slightly, and glowing lines extended from them, connecting to the other glowing grave markers. The shape of the lines was unmistakable, and in spite of John's attempts to rationalize what he was seeing, he felt a cold sweat in his armpits in spite of the coolness of the day. The glowing lines formed a pentagram. The five-pointed star that held such power for all those who believed in the occult.

He squeezed his eyes closed, turned away and looked around at the rest of the cemetery. Everything around him was as it always had been. The sun had started to drop in the sky. Shadows were lengthening. Trees waved in the gentle fall breeze, and a few yellow or red leaves danced as they fell from branches and then scudded across the grass.

When he turned around to face the Putnam burial plot again, the glow had faded from the headstones and the lines had disappeared. Yet now that he actually saw it, the pattern was undeniable. The five outermost gravestones, each of them among the oldest of the Putnam grave markers, formed the pentagram. They were white marble, and they leaned a bit like so many early markers. Even from here he could tell that their inscriptions were badly faded.

Now that he recognized the pattern he couldn't believe he'd never noticed it before because he had been to this cemetery so many times. However, when he blinked again, the five graves instantly fell back into the general rank of old Putnam graves. Almost certainly anyone else looking up this hill would see nothing unusual. The pentagram pattern was so controversial that if anyone had noticed it, they would surely have said something to other people and there would have eventually been articles in the newspaper or even a book.

While it seemed incredible that something so unusual had gone unnoticed for three hundred years, other nearby grave markers were larger and drew the eye. Then there was a Putnam mausoleum in one corner of the family plot. Even early on, when those five white headstones had been laid, there had been other nearby headstones that would have broken the pattern just enough to obscure it. He knew that if it hadn't been literally pointed out to him he never would have seen it, but now that he had, the pentagram was like a signpost.

As he thought about these things he reached back and touched the pint that sat heavily in his pocket. He knew he was pretty badly hammered. Were these real perceptions he was having or drunken visions? Even as he wondered, something else started to prickle his nerve endings. He looked at the pentagram again, convinced that he wasn't just inventing this, then turned slowly and gazed across at Gallows Hill. One point of the pentagram seemed to point in a perfectly straight line toward the top of the hill, the exact spot where the gallows had stood and where nineteen innocent women— one of them his ancestor—had been hanged as witches.

In spite of the scotch, John's mind started to race. Wishing he hadn't drunk half so much, he felt his news reporter instincts taking over. There had to be a story in what he was seeing. He hadn't yet gone to Julie's grave to put his roses in her vase, but now there was something he had to do first. He needed to look at the gravestones that made up the pentagram from close up. He needed to know whose graves they were, when they died, what the headstone inscriptions said.

As he started up the lane toward the Putnam family plot he wondered if living members of the family knew about the pentagram or whether the reason for its construction had died with earlier generations. As he neared his goal, the light breeze that had been blowing through the dry leaves seemed to drop. In the sudden stillness he thought he could hear the rumble of distant voices. He felt a chill pass through him, a sort of sixth sense warning him he was being watched.

He stopped and looked around the cemetery. There were no cars on any of the narrow roads and only a single person, a woman in a red jacket over a hundred yards away. Her head was bent away from him as she tended flowers in front of a gravestone. John chided himself and tried to shake off the feeling there was some kind of unseen threat nearby. He resumed his walk to the Putnam plot.

X

AS HE APPROACHED THEM, HE LOOKED AT THE grouped Putnam gravestones, some two or three hundred years old, others from the nineteenth century, some much newer, and he realized he could no longer pick out the grave markers that had so clearly delineated a pentagram. Up this close, the graves became clusters of family groupings, with grandparents, children, and grandchildren buried in close proximity to one another.

As he stepped onto the grass and began to walk amid the gravestones, he swore he again heard voices. They were very faint, like the sound that might leak through the walls of a crowded auditorium. He stopped and looked around, not seeing anyone at all, not even the woman in the red coat he had seen earlier. He pushed his fingers into his ears, but he knew the problem wasn't physical. It was mental. It was the second time today he had heard the sound of invisible crowds, but at least this time they weren't screaming in unspeakable pain.

As he looked around, unable to spot the markers that had stood out so clearly from lower on the slope, he thought about Ann Putnam, another of his ancestors. For reasons he couldn't explain he had never felt that his blood ties to the Putnam family were as strong as his ties to the Nurse side. Probably it was how things happened in every family, he thought, with emotional ties to some bloodlines much stronger than other. After all, hadn't his aunt insisted on keeping the portrait of Rebecca Nurse hanging on the wall all these years? As far as he was concerned he would happily have sold the ugly thing and collected a quarter of a million bucks, but some peculiar feeling of family loyalty had made that impossible.

Now, the same combination of scotch and reporter's curiosity that had driven him up the hill made him want to find Ann Putnam's grave. Was hers one of those that formed the pentagon? Even if it was what would it prove? He had no idea, but it struck him that an occult sign in a graveyard, in a *Puritan* graveyard, had to be incredibly unusual. It had to mean something, even though he couldn't imagine what.

He took another sip of scotch even though he'd had more than enough, and staggering slightly, started looking at the names on the oldest gravestones. Many were cracked, some broken, a number of them illegible, the letters of their inscriptions having been worn almost flat by years of wind, rain, and snow. He walked up and down, thinking there had to be a hundred Putnam graves, a large number but perhaps not surprising given three centuries of large families.

The granite mausoleum stood in the far corner of the plot, at one of the highest points on the hill. He moved up and back looking at the gravestones, drawing closer and closer to the mausoleum, noticing as he did that the sound of voices seemed to increase. By the time he had covered half of the plot, the voices had grown noticeably louder. Rather than finishing his search for Ann Putnam, he turned and headed straight toward the mausoleum, realizing that the voices seemed to be coming from inside.

When he reached the building the voices were distinctly louder. He started around it, first on the south side looking at the windowless gray walls. Steps ran up the front of the building, but a heavy black iron door barred the entrance. Iron bars covered the small window in the center of the door, and a detritus of old spider webs and the remains of the bugs and leaves the webs had caught rendered the window nearly opaque. The same accumulation filled the keyhole, giving him the strong impression that it had been years since anyone had opened the front door. The north side was also window-less, the granite covered with a slick of green moss.

Coming to the rear of the mausoleum he saw where a set of stone steps descended into the darkness, presumably leading to a lower level of Putnam family crypts. Drawn by his curiosity, he walked to the edge of the steps and looked down, realizing the voices here were louder than anywhere else. As he stood there, the sun went behind a bank of clouds, and the color seemed to leach from the world. Suddenly the whole world seemed as dank and gray as the granite that loomed over him, and he felt a chill run down his back.

As he squinted down into the darkness where the stairs disappeared, he heard the voice again from directly behind him. "*Go down.*" Given the eeriness of the setting, it startled him badly, and he spun around.

As he did, his foot slipped off the top step. He grabbed for the railing, missed and tipped backward, tumbling down the stone steps. Tucking instinctively, he took most of the damage on his arms, shoulder, and back, and came to rest at the bottom of the steps in a pool of absolute darkness. Pain shot from every part of his body as he tried to move. Wondering how many bones he had broken, he opened his eyes and squinted up the steps at the late afternoon brightness. He blinked, but the blurring would not go away. It told him he had a concussion, probably a bad one.

With a groan he rolled onto his knees. Partly from scotch and partly from the concussion his head whirled like some out of control carnival ride. He didn't know if he could stand or if he could, how he'd make it up the steps. Yelling for help would be useless. No one would ever hear him.

Wondering if his cell phone had survived, he reached into his pocket. His hands were so bruised his fingers barely worked, but after a minute of fumbling he managed to grasp the phone and pull it free. He pushed the button and looked to see if he had a signal and felt a touch of panic when he saw no bars. Realizing he must have fallen twenty feet or more, he cursed, thinking that with all the granite above him and the narrow opening of the staircase, no signal could reach him.

Ironically, the pint of Johnnie Walker was also intact. It was lucky because the broken glass could have cut him badly, but he was done with the drinking. Sure, that voice had startled him, but the real reason he'd fallen was he was drunk as a damn smelt. How had he let himself get to this point? Maybe the booze and the endless grieving and now the voices and the ghosts, maybe all of it meant his mind had finally snapped, and at some subconscious level he was trying to kill himself. What a fool, he thought. If he really wanted to die he should have jumped off a freaking bridge. All he'd done was bang himself up to the point where he'd probably need a couple days in the hospital, but otherwise nothing had changed.

Suddenly, he remembered the other thing. His white roses. The whole reason he'd come to the damn cemetery. He had a flashlight app on his phone, and went to it, turned on the light, and shined it around to find his flowers.

The first thing he saw was the blood. It was fresh, pooling under him. Touching his hand to his head and ear it came away wet and sticky. He was bleeding like a stuck pig. He felt a jolt of fresh anxiety but told himself that head wounds always looked worse than they really were. Even so, he needed to get medical attention before he lost too much blood.

He shined the light around the bottom of the narrow staircase. The roses were a few feet above him, balanced on one of the stairs. Moving the light around he looked for something he could grab onto that would help him get back to his feet. A metal door stood in the corner of the back wall. It was solid looking, its edges flaked with rust. Cobwebs fluttered from the handle and the lock hole, making it look as if it hadn't been opened in years.

Beside the door a metal shelf protruded from the wall. It was small but maybe solid enough to take his weight. John crawled to the wall, reached up, and grasped the shelf as solidly as his bruised fingers would allow. He tightened his muscles and started to pull himself up. Fiery pain shot out of every joint but he managed to get himself into a crouch and from there, inch by inch, he straightened.

Once he was on his feet his head spun so badly he nearly collapsed. He leaned against the wall, closed his eyes, and fought the nausea that roiled his stomach. Along with his blurred vision, the nausea and dizziness confirmed he was concussed, probably badly concussed.

Getting up the steps without falling was going to take everything he had. He turned on his phone flashlight again, wanting to find handholds for every step he needed to take. He would hug the walls and then grab the metal railing and half walk, half haul himself to the top of the steps. As he looked around something caught his eye. It looked like a handprint slightly indented into the wall to the left of the door. When his light stopped there, he could see that the indentation had a brownish red tint, as if it had once been painted.

He needed to get up the steps and to a hospital, but his reporter's curiosity held him in place. He shuffled a half step along the wall, and ignoring the sticky blood all over his palm, he pressed his hand into the indentation. Unlike the cold granite where he rested his cheek, the indentation was surprisingly warm. In fact when he touched it the stone felt as though it was a living thing.

In the next second he heard a loud snap, and the granite wall just to the left of the indentation began to move inward.

XI

THE DOOR SWUNG OPEN AND REVEALED AN
entrance into darkness so pitch black that at first it seemed
solid. John had almost forgotten about the steady drone of
voices he'd been hearing ever since he first set foot on the Putnam plot, but they rose to a muted roar as the door opened.
In spite of his dizziness and the pain that coursed through
him, John's curiosity sparked. He needed to know how it was
possible so many people had come to be underground here.
He staggered forward, leaning on the wall for support, until
he could put his head up to the opening and peer around the
corner. As soon as he did, several lights set into the inner
walls began to glow, increasing in brightness to reveal a stone
stairway that descended between rough walls hewn out of
the native granite.

He shuffled another half step, braced his shoulder against
the door and put his head all the way inside. A hard wind
was blowing up the stairway, flattening his hair and making
his eyes water. The wind also seemed to carry the sounds he
was hearing. It made them louder and louder until John had
to stagger away from the wall and bring his hands to his ears
to try and keep the voices out. It did no good. Dizziness and

nausea slammed him like a fist. He felt his knees giving way as he tumbled into blackness.

John knew he *had* to be dreaming because in the next instant he felt hands reaching out to grip him. It wasn't one or two hands but many, and they seemed to be lifting him out of his own body. He could look back and see his unconscious form lying just inside the entrance as the hands moved him along, deeper and deeper into the underground passage. The voices were all around him. They were loud, men's, women's, and children's voices, all speaking in an urgent babble that rendered them indistinct, more like the noise of a swollen river tumbling through a narrow gorge. He couldn't understand them, but he felt their unstoppable energy. They were voices that had been locked away for too long with no one to hear their tales.

He was being carried through a passage of complete darkness. He had a sense of motion, but there was no longer any wind in his face. In fact nothing touched him, there were no longer hands grasping. The voices had merged into one continuous roar, until he was being borne on a river of cathartic sound and an almost inhuman need to communicate. Remarkably he felt no sense of fear or threat. He understood that the voices *needed* him as if they had been waiting for someone to hear them for a very long time.

He wondered briefly how he could be moving down this dark passage because a dim memory told him his body was bleeding at the bottom of the stone steps. Moments earlier his physical body had been in great pain, but now he felt nothing at all but a sense of peace and acceptance. He could not have said how long the sensation of movement lasted, but at some point he realized things were slowing.

Up ahead a light appeared. It was soft and ethereal and seemed to emerge through thick curtains of mist. Gradually, the light became brighter and shapes began to emerge around it. He saw what looked like a house up ahead, and then seconds later he was moving through its walls. He felt nothing. It was as if the walls were constructed out of layers of mist. Incredibly, he knew exactly where he was, his old house, the one on Chestnut Street where he and Julie had lived before he inherited the big house on Pickering Wharf. He was still moving, but very slowly now. He had the ability to look carefully at what he was going past and to recognize details.

As he drifted toward the back of the house he began to see people, and then he saw something that shocked him even more. He saw himself. He was twenty years younger. He looked tanned and fit in worn khakis and a polo shirt. He was sitting on his porch, drinking a beer and smiling and watching something that was going on in the yard. Below on the grass he saw Julie. She was wearing a blue sundress, her blond hair pulled back in a ponytail. She was holding a garden hose, and Sarah was standing beside her helping to hold the hose. Water was splashing into a blow-up child's wading pool. The evening was hot. Dots of perspiration dotted Julie's skin. Her neck was flushed from the heat. Her legs were long, browned by the sun, and fit from running and biking. The untanned softness of her breasts peeked out at the sides of the sundress. He could see bugs flitting in the light of the lowering sun. He could smell freshly cut grass. He swore he could also smell the combination of perfume and heat and shampoo at the nape of Julie's neck.

He wanted more than anything to reach out and stop the motion. He wanted to hold her in his arms. He *needed* this. He wanted to stare, wave, shout, do anything to try and get Julie to notice him. He wanted to tell her he loved her and how much he missed her and how hollow his life had been since she died. He wanted to tell her that years in the future she should make sure never to drive on Route 128 on a rainy night in October. He wanted to tell her that if she just did that one thing they would grow old together. *Stop!* he tried to scream, but if his voice made any sound at all it simply blended with all the other voices. There was nothing to grasp, no way to anchor himself or counter the ceaseless motion.

Even as he tried to fight, he realized that his need, his loss, his urgency could not stand against this power that had already swept him up in its current. Whatever this force was, if profoundly human in some respects, it was at the same time inhuman. For the first time, it occurred to him that he might be dead. Perhaps he had died at the bottom of those steps. Perhaps this was the afterlife, a tortured, eternal drifting through the ashes of his life where he would experience his old desires and losses over and over.

Maybe the screams he had heard when he passed Abigail Putnam's Wicca Wonders were the cries of spirits driven insane by the torture of these repeated visions. A second later his questioning was interrupted when the light went out again and he returned to the rushing darkness. Some time later, maybe seconds, maybe minutes, there was light again, and he flowed quickly through other scenes from his life. He really was dead, he decided. He had to be. There was no other explanation for how he was seeing his memories rewind at high speed.

He revisited his stint as ABC's Washington correspondent covering the Pentagon and White House. It had been the biggest job of his career, the one just before he stepped off the fast track and took the executive editor job at the paper back in Salem so he could spend more time with Julie and Sarah. He even witnessed the moment when he had achieved his greatest fame, as he stood in the five-acre courtyard of the Pentagon, on camera row, reporting live less than twenty-five minutes after the two American Airliners flew into the World Trade Center towers. While fear and disbelief gripped the entire nation, he calmly told his listeners that another commercial jet was reported to be flying directly towards the Pentagon. At that moment most other networks were focused on the evacuation of the Capitol complex, but he had told viewers that he thought he could see the plane approaching. It was so low he could make out the American Airline logo. John winced, involuntarily reliving the moment as his videographer held the shaking camera and caught the plane hitting the building, capturing the fireball explosion of 10,000 gallons of jet fuel.

The images did not pause. He saw himself earlier in his career as a television reporter for a station in Bangor, Maine; then sailing during summers in college; walking to classes at the University of Vermont; playing on the football team in high school; playing street hockey with friends when he was ten.

As he finished rewinding his own life, the darkness became absolute, and he felt the speed pick up again. When the lights came again, he no longer saw scenes from his life but from what had to be his father's life. He saw old cars, old-fashioned clothes, men storming the beaches of France on D-Day. It felt like scenes from an old black-and-white movie. He saw his grandfather during the Great Depression; a man who must have been is great grandfather speaking at a rally for Theodore Roosevelt; the man who must have been his great-great grandfather hollering commands to his mates aboard a sailing schooner named *The Carolina*. John knew from reading his great-great grandfather's journals that the old captain might have been bringing his ship home from one of his multi-year voyages where he traded salt, furs, and spices in places like Capetown, Canton, and Calcutta before finally sailing home to Salem.

He was moving fast, speeding back through time, but unless he was badly mistaken, there was a sense of purpose in the rush, as if he was being carried toward some particular target. Only he had no idea what it might be. The light was constant now as he raced further and further back through the history of his family. There were sights and sound as well now, the shouts of seamen, the shrill scream of wind in the rigging, the odors of ship tar and dead fish and brine and the fetid stink of the close stale air below decks.

A tidy New England farmhouse appeared with smoke drifting from its chimney. Everything was in color now. The house was connected to the barn and surrounded by fields and orchards, but on closer inspection the corn in the fields looked brown and lifeless. Beyond the farm John could see rolling meadows and then pine and hardwood forest stretching as far as the eye could see, but the trees too looked like they hadn't had rain in weeks.

John moved toward the farmhouse, approaching the old oak door studded with nail heads. A sundial had been set into the wall above the door. He could see some letters that he couldn't make out and the numbers 1636. He passed through the thick door as if it was a curtain of gauze. Inside, the house was dark because the windows were small and let in very little light, and the air smelled of wood smoke, yeast, and baking bread. An open fireplace took up most of one wall, and the blazing fire made the farmhouse very warm. An old woman was bending over to peer into the open door of a baking oven set into the side of the fireplace. John could see several loaves of risen bread, their crust beginning to brown.

As he watched, the old woman closed the oven door, grasped a walking stick that leaned against the wall and shuffled to a rocking chair in one corner. She lowered herself heavily into the chair, wincing from the pain in her ancient joints, then picked up some sewing from the table beside her. In the opposite corner a younger woman sat at a wheel and spun yarn from a basket of wool on the floor. An infant slept in a cradle a foot or two away.

The women both wore long black dresses with high collars and tight cuffs. A flat white hat covered the younger woman's hair, and it was tied with string below her chin. The women's clothes were strangely familiar, as was the older woman's face. John knew he was looking at Rebecca Nurse. Her skin had a pale, sickly cast, and her cheeks and neck were folded into a maze of deep wrinkles. Age and hard living had made her fingers gnarled and crooked as sticks. They were deeply callused, her joints were swollen with arthritis, her fingernails broken. As he studied her, he realized he had misread the portrait that hung in his living room. For so many years he had judged her face to be cruel, but now he could see he'd been wrong. The face of the woman before him was hard, not because she was mean or indifferent but because her life had been incredibly difficult. She had endured a perilous sea voyage only to land on a savage coast where she and her fellow pilgrims had carved a life out of the wilderness.

Now as John looked at her he seemed to recall things he had read about Rebecca Nurse but paid little attention to. Founded fourteen years before her arrival, Salem had been little more than a small fort and collection of farms. She had married her husband, Francis, and then helped him scrape a farm out of the rocky soil. They had built this house, and for years she had cooked, sewed clothing, butchered animals, churned butter, and kneaded dough to feed a growing family.

She had borne eight children and nursed them and raised them. She had done the same with grandchildren. She had been a woman esteemed for her piety and sober judgment.

Now as he watched, apparently invisible to the two women, he heard a man's voice outside the house call out, "Becca." The voice trailed off but it carried a sharp note of alarm. Before either of the women could react a loud knock thundered on the door, and a group of armed men threw it open and crowded into the room. Behind the first group two other men looked on, helpless, held back by several other armed men.

The young woman at the wheel threw up her hands and screamed. She grabbed her baby from its crib and backed into the corner. The startled baby started to cry. Rebecca Nurse looked up her needlework, but she did not cower.

"What be the meaning of this, brother?" she demanded in a calm voice.

One of the armed men stepped forward, unrolled an official looking document and read. "Ye, Rebecca Nurse, be this day accused of practicing witchcraft and other deviltry. What say thee?"

She looked calmly at the man. "Edward Putnam," she said. "I have known thee for over fifty years. Thee hast seen me care for children and grandchildren. Thee hast seen me diligent and attentive on every Sabbath. I speak no ill of others and have worked no evil against any man or woman. Thou knowest me to be pious and true, so wherefrom doth this calumny spring?"

Unable to hold her stare Edward Putnam's eyes slid away. "Thou knowest what thou hast done, and thou shalt answer for it to the judges. Stand and surrender thyself and we will accompany thee to the meetinghouse."

"She is innocent!" one of the men cried from outside the house. John could see that the two men who were being restrained were probably in their fifties, and he imagined them to be Rebecca Nurse's sons or sons-in-law. The man who had cried out began to thrash violently, but his captors quickly wrestled him to the ground. Rebecca Nurse sat for another few seconds then struggled up out of her chair. She laid her sewing down on the table as if she expected to be returning for it shortly.

"Mother," the young woman said, tears streaming down her cheeks.

Rebecca Nurse reached for her walking stick then turned to the young woman. "Take thee the bread from the oven before it be burnt. See to supper. I shall return when my innocence be proved."

"Mother!" a man's voice called as an older man strode past the group of men gathered outside. He was an old man, probably Rebecca's husband, John thought, but he was vital and strong with big hands and muscles bunching like cords along his thick neck. His shirt was wet as if he had been doing some kind of strenuous work, and he carried an axe in one hand. He burst into the house before any of them could react.

"What is the meaning of this?" he cried when he saw men with drawn pistols and Edward Putnam with an unsheathed saber standing inside his threshold. The men nearest the door moved aside quickly and cast nervous glances at the axe.

Edward Putnam drew himself up. "Francis Nurse, we have been sent to arrest thy wife, Rebecca, under accusation of being a witch. We are ordered to bring her to the meeting-house to stand in judgment."

"Fie on thee. That is a black-faced lie."

John could see Francis's hand tighten on the axe handle, but Rebecca held up her hand. "Stay, husband. Let there be no wickedness in our home."

She turned and looked at the armed men who hovered uncomfortably, several with obviously shamefaced expressions. "As to this evil of which I am accused, I am as innocent as the child unborn. Surely, what sin hath God found in me unrepented of, that he should lay such an affliction upon me in my old age? I shall attest my innocence before the judges and the Eternal Father. Though I am fallen and as vile as any imperfect creature on this earth, I am no witch. God will prove the accusations mistaken."

"Mercy resteth in the hands of the judges," Edward Putnam said.

Rebecca bowed her head and appeared to say a silent prayer. The men shuffled their feet uneasily. After a moment, she raised her head and limped out the open door of the farm-house. She paused and laid her hand against her husband's cheek, then turned again and went out the door, moving slowly and with obvious pain in her joints. Even so she managed to maintain a mien of surprising dignity.

XII

JOHN WATCHED REBECCA DISAPPEAR FROM VIEW, and then he started to rise up toward the low rafters of the farmhouse, passing through the cramped upper floor and the roof. He was sure once again that he had not died because there seemed to be too much purpose to what he was experiencing. He also didn't think he was dreaming. It was more as if he was under the influence of some powerful hallucinogenic drug, but he hadn't taken any drugs. He'd fallen down some steps. He'd been injured. A wall had opened, and then the voices had come and grabbed him . . . and now he was here.

The voices were trying to show him something. But what and why? And whose voices were they? He also didn't think this was madness. In fact he felt quite the opposite, strangely more grounded than he had in years. His brain was coldly analytical and objective, ticking off lists of questions as he dug for the answers. He did not fight the experience, rather he focused on everything he could see, on memorizing every smell and sound, remembering every word.

He floated away from the farmhouse. It felt like a movie scene when the focus pulled back. He watched Rebecca as if from a great distance as she was led down a path that was little more than a pair of wagon ruts toward what looks like a small coastal village. As he watched the scene blurred once again and he realized the blurring had to represent the speeding up of time as whatever power had him in its grip moved him from moment to moment.

When images became clear once again and he started to descend, night had fallen. Below him a cluster of wooden buildings gleamed in the pale moonlight. Most had been built with rough-hewn logs, but he could also see a few newer looking buildings made of clapboard. The night was quiet, the silence interrupted only by the distant hooting of an owl. The people who occupied these buildings appeared to be indoors, and judging from the lack of light in the windows, asleep.

As John continued downward he was hungry for more details. He was now convinced that a story was being told, something was being revealed in this series of scenes, and the reporter in him was increasingly impatient to understand. He moved toward what appeared to be a house on the edge of the settlement. It was larger than the other homes, so he assumed whoever lived there was important or at least somewhat wealthier than his neighbors.

Just as at Rebecca Nurse's house he dropped through the roof, and then passed through a bedroom where a middle-aged woman slept alone on one side of a double bed. He came to a stop on the main floor of the house in a dimly lit parlor room. The only light came from a pair of candles on a round table in the center of the room. It appeared the candles had been burning for some time because large pools of wax had gathered on the table beneath them. Beside the candles lay a quill pen, but no accompanying bottle of ink. Heavy muslin drapes covered the room's three small windows and kept the light from leaking out.

Six men sat around the table, and flames from the fireplace threw their long wavering shadows into the corners. The air was close and stale, filled with smoke from the pipes two of the men smoked and from wisps that escaped from the fireplace. Right away John recognized Edward Putnam as well as several other men who had been in the party that arrested Rebecca Nurse.

The men were leaning on their forearms, their stomachs pressed against the table, and they spoke in conspiratorial whispers. At first, John could not make out their words. As he observed and tried to eavesdrop, Edward Putnam drew himself up so that he sat a little higher than the rest. The others noted this signal and immediately fell silent. As Putnam straightened in his chair, John noticed a large book in front of him that had been half-hidden between his arms. John continued to draw closer, an invisible presence in the room, and he watched Putnam open the book and remove a piece of parchment from its pages.

Putnam put on a pair of spectacles and prepared to read from the parchment. Before he did he looked slowly around the table, his steady gaze going from man to man, holding each of them for a few seconds as he appeared to search their faces for some sign of inner truth. Before he would move on to the next man, he gave each one a slight questioning nod then waited for the man to nod back. The first three men seemed resolute, however, when he came to the fourth, the man cast nervous glances at the men to either side and then cleared his throat.

"Do ye think we should reconsider?"

Edward Putnam's eyes grew hard. "We came to this wilderness to offer glory to God, but He hath given us drought and two bad harvests in a row. Our people are starving. Our animals grow sick. Your wife's milk dried up because she lacked sufficient nourishment, and ye lost a newborn last spring."

"Perhaps God tests us."

"Thinketh thee that ye can survive a third bad harvest?"

The man looked down at the table and after a second he shook his head. "No."

"Be ye with us?"

The man raised his eyes and nodded. "Yes," he said, his voice firm. Edward Putnam turned to the final man, who nodded without hesitation.

John's curiosity was on fire. It was obvious that Edward Putnam was making these men party to some kind of solemn covenant or pact. From the way they whispered and took pains to keep the light from leaking outside, this pact would be a closely held secret.

When Edward Putnam began to speak again, John felt a terrible chill run down his spine.

"Great Satan," Putnam began, speaking in solemn mono-tone that made the words somehow more terrible. "Hear us as your faithful servants, come before you. We six meeting on this sixth day of this sixth month, before the twenty-nine days of February, the month of death, hereby swear and attest that we shall sacrifice twenty-nine of our most God-fearing brethren in your name. According to thy will, we shall dutifully charge our children and our wives to aid us in carrying out these deeds in thy name. Our very courts and our pulpits will cast down God's own and judge them with utmost harshness and sentence them to hang. By so doing we acknowledge our imperfection and our error in worshipping Yahweh. Yahweh is not a generous God, but we know Satan is. We ask in return that ye shall grant us the bounties due to your most humble servants. Grant us respite in this God-forsaken place, Great Satan, so that seeing our obedience ye will make us fruitful once again and provide to us relief, suc-cor health, and a bounteous harvest."

John understood the enormity of what he was hearing: devil worship in the earliest days of the Salem settlement. Edward Putnam and these other men had falsely accused his own blood ancestor, Rebecca Nurse, of witchcraft, while they themselves had been the ones guilty of blasphemy and the practice of the dark arts. The question that came to him next was what was he supposed to do with this information. The crime had taken place hundreds of years earlier. People might care about the truth but only insofar as it affected their Halloween fantasies. Knowing that the Salem judges had framed and hanged an innocent woman would have no real impact three hundred years later.

Edward Putnam was not finished. He spread the parchment out on the table then reached down and drew a knife from a sheath on his belt. With his arm resting on the table, he unbuttoned the cuff of his shirt and rolled back the cuff to expose a muscular, hairy forearm. At a point about half-way between wrist and elbow he pressed the knife against his flesh until a small cut opened.

Allowing the blood to well to the surface, Putnam picked up the pen and ran the nib into the cut he had made. When it had collected enough blood, he used his bleeding arm to hold down the parchment and signed his name beneath the covenant he had read aloud just a moment earlier. Afterward, he handed the knife to the man on his right and the process repeated until each man had signed his name in his own blood at the bottom of the parchment.

John's attention had been so taken up watching the scene he reacted with alarm when he felt something touch his arm. Until that moment he had been able to smell, hear, and see, but he had pictured himself as being as insubstantial as a ghost, a sort of secret eavesdropper on the past. His head whipped around and saw the same ghostly presence he had seen in his office and in the library of his house. There was no mistaking Rebecca Nurse, however he realized that every characteristic he ever attributed to her from the old portrait in his living room had been wrong. He felt gentleness and compassion radiating from her, also wisdom and a capacity for endurance learned through long suffering.

"Why am I here?" he asked her. The words were spoken without sound, more as if he was communicating with his thoughts.

Instead of answering she took his arm and pulled him gently down toward the parchment on which the six blood signatures were drying. Still gripping his arm, she raised it and held it beside the candle flame. She was looking at him, and her eyes seemed full of sorrow, as if she was offering silent apology for what she was about to do. Strangely, while he sensed something important was about to happen, he felt no fear.

In the next instant he felt a blinding pain as she moved his arm until the tender flesh of his inner forearm brushed the tip of the candle flame. He gritted his teeth and rolled his eyes, but instead of fighting her and snatching his arm away, he submitted and let her run the flame up and down his arm until it felt as if his flesh had to be burning off.

Just when he thought he could not bear the pain for another second, she pulled his arm away from the flame and lowered it toward the parchment. With the same gentleness she had used to hold his arm over the flame, she pressed the burned flesh against the parchment, right on top of the blood signatures, and she rolled it slowly back and forth. For John the pain was truly unbearable, a sensation of burning far worse than the candle flame, as if the bloody letters were eating into his flesh, but still he allowed her to press his arm down and roll it back and forth.

The pain seemed to fill every atom of his being, but even as it did, he was moving again. He seemed to be hurtling at a breakneck pace back through all the scenes he had witnessed and then back up the dark stone passage and out into the October afternoon. He found himself suddenly back in his own body, the pain wracking every cell of his body as he struggled with the last ounces of his strength up the steps and out into the grass behind the mausoleum. The pain of the present and past seemed to merge inside him, and he fell to his knees and felt himself plunge toward blessed darkness.

CHAPTER TWO

October 19

THE NEXT THING JOHN REGISTERED WAS BRIGHT
light burning through his closed eyes like morning sunlight
coming through a closed shade. A second later the pain
slammed him. He arched his back against it, but his arms
and legs seemed to resist his attempts to move. He heard a
groan escape his parched lips.

"Thank God," he heard a voice say. "I think he's waking
up."

His eyelids seemed to be crusted shut. It took a moment
to open them and focus. In the first seconds he thought the
woman looking down at him was Julie. He tried to raise
his hand toward her face, but again he could not move. The
woman reached for him, gently touching his shoulder.

"Dad, be careful. You've pulled out your IVs once already."
It was Sarah's voice, his daughter, not Julie. "They've got you

restrained," she went on. "Just relax."

John blinked his eyes and rolled his head slightly. His neck felt like a broken hinge that had rusted shut. When he touched his tongue to his lips they were as dry as sandpaper.

"Where?" he managed.

"Salem Hospital," Sarah said.

He blinked again, and this time his eyes began to really focus. He could see Sarah dressed in sweat pants and a purple sweatshirt. Her hair was a mess.

"How long?"

"They brought you in yesterday afternoon. You've been unconscious ever since."

He closed his eyes briefly against the pain, then opened them again. A nurse put her head into the room, backed out, and returned a moment later with a doctor in a white coat. When the doctor stepped close, John recognized him and felt relieved. Sam Huddleston was tall, with a hatchet face, a full head of wavy brown hair, and an athlete's trim physique. A neurosurgeon and good friend, Sam sported a perpetual tan, even in New England winters. Given the way John felt, having his friend there was a big reassurance.

The nurse came over and put something on John's lips to moisten them before she held a glass filled with ice water and let him take a few sips through a straw. Sam Huddleston checked John's vital signs, spent a good bit of time examining his eyes, held up three fingers, and asked John to tell him how many he saw.

"Three. You think I forgot how to count?"

"I'm not sure if most reporters ever learned to count," Huddleston shot back. "Listen to the following words: yellow, ten, Tuesday, light. Keep them in your mind. I'll want you to repeat them to me when I ask you to in a moment, but first I'm going to ask you some other cognitive questions to test your memory."

"Yellow, ten, Tuesday, and light," John said. His voice was growing stronger, and the act of speaking was making him feel more alert.

"I didn't ask you yet. When was Sarah born?"

"December 4, 1981."

"What was your last column about in your paper?"

"People not cleaning up their dog poop in Salem Common. It'll probably win a Pulitzer."

"Repeat the string of words I just gave you."

John repeated, "Yellow, ten, Tuesday, light."

"What month did you lose Julie?"

"October, my favorite month," he said with a sardonic grin.

"What's your social security number?"

"012-28-1376. Do I pass?"

"What time did you go to the cemetery on Monday, and what did you have for dinner Sunday night?"

"I went to the cemetery after lunch on Monday. I don't know the exact time. And, for dinner on Sunday I heated up some pizza I'd picked up on the way home on Friday."

Sam looked down at him, seeming to think about whether he needed to do more checks.

"Hey," John said. "I think my brain's working as well as it ever does."

Sam smiled. "Anybody who's played as much hockey and gotten smashed into the boards as many times as you has got a soft head. Since you started out soft in the head, I can't be too careful."

"I'm going to call my lawyer. I think I've just been insulted."

Sam laughed, but then his expression became serious. "Do you have any recollection of what happened?"

"I fell down a long flight of steps."

Sam squinted at him. "Why do you think that?"

"Because that's what happened. I remember falling."

"How did it happen?"

John closed his eyes and pretended to think back. He remembered exactly what happened, but he wasn't going to tell his friend about seeing the pentagram or hearing the voices or the secret door or how he'd had some sort of astral experience where he'd been taken into the past by a ghost. If he said any of that Sam would probably stick him in a straightjacket and shoot him full of Thorazine.

He took a deep breath and let it out slowly. "Monday was the anniversary of Julie's death. Every year I go to the cemetery and put flowers on her grave, but every year . . . well it never gets easier. Before I went I had a long, liquid lunch with Richard to fortify myself."

Sam's face showed a flash of sadness. "That's not all you had. The ambulance guys found a mostly empty pint in your back pocket."

John felt his cheeks color and looked out the window, unable to hold his friend's gaze.

"Do you remember the particular steps you fell down?"

John nodded. "The ones at the back of the Putnam mausoleum."

Sam nodded. "I guess that makes sense. According the ambulance attendants you were found lying in the middle of the Putnam section of the cemetery."

"What were you doing in that part of the cemetery?" Sarah broke in.

He felt a twinge of guilt that he had to lie to his daughter. "I was just walking around, trying to summon the fortitude to go to your mother's grave."

"I should have gone with you."

"It's not your fault, kiddo."

Sarah's lip started to quiver, "Daddy, you had us all so frightened. I was afraid I might lose you." A tear broke from the corner of her eye and ran down her cheek. She didn't bother to wipe it away.

"Who found me?"

"A woman. She was there putting flowers on a grave and spotted you lying on the grass on her way out. It was starting to get dark, and the cemetery was about to close. If she hadn't seen you, you might have been out there all night."

He closed his eyes, recalling the woman in the red jacket he had seen. Then he tried to move his arm. "Why the hell am I tied down?"

"You weren't conscious, but you were thrashing around

pretty good," Sam said. "You ripped out your IVs. Can we trust you to behave now?" He reached over and unhooked the straps that held John's arms to the side of the bed, then did the same with the straps around his legs.

John hoped he hadn't also been shouting things about the crazy out-of-body experience he'd had at the cemetery, but even if he had he could explain it away as a concussion-induced dream. He knew that might be exactly what it had been, but he needed to go back to the Putnam mausoleum and see if that hidden door was really there. The rational side of his brain scoffed, telling him all he'd find would be a rusting metal door and cobwebs. The likelihood that the rational side was right frightened him most. It meant he was having some kind of serious mental breakdown.

That possibility brought a bolt of real fear. Maybe his emotional isolation, his failure to move beyond grieving for Julie's death and his drinking, combined with a concussion had really driven him over some edge. If that was really the case what was he going to do about it? Who was he going to tell? He shook his head and wished he had a bottle of scotch beside the bed.

"I asked, how are you feeling?"

John blinked. He'd been so taken up with his private thoughts he hadn't been listening.

"Sorry, Sam. I was just lost in thought for a second. I feel exactly like I fell down a set of cement steps. My head, my neck, my shoulder, arms, and hips, all of it hurts like hell."

"I want to watch you for just a little bit longer and make

sure you're okay neurologically. You seem fine at this point, but we need to be sure. Once we are, we can start you on some pain meds. Until then you'll have a bit of discomfort."

"You call this discomfort? What do you call natural childbirth, moderately unpleasant?"

Sam walked to the foot of the bed and made some notations on his iPad. "Sarah, I think your father is starting to recover. His sarcasm has reemerged."

He glanced toward John. "You weren't in very good shape when they brought you in, my friend. You'd lost quite a bit of blood, and you were out cold for more than twenty-four hours, which is serious. Your vitals were fine, but as in any case like this we worried about brain swelling, heart attack, or stroke. I sedated you to control your vitals and prevent swelling in the lining of your brain. Your blood pressure and pulse skyrocketed in the middle of the night and then again early this morning. That's when you tore out your IVs. We assumed it might have been because you were reliving some sort of trauma. The imaging showed you sustained a reasonably severe concussion. Give us a little more time to check out everything else. I'll get the nurse to bring you something for the pain."

"That would be great, Sam."

"Look, one more thing. You're not exactly the most obedient and reasonable patient I've ever treated. You need to go easy on yourself with this. I know you've had concussions on the ice, and you might already know what I'm talking about. But even so, realize that you might start feeling good and then feel worse after a few weeks. Teddy Johnson of the Patriots got a Grade 2 concussion and played out the season. The next season he could barely get out of bed, and those symptoms lasted for six months. Head injuries are quirky. You might be moody or angry for no apparent reason. Whatever it might be, give yourself a break."

"Why are you telling me this?"

"Because you *really* got whacked."

Sam turned and started to walk out of the room, but when he got to the door he stopped again and turned around. "Listen, I know the anniversary is a tough day for you, but as your friend and your doctor, I'm going to ask you to watch the drinking. You almost got locked into Harmony Grove overnight. This whole thing could have been a whole lot worse. And by the way a police report's been filed. It's standard operating procedure when someone is found unconscious under suspicious circumstances. So don't be surprised if the cops come to question you."

John shook his head, burning with embarrassment to be talked to this way in front of Sarah, but he also knew it was exactly what Sam was trying to do. "I guess I didn't realize how sloppy I was."

"You were sloppy. Your blood alcohol was way over the limit. Damn lucky you weren't driving. The booze isn't helping, John."

"Yes, daddy."

"I'm serious."

"I know."

11

An hour later the nurse had checked him twice more and finally given him a couple of Percocets. John felt them going to work almost at once, easing the pain that seemed to reside in every single part of his body. Sarah had remained there, and he could tell from her serious expression that she was trying to work herself up to have a "talk" about his drinking. It was a conversation he was eager to avoid. Sarah had inherited a need to impose order on her family and environment from Julie. While John had embraced Julie's ability to help control his own chaotic tendencies, he found the same character trait oppressive in his daughter.

"You might as well head out," he told her. "I'm sure you have plenty of things that need doing."

She gave him a tight smile. "I don't mind staying."

"I'm just going to lie here and sleep. I'll feel less guilty if I'm not being watched over."

She sighed. "You sure?"

"Positive.

She gave him a look, pressed her lips together, but finally relented. "Anything you want me to ask the nurses on my way out?" she asked as she gathered her things.

"Yeah, how much longer do I have to stay here?"

"Sam said that if they don't see anything bad like brain swelling, they'll let you go in a day or two."

John let out a sigh. "Thank heavens. I hate hospitals."

Sarah gave him a wry smile. John knew they were both thinking about the night Julie had been killed. He had come to this same hospital to identify her body.

"Well, don't let me keep you. I know you've probably got an incredibly busy day tomorrow. Morning broadcast, right?"

She nodded as she bent over to kiss his forehead. "Got to get my beauty sleep, right?"

John smiled. He knew the game, having spent twenty years on the television news fast track. His last TV job, the one that had burned him out, had been as ABC's Washington correspondent. He didn't miss it, but he was glad he had done it. And he was proud as hell of Sarah who had chosen to follow in his footsteps.

He watched her straighten up. Sometimes in a certain light she looked so much like her mother it almost took his breath away. He looked at her for a long second, thinking of Julie and suddenly fearing something might happen to Sarah just the way it had to Julie, something random, completely out of the blue. It had almost killed him the first time, and he didn't think he could take it if it ever happened again.

Sarah was looking down at him, and suddenly her eyes tightened. "You okay, Dad?"

"Yeah, other than the fact that every single atom in my

body hurts. Why?"

She shook her head. "It's weird. Please don't take this the wrong way, but you look spooked. The only other time I've ever seen you look like this was the night after you reported from the Pentagon on 9/11. You remember that?"

She had caught him by surprise. He wanted to deflect he comment, but he could only nod. "Yeah."

"The day that plane crashed into the Pentagon I'll never forget it."

"I'm not sure what you're getting at."

"When you were reporting," she stopped, looked up at the ceiling and blinked back tears. "God, I can see it like it's yesterday. You were right there in Camera Row with the other reporters, but when that American Airline's plane started coming toward the building and other people started running you just stood there and reported. Your cameraman was shaking so badly he could barely aim the camera, but you sounded like you were doing a regular evening broadcast. And then after the plane hit, you just turned back toward the camera and said in this super calm voice, 'The Pentagon has been attacked by a civilian jet. Reporting live from the Pentagon, I'm John Andrews. Please excuse me, I need to go.'"

John winced. Talking about those moments was something he had studiously avoided ever since that terrible day. "Why are you bringing this up?"

Sarah balled her fists. "Because we *never* talk about things like this. You keep everything locked up inside. I know you suffer and hurt every single day because you miss Mom so much, but that's not how I'm built, and I can't do that, right now especially. I just spent the last twenty-four hours thinking that you might die, and now I need to talk, so just shut up and listen to me.

"We never talk about the fact that what you did next is still seared into my brain. Instead of running away like any normal person, you dropped your microphone and then ran right toward the fire."

John shook his head. He didn't want to talk about it, and he had successfully refused to speak of it with anyone for all these years. For months afterward people had wanted to interview him or write articles about him, but he had steadfastly refused. He remembered the destruction and the terrible heat, the absolute unreality of the moment, and his compulsion to try and help. He found a wounded officer stumbling half blind through a hole the plane had punched in the wall, and he helped drag him to safety. He tried to go back for others but by that time firemen were there with oxygen and fire suits, and they pulled him away. Still, there was no way he would ever forget the smell of burning jet fuel and the smell of roasting flesh.

"Please don't," he said. "Let it stay in the past."

Sarah shook her head. "I would but there's something else. I'm bringing it up for a reason. It was the way you were afterward. You were different, like you'd seen something too horrible to discuss. I understood, and so did Mom. We didn't try to talk to you about it, and we understood why you didn't go on *60 Minutes* or any of the other shows to talk about what you'd done. I get all that, and I'm sorry to bring it up now, but I have to tell you something."

John knew what was coming next, and he looked away from her.

"You're acting the same now." Sarah paused, maybe waiting for him to react or maybe searching for words. "I know you've got a concussion, and you're all banged up. I also know you've been drinking too much, but that's not it. I think something happened to you that's got you really, really shaken up." She paused again. He still didn't speak. "I don't think you told Sam the truth about what happened in the cemetery. Maybe . . . maybe you really don't know yourself because your memory is screwed up, but *something* happened. You saw something or something happened to you. I know it's your instinct to keep it buttoned up like a good New Englander, but I wish you'd let me in. Please?"

John forced himself to look at his daughter. He felt his guts twist, partly out of love that she was reaching out to him like this, but also partly out of sadness that he could not reciprocate. How could he tell anyone what was happening to him? How would he react if Sam or some other friend of his told him about voices, a secret door, and a ghost who had taken him on a tour of the past?

"Kiddo, I've just gone through a fall that kicked the crap out of me, and I'm probably having the typical reactions Sam talked about. I really appreciate your concern, and if I can dredge up anything I need to share, I'll tell you."

Her lips twisted as she studied him. "Promise?"

"I promise," he said, feeling the knife twist again.

She leaned over and kissed his forehead once more.

"Feel better. I'll stop in tomorrow afternoon when I finish at the studio."

When she left his room, he lay back against the pillow and closed his eyes, hoping sleep would come. The Percocet was working its magic. The pain in his neck, joints, and bones had receded to acceptable levels, and he felt a pleasant drowsiness taking hold of him.

He was thinking that perhaps tomorrow he would get Amy to bring his laptop to the hospital, and he would begin the process of searching for a good therapist, someone to whom he could confide the strange things that had happened to him. He was actually feeling comforted by Sam's explanation of the mental strangeness that could accompany a concussion. Perhaps his mind, lubricated by alcohol and overwrought by the prospect of visiting Julie's grave, had written its own story to fill in the blank spot created by his fall. Perhaps he wasn't going crazy, after all.

He smiled to himself. That explanation *did* seem a great deal more scientific than the alternative. He lifted his left arm off the sheets, thinking now that his pain had subsided he would reach for the ice water in the plastic cup on the bedside table and have another sip before he dozed off. What he saw made his momentary comfort vanish and his teeth clench in horror. Without realizing he started to hyperventilate and felt his blood pressure begin to spike.

He struggled to calm his breathing and reduce his racing

pulse, afraid the monitor attached to his finger would set off an alarm and bring nurses and doctors sprinting to his bedside. He felt sweat break out along his hairline and cold lines of perspiration run from his armpits down the sides of his body.

Little by little he managed to bring himself under control, but his eyes remained riveted on the inside of his left forearm and the dark purple scrawling or scarring or whatever the hell it was that showed like some lurid tribal marking or burn mark or bruise. Only, despite his futile attempts to question what he was seeing, he knew *exactly* what it was. After a few more seconds he closed his eyes and relented as his memory ran back to the moment when the spirit of Rebecca Nurse had taken his arm, heated it over the candle flame then rolled his blistered flesh across the bloody signatures.

When he opened his eyes again, the signatures were still there. He touched the discolored flesh with the fingers of his other hand. Strangely he felt no pain. Whatever the hell had put the letters there, he felt no sensitivity and no scarring.

Then he thought of one other thing, and he didn't know which one frightened him more. A few minutes earlier Sam and the nurse had checked him over carefully. The nurse had adjusted the small monitor on the end of the third finger on his left hand, and she had rolled his arm over to do it. She hadn't noticed a thing, nor had Sam, nor had Sarah. There was only one possible conclusion: the letters were just figments of his imagination. That meant it hadn't just been the booze and the fall and the concussion. He was going crazy.

Thankfully, in spite of his mental turmoil, he finally found the pull of the Percocet too difficult to resist, and he closed his eyes and dropped into a fitful sleep. Even in sleep, however, Rebecca Nurse continued to occupy his thoughts. She appeared in his dream, and he was convinced she was struggling to warn him about something with her eyes, which were hooded and full of foreboding. She was telling him he was in danger, but try as he might he could not understand anything more specific.

III

ABIGAIL PUTNAM ENTERED THE ROOM AND went to the last empty chair at the table. She seated herself without ceremony and flashed a scowl around at the five others who had arrived before her. She had kept them waiting for twenty minutes to help make her point. She was furious, and she wanted to them to know it and worry.

Abigail was sixty-two years old, short, and heavyset, but her size did not suggest fat as much as power. In spite of stumpy legs and wide hips she moved with the speed and determination of a much younger woman. Though it was shot through with gray, she wore her hair long, bound in a simple ponytail that hung down her back in the style of a much younger woman. Her face was round, her cheekbones pronounced in a way that might have made her look jolly except for the bottomless pools of her dark eyes. They were emotionless, lacking any vestige of empathy or compassion. When she was angry, as she was at this moment, they seemed to swirl with caustic energy and reminded people of the implacable will that made most of them unwilling to cross her.

The man to her immediate left, Senator Austin Hallowell,

was in his mid-fifties, tall, and elegantly dressed in a charcoal pinstripe suit, with gray hair combed straight back from a high, narrow forehead, an aquiline nose perched above a precise mouth.

The woman to the senator's left, Amanda Putnam Pendergast, had icy blue eyes and blond hair just starting to go gray. She might have passed for forty-five except for the wrinkled skin and blue veins on the back of her hands, well camouflaged by eye-catching diamond and sapphire rings, and the tight skin around the corners of her eyes and mouth that might have been burn scars but were the telltale signs of significant plastic surgery. In reality Amanda's age was north of sixty-five, but even though others might suspect it, only her most intimate confederates, including the people around this table, knew it for sure.

On her other side sat Cabot Childress Putnam, VI, a large man whose name implied pedigree beyond words, but whose oversized head and massive body implied even more strongly an ex-college football jock. "Cabby's" short hair, cut down to little more than stubble gave his thick features an aura of truculence, which helped to intimidate anyone who might guess him to be effete because of his name, or the criminals he ran into daily in his work as a Salem police detective. His beefy shoulders and biceps bulged the arms of his suit coat, but the beginning of a gut pushed his tie outward and testified to the onset of middle age.

The fifth man, the Very Reverend Staunton Winthrop, was thin with wispy flyaway hair that always looked like it had just been tangled by a windstorm. His suit coat hung loose from bony shoulders, and a prominent Adam's apple bobbed in his skinny neck above an ecclesiastical collar worn about two sizes too large. The man's hollow cheeks and the yellowish tint of his skin testified to the chemo treatments he was undergoing and the cancer that continued to eat his insides, in spite of the prayers of his parishioners and the best efforts of his doctors.

She sat silent for several long seconds, allowing the tension level to rise around the table. "You," she said at last, taking in all five of the people in a sweeping glance, "have made a serious mistake. This girl is not some homeless waif. She's a high school student from Beverly. An honor student at a Catholic girl's school, for Pete's sake. Her disappearance is in all the papers. What the hell were you thinking?"

Cabby Putnam cleared his throat. "We caught sight of her when she got off the train. You've seen the clothes she was wearing. She looked like another runaway: worn out shoes, torn clothes, no sense of style in any of it, just ragged."

Abigail turned and burned him with her eyes. "Are you telling me that there's a uniform for homeless kids? Some way to unfailingly recognize them?"

"No," he stammered. "I'm just saying—"

"How much did she spend in the shop?"

Amanda Putnam Pendergast said, "Thirty-five dollars."

"Does that sound like a homeless kid to any of the rest of you? Anybody think a lot of homeless kids spend that kind of money getting ready for Halloween?"

The others looked down and studied their hands. No one would meet her eyes.

"We've been operating for over three hundred years, and in all that time hardly anyone has noticed the people we take. We've been careful. We've had a few close calls, but we've hardly ever made mistakes like this. And that's not even the worst part."

She paused, looked around the table, and waited until she was sure she had everyone's absolute attention. "John Andrews is becoming *aware*. His astral signature was so powerful he was glowing like a beacon when he walked past my shop the other day. I couldn't miss him."

Everyone froze and stared at her. "How is that possible?" Senator Hallowell asked after a few seconds. "We were told he's an alcoholic. Alcoholics don't have the sensitivity to become aware."

"I think he's a man who drinks to dull his grief, but I think he also possesses a profound sensitivity."

Amanda Putnam Pendergast cleared her throat. "Is someone trying to contact him?"

Abigail looked down at the table and shook her head. "*Of course!* He is descended from Rebecca, and she is *always* trying."

"Don't forget that he is also descended from Anne Putnam," Senator Hallowell added.

Abigail looked at him, wondering how it was that the coven had operated successfully for over three hundred years with such nitwits as judges. "Thank you for that insightful comment, Austin," she said. "Do you think we would care in the slightest if Rebecca Nurse contacted John Andrews if he was not also descended from our bloodline? In combination with Rebecca, this man can *penetrate* us," she said, belaboring the obvious.

Reverend Winthrop started to shake his head. "I don't agree. His drinking should have insulated him from spiritual contact. His sensitivities are just too dulled."

"We can't afford to take the chance that you're right," Cabby Corwin shot back. His small, piggish eyes were half-closed as he looked at the reverend.

The reverend's lips tightened, but he said nothing. Senator Hallowell asked, "Is Andrews starting to make trouble in other ways?"

"He's started looking into Melissa Blake, for starters. I'm told he noticed the disappearances and suspects a bigger problem. He wants to do a series of articles on them."

Her eyes continued to pan over each of the people. "We have talked about John Andrews in the past. We have always known the danger he represents."

Reverend Winthrop cleared his throat. "There were two previous occasions when he began to develop *awareness*. On each occasion we attempted to deal with the problem."

"And failed," Abigail snapped.

"Failed to achieve a permanent solution."

Amanda Putnam Pendergast shook her head, her voice becoming shrill with anxiety. "Why have we waited this long? Anyone related by blood to our coven and *her* is a risk.

If they become *aware* they could be a terrible danger!"

"True," said Senator Hallowell. "But most of them never actually become *aware*, and therefore they don't threaten us."

"You know our policy, Amanda," Abigail said. "We monitor the people who have the bloodline, but we don't actually kill them unless they become *aware*."

"Well, maybe we should start."

"We have determined that the risks would be far greater that way," Cabby said.

"And why is that again?" Amanda demanded, her eyes going wide with anger.

"Because killing people draws unwonted attention," Abigail snapped, her eyes going to Cabby. "Just the same as kidnapping the wrong people."

Cabby's cheeks colored, but he said nothing.

"Is it possible *she* knows of our plan?" asked Reverend Winthrop. "And if she does, has she found a way to break through and speak with Andrews?"

"I go back to my original question," the senator said. "Why Andrews? Why him?"

Abigail sighed. "He's a journalist. It's his nature to dig. I hate to say it, but he's also courageous. He's the one who ran into the burning Pentagon right after the terrorists crashed the plane on 9/11."

"So, you've answered the question," Amanda insisted. "He's a courageous researcher who won't stop going after the truth. If Rebecca Nurse was going to try and contact any particular person in this bloodline, it would be him. He's a problem. We need to take care of the problem."

"As I already mentioned, we tried twice," Reverend Winthrop said. "Don't you remember? In spite of looking much younger, you've been a judge almost as long as I."

Amanda nodded. "The fire, and somehow he got out of it. Then that car accident four years ago. We thought he was the one driving."

"How were we to know he would send his wife at the last moment?" Cabby Corwin demanded.

"Simple," Reverend Winthrop shot back. "Someone should have watched his house."

"I can't assign officers to watch somebody's house without a paper trail, especially when it's the executive editor of the damn newspaper. I have to have grounds for suspicion. Otherwise word will get out, and people will start to talk, and then some smart guy will start to make inferences. John Andrews isn't the only smart guy out there."

"No, but he may be the only smart guy who's related to one of the judges *and* Rebecca Nurse *and* who is becoming *aware.*" She glared at Cabby. "Think about that, *Lieutenant,* and tell me what you intend to do about it."

THREE

October 20

THE NEXT MORNING, AFTER A TEAM OF DOCTORS and nurses, including Sam, came in to check his cognitive memory function and vision, he was given a CAT scan to look for any evidence of brain swelling. The whole time they were checking him, John kept hoping one of them would notice the strange brownish swirls on his left forearm. He glanced down at his arm several times, but he saw nothing. The letters seemed to have disappeared. When all the tests came back negative, the nurses moved him from ICU to a private room on one of the post surgical floors. Shortly after the nurses got him settled, made him walk to the bathroom and back, then reattached to his monitors, Sam came into the room.

"When am I getting out of here?" John asked.

"I want you here one more night," Sam told him.

"Why?"

"Whether you want to admit it or not, this fall has set you back a bit. I can see it in your eyes."

John felt a surprising flash of anger. "Why don't you try diving down a steep set of cement stairs and see if doesn't screw up your day a bit?"

Sam tipped his head and gave John a look. "Listen to yourself, my friend. That's the concussion talking. Give yourself a day or two of rest. Trust me on this. You need it."

John looked at Sam. There were so many things he wanted to say—that he needed to get the hell out of there to start figuring out whether he was going insane or whether, as outlandish as it sounded, Rebecca Nurse was real and was trying to warn him about something—but he didn't dare say it to any of them. In the end he just nodded and grumbled, "Okay."

"I've got rounds to finish. I'll check in later."

Sam went out, and a minute or two later Richard Harvey breezed into the room holding a bunch of newspapers and magazines and a small wrapped package that looked like a book. He stopped and looked at John and shook his head very slowly.

"Looks like you beat yourself with the ugly stick," he said. "Did you break the stick?"

"Your college humor never ceases to amaze me."

"I can do even better if you challenge me."

"Please don't."

"So, what the hell happened to you? The rumor mill says you got mugged."

John shrugged. "Nothing so dramatic. I fell down a set of cement steps."

"In the cemetery?"

"By the Putnam mausoleum."

"What were you doing there?"

"Just wandering around."

"Bad idea, wandering around in cemeteries."

"Yeah." John regarded his friend. Rich was a professor of theology. Maybe he would listen to what John had to tell him and somehow reserve judgment.

"Hey, let me ask you a question," he said. "In your studies have you ever run across rites where people sign their names in blood?"

Rich smirked. "Does this have something to do with your current condition?"

John shot an involuntary glance at his forearm where the letters remained invisible. He realized they might have been a product of his imagination the night before and might never appear again. "No . . . I was just curious. Something I read."

"Blood signatures were usually used in occult ceremonies," Rich said.

"Occult?"

"Witchcraft or devil worship, that kind of thing."

"Is witchcraft different from devil worship?"

"Today? Completely. Wicca, the term used today to describe those who believe in magic and witchcraft, is what we would call a modern pagan religion. Wiccans don't subscribe to any particular theology or religious cannon, but many of them tend to venerate both a god and a Triple Goddess. They—"

"Sorry to interrupt, but was there a point in the past when witchcraft and devil worship were the same?"

Rich screwed up his face in a look of suspicion. "You should know the answer to your question, old boy. You are a direct descendant of a woman who was hanged for just such a crime."

"I *know* that, but I'm asking because I never understood the actual supposed mechanics."

"Uh-huh. Have you been having weird visions or something? It's typical of people who have had their brains mashed, they tell me."

"I haven't had my brains mashed," John said with a touch of anger. "I just wanted the answer to a simple question."

Rich looked at him as if he was humoring someone whose mental stability might best be described as delicate. "Well, the belief at the time, back in the mid-1600s was that witchcraft and devil worship were basically the same thing. But it's rather difficult to speak factually because the people doing the accusing were themselves religious hysterics, and were usually either dunking the accused in a pond using what might be called an old-fashioned version of water-boarding or crushing them under a load of rocks. The accused for their part usually tried to hold out and deny everything, because to admit to witchcraft meant they were going to be hanged or burned at the stake. Unless, of course, they were mad as hatters, in which case they often gave the accusers vivid descriptions of their supposed occult rites. Does that answer your question?"

"No, you didn't talk about using human blood to sign covenants."

With a quick headshake Rich said, "Covenants of that type were rumored, but I don't believe any were ever actually discovered because I'm not sure any actually existed."

"Thank you."

"You're welcome." Rich stood up and laid the magazines on the mattress where John could easily reach them. "I've got to get back and prepare for my next class. Rest well."

John glanced down at his arm and his unmarked white skin. "Thanks for the reading material and for what looks like a book."

"Something cheery to distract you from thinking about blood signatures. You know, it worries me that all this blood and witchcraft stuff may be a line of thinking produced by the medical care you're receiving here. Remind me to keep my sorry ass out of this particular hospital when I get sick."

IV

JOHN DOZED FOR TWENTY OR THIRTY MINUTES before he was awakened by the sound of his door latch. He cracked his eyes to see Amy Johnson peeking around the door, gazing at him with a worried expression. Seeing her, he opened them all the way.

"Hi," he said.

"I didn't mean to wake you."

"You didn't. Come in."

She opened the door the rest of the way then turned back to pick up two heavy canvas bags that she lugged into the room and put down next to his bed. "I heard what happened," she said in a rush. "I feel so bad. Are you okay?"

"They tell me I'm going to live," he said, trying to sound tougher than he felt.

He pointed to a chair beside the bed. "Please have a seat."

As Amy turned and pulled the chair toward the bed, John couldn't keep his eyes from running up her slender legs and noticing the way her knit dress molded to her thighs and rear. It wasn't the first time he had reacted to her this way, but he always felt a twinge of guilt, as if he was being unfaithful to Julie, even though part of him knew that was ridiculous.

What he knew wasn't ridiculous was the fact he was nearly eighteen years her senior. He was a geezer. Amy was only eight years older than Sarah.

She sat down, flashing a quick peek of a very fit thigh before tucking her skirt demurely. "I brought a bunch of stuff from the office in case you felt well enough to tackle some work," she said.

"The laptop is great," he said, bunching his pillow and sitting a little higher in the bed. "I have an editorial to work on. Maybe I'll write one about the dangerous cement steps at Harmony Grove Cemetery. I think they're trying to snare unsuspecting members of the living public."

Amy gave him a bright smile. He liked the way she seemed to appreciate his sense of humor.

"So what happened?"

"I really did fall down a set of stone steps."

She studied him, and he could see something unspoken going on behind her eyes.

He shrugged. "People fall," he said.

She nodded, still not saying anything.

"What?" he asked.

"Don't take this the wrong way," she said, "but you look like something worse happened. I don't mean you're not banged up pretty well. But it's your eyes, like you're brooding about something."

"My daughter said the same thing."

Amy just shrugged. "There you go."

"What if I told you I was thinking about quitting the paper?"

She blinked as if she was sure she hadn't heard him correctly. "I beg your pardon?"

"You heard me. I may need to take a leave of absence, or maybe even resign." He took a breath and let it out. A voice in his head was telling him not to lie to this woman. *Lie to everyone else*, it said, *but not to her.*

"What's happening, John?"

"I think my gears are slipping."

"That's a macho term for the fact that you think you're losing it?"

He tried for a smile but felt it slip almost right away. "Something like that."

"What really happened?"

"I—" he stopped when he felt something pulse in his left forearm. It was lying loosely in his lap, and he rolled it slightly, shocked to see the dark reddish brown writing was once again unmistakable.

"John? Everything okay?"

He tore his eyes from his arm. "Sorry, I lost my train of thought."

His mind was racing. Why were these weird letters suddenly visible again? Were they visible to anyone else? If he showed his arm to Amy would she even react? If she did, what then? If he was honest with himself, he sensed Amy had a crush on him and had for a long time. He passed it off as over-idealization on her part because of his television correspondent past and because he was her boss. What he saw as her vulnerability was probably why he had always been a little bit formal and distant around her, even when his own loneliness might have made him weaken. He believed that any relationship between them would be doomed from the start because of the difference in their ages and because he was her boss. If things didn't work out it would be likely to hurt her deeply, and he cared about her enough that he never wanted to risk it.

In spite of all those oft-repeated cautions, another thought pulsed in his brain. Precisely because Amy cared for him and respected him the way she did, she might be the only person who could listen to the true version of what happened and find a way to consider it something other than the ravings of a disturbed mind. He thought that when it came down to it, Amy would be likely to give him the benefit of the doubt even more than Sarah would.

Making his decision, he slowly rolled his arm so she could see it, then he waited.

It took only a second. Amy glanced down and gasped. "What is that?"

He struggled to contain his surge of nearly pathetic gratitude. Until she'd seen the writing on his forearm he had not admitted to himself how much he feared she wouldn't.

"Thank heavens you can see it," he whispered. "I was afraid I was going mad."

"What are you talking about? I can see it plain as day."

He nodded.

"Is that what happened to you when you fell?"

"I think so."

She stood up, came over to the bed and reached for his

arm. Cradling it very gently she looked at him. "Does it hurt?"

He shook his head.

"May I touch it?"

He nodded, and she ran her fingers over the writing. "What do the doctors say?"

"They haven't seen it."

She looked up at him, her face wrinkled in question.

"It, um, disappears sometimes, but then it comes back."

She looked down at his arm again and ran her fingertips along the swirled writing. "It doesn't seem to be a scar or a burn. Could it be at tattoo?"

He was more aware of her touch than he wanted to admit. "I don't think so. Don't tattoos scar over right after you get one?"

She smiled. "I wouldn't know. I don't have one."

He felt his face color and couldn't hold her gaze. In spite of his best efforts to do otherwise he was picturing a butterfly tattooed on her ass. He hadn't thought about a woman's body this intensely since Julie died. "Me neither," he managed.

"Then what it is? You have any idea?"

"No . . . well, maybe."

She waited, and her brows wrinkled as she watched him struggle with his answer. "What, John?"

He took a deep breath and raised his eyes to her. "I haven't told anyone else what really happened because it's so weird I'm afraid people will think I'm crazy. I even worried that the writing on my arm was something only I could see."

Amy was nodding. "You have to tell somebody eventually. Right?"

He nodded. "I just don't want you to think I've gone around the bend."

She shook her head. "I couldn't."

John took another deep breath and began to tell her everything that had happened to him in the cemetery.

V

AMY DID NOT INTERRUPT HIM UNTIL HE FINISHED. "So?" he said at the end. He didn't know how to read her silence and wondered whether it meant she was fascinated by the story or horrified by what she deemed to be his insanity.

She opened her mouth but then closed it again without speaking. He felt a growing sense of dread, but then instead of saying anything she fumbled for her purse and pulled out her iPhone.

"Roll your arm," she commanded as she hit the camera app and prepared to take a picture. "Before this thing disappears again, I want to get a couple pictures."

He obeyed, and she put the phone close and took several different shots, trying to get each aspect of the scrawled letters.

"What are you going to do with them?" he asked when she finished. He had a sudden jolt of panic that she wanted to show them to other people.

She put her phone away, then sat and looked at him. "Let's just assume for a moment that everything you told me really happened. It's not something I can go out and tell other people. You agree?"

He nodded.

"So, the first thing I need to try and do is find out if those marks on your arm that look like signatures can be matched to any actual historic signatures."

"I know one of these is Edward Putnam. He seemed to be the leader of the group."

"Then I need to find something else, some old document that Edward Putnam signed."

"Like what? How are you going to do that?"

"I don't know yet."

"I know," John said. "I'll call my friend, Richard Harvey. He's a theology professor at Salem State. I'll tell him we're trying to authenticate some old Puritan documents and ask if he could help."

"Okay, that's a good start," Amy said.

"Not really. Nobody except me and possibly you is going to be convinced by the fact that a letter on my arm seems like some old signature from the 1600s."

Amy's eyes hardened. "You have any better ideas?"

Surprised at the way she was assuming authority, but grateful at the same time, he glanced down at his arm and shook his head. "No." He remembered he way it had felt when Rebecca Nurse held his arm over the candle and then pushed his seared flesh down on the parchment.

And then the thought hit him. "You know I'm pretty sure this wasn't the first time I've had a strange experience relating to Rebecca Nurse," he blurted.

"What are you talking about?"

"When I was in college, my roommates and I had gotten a keg, and I'd gone to bed drunk. I remember waking up in the middle of the night. I was really dizzy and everything felt wrong. I was thinking it was probably the beer and that I was going to get sick. I was alone in my room, but it seemed as if somebody else was there with me and she woke me up."

"Your girlfriend?"

"No, it was an old lady. I never saw her. I just heard her voice, and she was screaming at me to wake up. I finally did, enough to smell the smoke and realize what was happening, and I woke my roommates and a few other people and we all got out okay."

"But an old lady woke you up?"

John shook his head. "I was drunk. I just assumed it was the alcohol and some kind of weird dream, only . . ."

"What?"

"Well, the next day when the fire was out, they let us back into the dorm to go through our stuff and salvage anything we could. I went into our old room, but everything was either charred or waterlogged from the fire hoses except this one thing. I'd been writing a paper for one of my classes. I even remember the title, 'Rebecca Nurse: A Wrongful Death in Salem's Witch Trials.' It was on the floor under my desk, and it was a little wet and a tiny bit singed, but otherwise it was perfect. Everything around it was black and soaked."

John took a deep breath. "There was one other time I saw Rebecca Nurse, and that was just before Julie's accident. I never saw her again until two days ago."

Amy was shaking her head. "I don't think you're crazy, John. I've always been a cold-hearted rationalist and never bought into paranormal ideas, but I really think this is different. You need to figure this out because I think somebody is trying to tell you something."

VI

AMY LEFT TO GO BACK TO THE PAPER. WHEN she did John climbed from bed and walked to the bathroom and then made his way back to bed. He was still shaky and surprisingly weak, and every joint and bruise in his body was still screaming. He tried to ignore the discomfort, took his laptop from the table, fired it up, and composed a quick email to Rich Harvey. He told Rich that he and Amy were working on a human interest story about a man who had found some old parchments in the attic of a deceased relative. Before they could print the story they needed to authenticate the signatures, particularly one that seemed to be Edward Putnam's, and therefore Amy was going to be calling Rich to see if he could show her something in the university's ancient books and documents collection that had Edward Putnam's signature.

When he finished the email and hit send he felt as tired as if he had done a fast five-mile run. He put the laptop back on the table and was climbing back in bed when a nurse came to check on him and refill his water pitcher. She offered him a Percocet, and since his pain had spiked from his slight exertion, he took it without argument. As the nurse walked out of the room he lay back, tilted the bed flat, and closed his eyes.

As he felt the drug begin to kick in, washing the pain away like an outgoing tide, he wondered if he had done the right thing by telling Amy. She had seemed to believe his story in spite of how absolutely ridiculous it sounded, even to him. He suddenly saw himself not as the one holding all the cards where their relationship was concerned, but as a besotted older man with a hopeless attraction for a beautiful younger woman, who makes an absolute ass of himself in the process. He had read about such things in books, seen it in plays. Was he becoming such a caricature? He wondered if he should trust Amy the way he did. Was it possible that even now she was on her cell phone talking to her friends and colleagues at the *Salem News*, telling them her boss was a raving lunatic. Even as he thought it, he knew that wasn't the case. A genuine bond connected them. Part of it was professional respect. Part friendship. Those things were real and incontrovertible. Was it possible there was something more, as well? Or was he just a lonely older man fantasizing about an unattainable younger woman?

The Percocet was making him sleepy, but before he drifted off, he glanced around the room. In the far corner, sitting in a chair by the window was Rebecca Nurse. Dressed in her usual high-necked, black dress, she sat with her head bent as she worked on her embroidery. As if she sensed his gaze, she stopped working and raised her head. The harsh disapproval he had always seen in her eyes when he gazed at the portrait was gone. Instead he saw kindness and wisdom and strength. To his surprise her lips lifted in a smile as if she was telling him he was doing the right thing.

When he looked down at his arm, the letters had disappeared again. He closed his eyes and slept.

7.

WHEN HE WOKE, THE LIGHT COMING THROUGH his window had faded. It was rush hour, and a line of slow moving cars was visible in the distance, their headlights creating bright halos as they crept through the heavy fog that had rolled in off the ocean. He heard the clicking of someone working on a laptop, and when he turned his head he saw Sarah had returned.

"Hey," he said. "How long have you been here?"

She looked up from her keyboard. "A couple hours. I hope my clacking didn't wake you."

"Not at all." John blinked his eyes, then reached for the button to tilt the bed higher. He actually felt better. The pain was no longer as sharp. "I hope you're not neglecting your work to sit here in my room and watch me sleep."

"Not at all. I did my newscasts and now we're just emailing back and forth with ideas for tomorrow's show. It's the Internet age, no need for me to sit in meetings."

He glanced toward the other corner to see if Rebecca Nurse was still there, but she was gone. Rolling his arm slightly he looked for the marks, but they, too, were invisible. He was just starting to relax when his door opened, and Amy bustled in.

"Hi," she said in a bright voice. Then she noticed Sarah. "Oh, sorry, I didn't know you had company."

She was wearing blue jeans and a red down vest, and for the second time that day he was struck by how beautiful she was. Walking in the fog had formed small drops of moisture that sparkled in her straight black hair, and her blue eyes seemed to light up the room. She carried a bulging accordion file full of papers from the office, but her gaze was on Sarah and it held an arctic coolness he had never seen in her before. If he didn't know her better, he would have sworn what he was seeing was jealousy.

He swung his gaze toward Sarah and saw the same coldness written in her features. "Sarah, this is Amy Johnson, my associate editor. I think you two have met, but it was a long time ago," As he said it, he was thinking that he knew exactly when and where they had met. It had been at Julie's funeral. "Amy, this is my daughter, Sarah."

Amy put the accordion file on the foot of the bed then stepped over to Sarah's chair. She put out her hand. "Nice to see you again," she said with a pleasant smile but a slight edge in her voice.

"Nice to see you, as well," Sarah said. When he glanced at his daughter he saw a gleam in her eyes that reminded him of a guard dog when someone gets too close to its master. He wondered what unspoken communication was going on between these two women.

"I just brought you a bunch of stuff from the paper, in case you feel well enough to dig into your correspondence.

I didn't mean to interrupt," Amy said, as she turned and headed back toward the door.

"You're not interrupting," he said quickly.

"You're not," Sarah said, not as convincingly.

Amy stopped and turned. "Well, how are you feeling?"

"Better, thanks. I managed to make it to the bathroom on my own and got an email off to Richard Harvey. Did you get a chance to call him on that question we discussed."

"Yes. We're getting together tomorrow morning."

He could feel the curiosity in Sarah's eyes as he spoke, but he wasn't going to bring her into the conversation. No way. Sarah's tolerance for the unusual, her ability to suspend disbelief didn't begin to compare to Amy's.

"Well," Amy said, still standing by the door. "I'll get in touch with you tomorrow after I've met with Professor Harvey." She gave him a quick smile. "Night." Then a less friendly glance in Sarah's direction. "Good night."

Amy walked out. As the pneumatic hinge pulled the door closed behind her, silence settled into the room interrupted only by the occasional faint sound of car horns still crawling along the highway.

"Something bothering you?" John said at last.

"No," Sarah said, much too quickly.

"Sarah."

"I didn't know you two were dating."

John blinked at his daughter. "I beg your pardon."

"Please, Dad. I wasn't born yesterday. When she walked in there was suddenly that kind of you-know-what tension in the room. You could cut it with a knife."

"What kind of tension?"

"Are you playing games with me? Sexual tension."

John opened his mouth to speak, but Sarah cut him off. "Look, Mom has been dead for four years. You have every imaginable right to start dating again. You probably should have started a long time ago, and you don't owe me any explanations or need to tell me who you're seeing until you're ready, but . . ."

"But what?"

"It would be nice it you picked somebody a little closer to your age. She could practically be my sister."

"Well, let me correct you on two things. First, you're twenty-eight, and she's thirty-six. Second, we're not involved."

Sarah huffed out a humorless laugh. "I think you seem to be the only one who hasn't figured out that you are."

VIII

JOHN LAY WITH HIS HEAD ON THE PILLOW, his eyes turned to the window where he watched the occasional pair of headlights wind its way through the misty dark. He thought about what Sarah had said about him being the only one who didn't seem to know he and Amy were involved. He wondered if Amy knew. He supposed she must, since women always seemed to know about these kinds of things before men had a clue. And if she did know about it, he probably had to assume she must like the idea.

He thought about Julie, about how much he had loved her, but he also thought about spending the past four years alone, endlessly grieving for someone who could never return. Julie had been very much a woman, with all the sensitivity and compassion that implied, but she had also been tough-minded and practical. She would have seen four years of solitude and mourning as an absolute waste of his precious time on earth, and Julie had never wasted anything. She hadn't wasted water or electricity or heat or money, and she certainly hadn't wasted time. She had been a multi-tasker of the highest order. If he was honest with himself, he had to acknowledge that she would have been angry with him, furious even, that he had been allowing time to pass the way he had, directionless, wallowing in his misery, sucking down single malt scotch in embarrassing quantities to alleviate the pain. She would have kicked him in the ass and told him to go out and find a pretty girl to take to dinner.

And here he'd had one staring him in the face every day for the past four years, and he hadn't been able to see it. Well, that wasn't exactly true. He'd seen it, and now he had to decide what he was going to do about it. He'd been with Julie for so many years, he didn't even remember what it was like to go on a date, to reach for a woman's hand when you weren't sure she wanted you to, or to try and kiss her. Or to make love. Holy crap. He felt a hot flush in his loins, but at the same time his stomach went cold at the idea. How could he start all of that confusing intimacy with a new person? He knew he could *do* it physically, but mentally and emotionally he wasn't as certain.

What was wrong with him? Weren't women the ones who were supposed to have all the emotional uncertainty about sex? Men were supposed to hop on, hop off, then ride off into the sunset. Slam, bam, thank you, ma'am. Only that wasn't him. Maybe it had been him once, but it wasn't any more. It was like he'd turned his wizened old heart over and found a tender new shoot growing where he didn't think any new growth was possible. He wanted to protect it and make sure it didn't get trampled.

He turned his head away from the window and saw Rebecca Nurse sitting in the chair in the corner, working on her embroidery as always. As if she felt his gaze, she looked up. "Were you ever as confused as this?" he asked.

She gave him a gentle smile, as if telling him, *Of course.* But then her smile faded, and her eyes became pinched.

"More things are going to happen, aren't they?" he said to her. "I can't just become a lovesick puppy and act like nothing else matters, can I?"

She raised her eyebrows slightly, as if telling him he was exactly right.

When the nurse came in a few minutes later with a Percocet, he gobbled it greedily, wanting to close his eyes and enjoy a dreamless sleep, free of all his confusion.

FOUR

October 21

THE NEXT MORNING JOHN'S CELL PHONE SHOWED an early call. It was Richard Harvey.

"I know you're up because they don't let you sleep in hospitals. You've probably had three enemas already."

"How did you guess? Were you hoping to watch them give me one?"

"Hardly. I wouldn't pollute my senses that way, not after my eyes have been feasting on your truly delectable little friend."

"Did you show her what she wanted?"

"Yes. Sadly all she wanted to see was Edward Putnam's signature. I would have shown her so much more if she had just asked. The body of an aging college professor can drive women into paroxysms of orgasmic bliss."

"How shocking she didn't understand that."

"Yes. Tell me, what does she really do for you?"

"She's my associate editor, dirtbag. She's smart, and she's professional, and she's got a lot better options than you or me." Even as he said it he felt a twinge of jealousy, knowing it was true and wondering again if he was just an old fool falling for a beautiful younger woman. "Now, if you want to talk about somebody young and less discriminating, we have a new copyboy."

"Very funny. I'm just trying to say I've been under the impression that you've been living in the desert as far as your exposure to beauty is concerned, but it's not the case."

"Why would I mention her? Half the time all you can talk about are the coeds you spend your days drooling at."

"It's my cross to bear."

"Yes, well, thanks for helping out with the signature." As he said it, John glanced down at his arm. The letters that had been created by rolling his burned flesh in drying blood were not visible. Even though he couldn't see them, he knew they were there because Amy had seen them, too. In spite of his initial skepticism he was starting to think they might be a clue of some kind, maybe even part of a map directing him toward some as yet undiscovered purpose. What were they trying to tell him? Why was the ghost of Rebecca Nurse now at his side for so much of each day? He felt as if invisible walls were closing in on him, forcing him to move along a predefined path. If he concluded he wasn't going insane, then didn't he have to also conclude there had to be a purpose to all of this? But if there was, what was it? Was there something he was supposed to be doing? How was he going to discover the answer?

Rich interrupted his train of thought. "No problem. When are you getting out of there?"

"Hopefully today or tomorrow. Whenever they determine that my brain's not swelling."

"Let me know if it does. Maybe if it did you'd be smart enough to become a college professor."

"Eat me."

"So long, lowbrow."

As John punched off the call, in spite of everything that was troubling him, he realized he was smiling.

II

TWENTY MINUTES LATER AMY PEEKED HER HEAD into the room, and upon seeing him alone, breezed inside. "Morning. How are you feeling?"

At the sight of her face John felt a sudden giddiness that surprised him. The thought flashed through his brain that he was "involved" with her. But what did that mean? How was he supposed to act? "My brain is swelling," he said, trying to cover his confusion. "I feel like a college professor."

She stopped and looked at him in alarm. "What?"

"Bad joke. Sorry. Rich Harvey called a little while ago and told me you two had gotten together."

Amy nodded, her face serious. "I saw the signature."

"And?"

She stepped over to the bed, took his arm, rolled it over, and looked carefully at the blood-colored letters that once again stood out clearly. "It's absolutely identical."

When she let go of his arm, John sat back and closed his eyes, feeling a huge thrill of relief. It was one more indication, albeit a small one, that what he was going through was grounded in some semblance of rationality. When he opened his eyes again Amy was looking at him, her eyes pinched in concentration.

"What?" he asked.

She pulled up the bedside chair and sat down. She put her hand out and laid it atop his right arm. All his senses seemed to be aware of her touch. "We have to figure out why this is happening to you and not to someone else and what it means."

"I agree," he said, feeling almost light-headed at her use of the word "we," as if they were unquestionably a team in this.

"But even more important," she went on, "we have to figure out why it's happening *now*. Why not ten years ago? Why not next year? There have to be reasons. Do you have any idea what they could be?"

He thought for a second, but then shook his head. "Not a clue," he admitted. "Other than every time I saw Rebecca Nurse it was almost Halloween, but that could be totally coincidental."

"Did you actually see her in college?"

"No, I don't think so. I just heard her telling me to wake up."

Amy nodded. "But you didn't see her last year or ten years ago?"

"No."

"So, why now?"

He shrugged and shook his head. "No idea." He took his other hand, laid it on hers and squeezed gently. She did not pull her hand away. Rather she opened her fingers and let them intertwine with his. "We also have to understand why you can see these letters on my arm."

"No one else can see them?"

"I don't think so. They seem to disappear when anyone else is nearby, but not with you. Doesn't there have to be a reason for that?"

She looked at him for a long time. "What would that be?"

He looked at his arm again with the signatures etched in the color of dried blood and then at the corner chair. Rebecca Nurse was back with him, working calmly on her embroidery.

"Why do you keep looking at that corner?" she asked him after a moment. "Is it Rebecca Nurse?"

He nodded. "She's there, doing her embroidery."

"How do you know who she is?"

"Her portrait hangs in my living room. It's been handed down in my family for generations. It's a big deal. My great aunt made me promise I would never sell it or take it off the wall as long as I owned the house. I used to hate the painting because it struck me as so grimly Puritan, this old woman sitting in her harsh black dress and her humorless, judgmental eyes." As he said it, he looked again at Rebecca sitting in the corner chair. "I realize now that I was wrong. She was actually kind and wise and strong. The painter just didn't bring those qualities out very well."

"Does she speak to you?"

He turned back to Amy. There was no trace of doubt or mockery or disbelief or any of the other things he might have expected, things that he might have felt if positions were reversed. "Nothing you can actually hear. Several times she's managed to throw some words into my head, but she doesn't do it very often. Mostly it's like she's waiting for me to discover something, maybe investigate it, but she can't do the work for me. I have to do it, or *we* have to do it."

He shook his head. "Why is it you believe I'm actually seeing her? Why don't you think I've gone bonkers?"

She gave him a gentle smile. "You've got your own basket of faults, John. You drink too much. You mourn Julie, but it's a lot more than that. You blame yourself for what happened."

"I don't—"

She held up a hand to silence him. "You were giving a Halloween party for the staff of the paper that night, remember? You forgot to pick up a case of wine you'd ordered, and you couldn't send out anyone at the office because we were all rushing to make deadline. Julie's car was in the shop, but she walked in and got your keys and took your car. Don't your remember?"

He closed his eyes and tried to pull together all the things about that day that he'd forgotten in the horrible aftermath. Amy was right. He *had* forgotten the wine and Julie had agreed to go get it. She had taken his car, his new Audi with the all-wheel drive that was supposed to be so safe in rain and snow. As he recalled the details he realized they had been locked in a part of his subconscious for the whole time since the accident. As if he was some kind of wild-eyed Biblical penitent, he had flayed himself over and over with those details until he didn't even recognize what he was doing. He had gone well beyond mourning his wife's tragic death. His subconscious was loaded with accusations as if it was entirely his fault because through an act of callousness or venality he had put her at risk and let it happen.

"John?"

He opened his eyes and looked at her, realizing he'd been hyperventilating. "I didn't . . . I forgot . . ."

"You didn't forget anything." She nodded. There were tears in her eyes. "It's time to stop punishing yourself. You didn't do anything wrong, but only you can take yourself off the rack."

Even as she said it, he felt something lift, as if he had been on a very long and punishing hike and was finally taking off his heavy pack. "Is it really that easy?" he asked.

Amy smiled, and a tear broke loose and ran down her cheek. "I think so."

He reached out without giving it any thought and gently wiped the tear. Out of the corner of his eye he could see that Rebecca Nurse had looked up from her embroidery. She was smiling, and he knew it was her way to telling him he was moving in the right direction.

III

MELISSA BLAKE HEARD SOMEONE PULL THE BAR from the door of her prison, and a second later the blinding light caused her to put her hands in front of her eyes. The person, the jailer, whoever the hell they were, stepped into her cell and took the bucket Melissa had put beside the door. A second later she heard a clank as a new bucket was placed on the stone floor, and then the door closed again, and the bar banged back in place.

Melissa had not even tried to speak or beg or ask questions. It never did any good when she did. No one had spoken even a single word to her since the first day when the woman told her what to do with her daily bucket and that no one cared about her. Since that time—had it been morning or night? Melissa didn't know—they had replaced her bucket four more times. Did that mean she had been here four days? Would those be twelve-hour days or twenty-four hour days? She had no idea. She wasn't even sure how many times they had replaced the bucket, not for certain.

After the bucket had been replaced the first time she had stood up and explored her cell. Its walls were stone, rough and damp and timeless as the walls of a cave, and they felt as if they had been chiseled out of solid rock. The floor was also stone, but it felt in places as if the material was different, and she wondered if her captors had poured cement in some spots, perhaps to make the surface even. The only thing that wasn't stone was the door, which seemed to be made of oak or some other hard wood and hinged with huge, wide strips of steel or iron. When she hit the door with her fists it made almost no sound. It was like hitting a tree.

The one thing she had discovered in the opposite corner was a blanket and pillow. The blanket was neatly folded when she first stumbled across it, and to her amazement it smelled clean. The pillow even had a pillowcase and also smelled clean. Cocooning inside the blanket and using the pillow to keep her head off the damp floor had at least allowed her to stop shivering and get some sleep.

Rest and food had allowed her to think, but thinking didn't do her any good. She tried to figure out why she was here. Were they hoping to get ransom? If that was the case why hadn't they asked her how to get in touch with her family? Did they already know how? If it was a kidnapping, wouldn't they have had her speak on the phone to her parents to let them know she was unharmed? If it wasn't a kidnapping what did they want with her? Thankfully they hadn't tried to rape her.

As she was puzzling all of this out, going through the circular logic for the hundredth time since she found herself here, she heard the first sound that didn't seem to be part of the usual prison routine. A voice. Someone was screaming.

Melissa moved through the darkness to the bar of light that showed underneath her door. She lay on the ground, put her ear up to the crack and listened. From someplace nearby she could hear someone shouting just the way she had shouted when she first arrived.

"Hello? Are you out there? Let me out of here dammit! Let me out! Let me out!"

It was a male voice. He sounded young, maybe her own age or a bit older, and he sounded lost and scared, and she knew he was a prisoner just like her.

IV

THE MAN WORE BLUE JEANS AND A BLACK hoodie. Wraparound sunglasses and a costume beard covered much of his face. He stayed off the sidewalk, avoiding people as much as possible, and walked with his head down and his hands in his pockets, not because he was deep in thought but because he was trying to keep other people or security cameras from seeing his face or his hands. He had dark latex gloves on his hands to keep him from leaving prints and to make him look like a black guy if his hands were the only part of him anybody saw.

He'd been told to do things *exactly* this way, and the people who told him ought to know because they were the same guys who'd be trying to catch him if somebody fingered him. They'd also told him to come here completely clean, no drugs in his system. They said they wanted him able to think clearly. How the hell was he supposed to think clearly when he was coming here to kill a guy? *Want to tell me that, you idiots?*

He was here because yesterday he'd gotten busted with ten grams of coke that he'd bought from his supplier and re-cut and was getting ready to peddle on the street. He was already out on parole after his second hitch on a felony possession with intent to sell, and he knew a judge and jury would send him back for twenty more with no chance of early release. Only the cops hadn't taken him to the station. They'd taken him to a motel and told him what he needed to do if he wanted to get his dope back and stay free. So, that's what he knew. He was here to kill a guy, but he had no idea *why* the cops wanted this guy dead. The nice thing was, as long as he got to stay on the street, he really didn't care.

The day was rainy and cold. Cars went past, their tires hissing on the wet roads, their windshield wipers on high. Hardly anybody was walking, and those who were had umbrellas over their heads and were looking down at their feet to make sure they avoided puddles. *Perfect.*

He walked around the back of the main hospital building toward the metal door that was near the delivery entrance. It was supposed to be locked, a fire exit door or something like that. There wasn't even a handle on the outside, but just like he'd been told to expect, the door was propped open. He swung it back, stepped inside, and kicked the rubber door-stopper free. The door closed behind him, and he looked around at the rough cement floor and naked cinderblock walls and the fire stairs that rose to his right. There was nobody around but he could hear the faint sounds of the hospital behind the closed doors.

His hands were sweating, and his breath came in uneven gasps. He was too rattled to bluff his way out if somebody came through the doors and challenged him. He had a gun in his pocket, and he was ready to use it because nobody in the world would ever believe that cops were the ones who had told him to come here. If he got busted he'd never survive the joint for more than a couple weeks. That's how dirty cops covered their tracks.

He took the one-hitter out of his pocket, twisted it open, put the end in his nostril, and inhaled deeply. He repeated the process on the other side, then twisted the bullet closed and slid it back in his pocket. He felt the burn as the coke raced up his sinuses, hitting his system like an accelerator. *Putting the pedal to the metal*, he thought. *Putting on my armor.* He loved coke. It always made him feel like the risks had gone away, like there wasn't anything he couldn't do.

He started up the stairs. Fourth floor, he recalled. Room four-twenty-eight. Single room. White guy, fifty-something. He reached into his pocket and looked at the picture they'd given him. The guy looked younger than what fifty ought to look like. He had dark hair, not much gray, skin tight across his jaw and cheekbones. His eyes were full of energy, the eyes of a guy who didn't take crap. His neck was thick, and from the set of his shoulders he could hold his own in a fight. None of that was good, but the guy was in the hospital. They'd told him the guy was recovering from a bad fall—concussion and serious bruises. Good chance the guy would be asleep, but in any case the guy wouldn't have any fight. That's what they told him.

He reached into the pocket of his hoodie and touched the hypodermic. It was empty. The whole job was to get on top of the guy, stick the needle into his vein and push in some air. The cops said it would cause an embol-something-or-other and kill him, and the hospital would probably think it had something to do with his head injury. And even if they didn't, so what? As long as he got out without looking at a security camera or getting face-to-face with a nurse, they'd never know who did it. And if something went wrong and he couldn't get the needle in a vein or if the guy was awake, he could strangle him or if things really got bad, he could shoot the bastard and run like hell.

When he got to the fourth floor landing, he stopped and took a deep breath. The coke was working, but not well enough. He took his bullet and gave himself another couple snorts. He was getting low on dope, but tonight he'd be flush and he'd also get his ten grams back.

He opened the door and stepped into the hall. He remembered to keep his head down as he turned left the way he'd been told. A door up ahead of him opened, and he heard the click of high heels coming down the hall toward him. Not a nurse. Their shoes squeaked. The woman went past him without slowing, but he got a peek at a pair of great legs. Behind him now, her heel clicks faded.

Counting the doors he went to the seventh room on the left. He opened the door without knocking and saw the guy lying in bed. The guy was awake and turned his head toward the door.

"Did you forget something—?" he started to ask. Then when the other man stepped all the way into the room and shut the door, the guy's face darkened, and he demanded, "Who the hell are you?"

The man said nothing as he made it to the edge of the bed in two long strides. He reached into his hoodie pocket came out with the hypodermic and thrust it at the guy's neck. For an old man who was supposedly hurt pretty bad, the guy was fast. He saw the needle coming, grabbed his attacker's wrist and twisted. The man realized belatedly that his intended victim was also strong as he found himself forced sideways and down by the twisting leverage on his arm.

He started to panic and tried to slug the guy with his other hand, but the guy in bed hunched his shoulder, making it hard to hit his face, and twisted harder on the man's wrist. Neither of them had made a sound. At least the guy in the bed wasn't calling for help, not yet, but it was only a matter of time.

The man gave up hitting and jammed his hand into the pocket of his jeans. Finding the grip of the pistol, he tried to pull it free, but the guy in the bed seemed to sense what he was doing. He couldn't have known whether it was a gun or knife, but he knew it was something, and jammed his hand down, trying to keep whatever it was from coming free. The man stopped trying to pull his hand out and jammed it farther into his pants. He had a good grip on the pistol now, and because the jeans were baggy, he just had to tilt it up and pull the trigger. At this range he couldn't miss.

He started to bring his wrist up, but the other guy stuck his hand down into the man's pocket, got a grip on his hand

and started to force his hand back down. The man couldn't shoot yet. If he pulled the trigger now he would only hit the mattress. And the guy in the bed was strong. He was bending the man's wrist down again, and he couldn't pull the trigger now because he'd shoot himself in the leg or the foot. Then the guy in the bed did something the man never expected.

He head-butted him, right in the damn nose. The pain was blinding and instantaneous. His nose was already bad enough from all the coke he did, and he felt the cartilage shatter. For an instant he forgot about the gun, and that was when the guy's hand found his trigger finger and curled it against the trigger.

The man felt the impact, but he felt no pain. It was more like a deadening shock that ran all the way from his thigh down to his foot. His eyes were tearing but when he looked down, even though he couldn't see much, he saw the blood. It was like he was standing in a puddle of it, and it kept spreading, getting wider and wider.

In the next couple seconds it was like somebody had turned the air conditioning on real high. He felt himself getting cold, really cold. People were in the room behind him now. He was already getting lightheaded and knew he'd shot himself, but he wasn't going to get caught. He turned to run, but as he did his feet slipped on the blood. He splashed down in the puddle but managed to get his pistol out of his pocket. He saw two nurses and a guy who looked like a doctor. He aimed the gun at them, and they backed around the corner.

He turned and looked for the guy in the bed, but he

couldn't see him. Had he jumped out and made a run for it? He wasn't sure. His brain wasn't working right, but he knew he couldn't get caught. *He couldn't.* The cops would put him back in the slammer, and then they'd have some hard-timer shiv him in the chow line or shower or exercise yard.

A head came around the corner. He squeezed off a shot, but it just punched a hole in the wall. He tried to crawl toward the door. People would run when they saw him. He'd get to the stairs, and then out to his car. He'd drive somewhere he could tie off his leg and stop the bleeding. He just had to keep moving, but he was so damn tired and cold. He went from his knees onto his belly. He was a mess. Blood was everywhere. He sighted along the pistol, waiting for someone to come into his sights. He just needed to rest for a second or two, then he'd get up and make a run for it. Just rest. Just rest for a second.

V

WHEN THE GUN WENT OFF, JOHN FELT THE SHOCK run through the man's body. He knew from the position of his own hand that the pistol had been aimed at the man's leg. The shock confirmed it and so did the almost instant coppery odor of blood. It was a big odor, and John knew even without seeing that it meant a lot of blood. Without meaning to he released his grip as the man looked down at his leg. A second later the man must have slipped on his own blood, because he tumbled out of sight.

Not knowing what else to do, John rolled to the far side of his bed and lay pressed against the bedrails. He tried to keep his breathing under control. He didn't know if the man was unconscious or maybe had forgotten about him. A pair of nurses and a doctor came rushing into the room, looked down at the man on the floor and ducked back out. John wanted to run, too, but he couldn't risk getting out of bed, making his legs into targets and trying to run for the door.

A doctor put his head into the room and looked at John from around the corner where he was out of sight of the gunman. John made a gun symbol with his hand and pointed and the doctor nodded. The doc crept forward and started to put his head around the corner, but he jerked it back as a shot went off. John's ears rang because the shot was much louder with the gun out of the man's pocket. He saw the hole in the white wall.

A second later as his hearing returned, he heard the man moving. At first John feared he was going to hoist himself up on the bed and shoot him pointblank. There was nothing John would be able to do. The sounds continued. John realized after a few seconds that they seemed to be getting a little farther away, heading toward the door. The man was trying to escape.

Another few seconds went by, and then John heard a sort of splash as if the man had collapsed. He risked a peek, and saw the man lying on his stomach, trying but failing to keep his gun aimed at the doorway. Below his waist was a sea of blood. John thought the amount was almost unbelievable. How could so much leak out of a person so quickly?

The man had just tried to kill him, but John thought there was little risk he could even pull the trigger now. He didn't want the guy to die because he wanted answers, namely who had sent him. He didn't think for a second that this had been a random event. No way.

He unlocked the bars on the far side of the bed and slid them down. Putting his feet on the floor, he moved as silently as he could, taking care to avoid the pool of blood, until he was right behind the guy. Then he took a deep breath, stepped into the blood, and dropped onto the guy's back. His knees slammed the man's shoulders and pinned him to the ground. In a quick grab, he took the pistol from the man's nearly inert fingers.

"I've got the gun!" he shouted toward the door. "It's safe! Get in here and see if you can stop the bleeding! Hurry!"

A second later, a doctor put his head around the corner, saw John kneeling on the guy's back and signaled for others to follow him. He rushed into the room, pulled a rubber strap from his pocket, and as John rolled onto his knees in the pool of blood, the doctor wrapped the strap just below the man's groin and pulled it tight. A second later he rolled the man over while one of the nurses sliced off his pant leg. The blood pressure seemed to have dropped because not as much seemed to be flowing as a few moments earlier. John could see a hole high on the man's thigh and then a few inches below it a long furrow that had laid the lower thigh completely open. The doctor said something about the femoral artery, and plunged his finger into the bullet hole.

He shouted for a gurney and three units of type O. The gurney and the bags of blood arrived in only seconds, and they lifted the man up, plunged a needle leading from the bag of blood into his arm and ran out with him toward what John assumed had to be the emergency room.

As soon as the man had been taken away, several doctors rushed in to check John. His heart was racing, his blood pressure was high, and he had a red mark on his forehead from where he had head-butted the other man and broken his nose, but otherwise he felt remarkably good. Sam Huddleston hurried in a minute or two behind them.

"Did I hear this right? You head-butted the guy?" he said as he stepped into the room. A half-second later he stopped, his face taking on a look of shock as he saw the lake of blood and the doctors already crowded around the far side of John's bed where they could keep their feet dry. "Hell fire," he muttered.

John looked at his friend. His own legs were sticky with the man's blood. Even so, his pulse was beginning to slow, and a giddy feeling that he'd not only survived the encounter but come out victorious was starting to replace the near-shock he'd felt only moments ago. "If you could just keep insane killers from roaming the corridors of your hospital, maybe a person could recover from a concussion in peace."

Sam shook his head. "We're going to get you cleaned up and into a fresh room and then I want a CAT scan done to see if you've reinjured anything."

John held up a hand. "Honestly, I feel remarkably good. I don't even have a headache, which is more than I can say for the past few days."

"Still, we're not taking any chances."

After a long hot shower, John endured another CAT scan, and when it was over, he found himself being wheeled back to a different room, one that thankfully did not reek of freshly spilled blood.

A few seconds later, Sam followed him into the room. "Well," he said, "your head appears to be remarkably hard. You ought to give it to science when you die so we can try to figure out how your brain has been able to take the abuse you dish out without turning to jelly."

"I'm a journalist. We're hard headed. Goes with the territory."

"Apparently, like cockroaches, you can survive anything. As a group you're about as well loved as cockroaches."

"What about the other guy?"

"Not a cockroach, I'm afraid."

John scowled. "He died?"

Sam nodded. "That gun in his pocket was loaded with 9mm hollow points, nice little bullets that expand when they hit their target. The shot went through his femoral artery, hit the bone, flattened and ricocheted down along his leg, which is why it looked like you attacked him with a sword."

"You couldn't stop the bleeding?"

"We should've been able to, but we also found a little plastic thing filled with what we think is cocaine. The ER docs said his heart was pumping double-time, supporting the thesis that our boy had gotten himself jacked up on something just before he came into your room. It looked to them like he bled out in about half the normal time."

"Dammit," John muttered. "I wish we could have talked to him."

Sam studied him. "You don't think it was random?"

"A guy breaks into my room and tries to stick a hypodermic in my neck, and when that doesn't work he tries to shoot me? The guy had to sneak in, get up four flights of stairs, come down a hallway where there were lots of other rooms to choose, but he comes into my room?" John shook his head.

"No, I don't think it was random. What was in the syringe?"

Sam shook his head. "Nothing. It was empty."

"*That* doesn't make any sense."

"Well, if it really wasn't random, maybe in a weird way it does make sense. The guy might have been trying to inject air into your veins. It would probably kill you pretty fast, and when we looked for cause of death, we might have decided it was from natural causes. That would be pretty sophisticated and pre-meditated." Sam raised his eyebrows. "John, have you been a naughty boy, like maybe porking some mob guy's wife on the side?"

"Hate to disappoint, Sam."

Sam opened his mouth to say something else when a voice broke in. "Am I interrupting?"

John glanced over and saw a face he knew. "Lieutenant Card," he said. "Is this official business?"

"It's actually Captain Card," Brad Card said with a smile.

"Congratulations on the promotion," John said.

"Congratulations on staying alive," Card said, his expression becoming serious.

He was a Massachusetts State Police detective who had overseen the investigation into Julie's accident. Even though there had been no conclusion other than that bad weather and bad luck had caused the fatalities, Card's intelligence and no-nonsense style had impressed John. They had become friends in spite of the terrible circumstances.

Now, realizing that he hadn't seen Card in the past year, he asked, "What brought you here so fast?"

"I was in the area when I heard the call go out, and when I heard your name, I figured I'd come on by and see what was going on. I'm glad to see you're okay."

"Thanks, me too."

"Had you ever seen your assailant before?"

John shook his head. "Who was he?"

"His name was Kenny Dubrowski, a punk from South Boston who'd gone up twice on felony convictions, once for armed robbery, once for dealing cocaine. He was out on parole for his last bust, but . . ." he shook his head. "I didn't think something like this was in his repertoire."

"What was 'this'?" John asked.

"Well, we can't prove it, of course, because Dubrowski's dead and we can't ask him, but it looks and smells like a paid hit. And then of course the question arises: who tries to hit a newspaper editor. You working on any investigative stuff that might invite this kind of response?"

John shook his head. "Not that I know of."

"I already asked him if it might have been a jealous husband . . . or wife," Sam said. He crossed the room, held out his hand and introduced himself.

"Funny, Sam," John said.

"You a friend of his in addition to being his doc?" Card asked.

"In a manner of speaking," Sam replied. "John likes me. I can't stand him."

"Join the club," Card said.

"Have a little respect. You're talking to somebody who

just narrowly survived an assassination attempt."

Card nodded. "You really have no idea at all why somebody would want you dead?"

John glanced down at his arm, saw that the blood-colored letters were invisible, then looked back up and shook his head.

Card gave him a blank look that said he wasn't buying it, but he shook his head at the same time. "Even though you claim you don't have any idea why this happened, I'm going to put an armed officer outside your door until you're released. If you decide you can tell me more about this at some point, that would be great."

As Brad turned and walked out, John felt a sharp twinge of guilt that he lying to his two friends. But he couldn't imagine telling a police captain and a doctor the only reason he could think of somebody wanting to kill him had to do with a woman who died three hundred years earlier.

VI

AMY CAME RACING THROUGH THE DOOR OF HIS room about an hour after Captain Card and Sam left. Her face was white with worry, and she let out a huge sigh when she laid eyes on him.

"There's a policeman outside your door, and you're in a different room, but you're okay?" she demanded. She came over to the bed, looked down at him, and took his hand in hers.

"Perfectly fine," John said.

"What happened? They had the police scanner on in the pressroom, and I heard something about a shooting at the hospital." She closed her eyes and shook her head. "Somehow, because of everything else that's been going on, I knew it had to be you."

"A guy broke into my room."

"And he tried to kill you?"

John nodded.

"Why? Who was he?"

"Since I'd never seen him before, who he was would seem to be unimportant, but understanding why he came is critical."

"What do the police think?"

"They don't have any motive. They think it might be because of some article we're writing at the paper." He looked down at the writing that was now clearly visible across his forearm then at Rebecca Nurse, working diligently at her embroidery in the corner chair. "But we both know it has to do with this writing on my arm and that woman sitting over in the corner." He looked directly at the ghostly figure. "Can you tell us anything about why this happened, Mrs. Nurse?" he demanded.

Rebecca Nurse raised her head and gazed at him. Her somber expression seemed to say that he shouldn't be surprised by what had occurred. He studied her for a long time before he turned back to Amy.

"Remember the questions we talked about last night? Why me? Why now? And why you are the only other person who can see these letters?"

She nodded.

"Well, as I've been lying here attempting to make sense of this, I've come up with some pretty crazy answers. Let me try a couple out on you. First, why me? The only answer I can come up with is I'm descended from both Rebecca Nurse and Ann Putnam. That scene that Rebecca took me back to related to both sides of my family. So I'm wondering if my bloodline gives me some kind of innate sensitivity to this stuff. Perhaps Rebecca Nurse needs this blood relationship to reveal herself. And—I know this sounds nuts—but I'm wondering if my blood relationship with Ann Putnam was what allowed me to open the hidden door in the Putnam mausoleum."

John looked at Amy to try and gauge her reaction. She was gazing at him intently, her expression void of skepticism. She nodded. "Keep going."

"So if that's true, why now? Why didn't this stuff happen to my father, who was also related to both women, or to his mother or to my great grandmother?"

"How do you know it didn't?"

"I guess I don't, but I also suspect I might have heard about it if it had." He let out a sardonic laugh. "I mean, they probably would have been committed to an institution for the mentally ill, and that would be in our family lore."

"John, you're not going insane."

"Please keep telling me that." He smiled and gave her hand a squeeze. "So anyway, assuming I'm not totally nuts, I have to assume there is something going on in the present that relates to what Rebecca showed me in the past. That's the only way this all makes sense, isn't it?"

"But that still doesn't tell us why some stranger tried to kill you, unless . . ."

"Unless what?"

"If we assume your suppositions are true, then we have to also assume that the attempted murder was related to Rebecca Nurse. Unless maybe you tripped some kind of alarm . . . or something."

"I'm not following you."

She went to the table and brought John's laptop back, then

sat on the side of the bed, woke up the computer, and started typing. "There's too much stuff here to try and understand it without a list, so I'm making one." She turned the computer so he could see it as she typed.

1). John Andrews—descended from Rebecca Nurse and Anne Putnam.

2.) College dorm fire. Saved by Rebecca Nurse. Term paper on Rebecca Nurse did not burn.

3.) Wife killed in accident in his car four years ago. Person driving other car was Richard Putnam.

4.) What do we know about Richard Putnam?

5.) John Andrews hears screams outside Wicca Wonders, owned by Abigail Putnam.

6.) What do we know about Abigail Putnam?

7.) John Andrews hears voice, saves baby.

8.) John Andrews injured in cemetery, goes through secret door in Putnam mausoleum. Sees Edward Putnam and others in pact with devil.

Amy looked at what she had just typed, then she held up a finger. "Forgot a couple things."

9.) John and Amy had considered writing an article about young people disappearing in Salem area. Melissa Blake is most recent disappearance.

10.) Who else knew about the article?

11.) Amy is only other who can see letters on John Andrews' arm. Why?

She stopped typing again and turned to look at him. "I have a strange question for you."

"Shoot."

"How did your parents die? How old were they?"

"They died in a skiing accident in Switzerland, an avalanche. That's why I'm living in Great Aunt Eleanor's house and not them."

"How old were you when that happened?"

"Eleven."

"Any other people in your family die under strange circumstances?"

John shook his head. While it had certainly been tragic, he had never before thought of his parent's deaths as "strange." He shrugged. "A lot of my ancestors were sea captains. It was a pretty risky profession, and some of them died at sea."

Amy nodded and made several more notations.

12.) Strange deaths in John Andrews' family.

13.) Genealogy—Amy's and John's. Also, who are the descendants of the names on John's arm?

14.) Appearance of Rebecca Nurse to John—why now? What are we supposed to discover?

When she finished they both looked at the list, and after a few seconds John shook his head. "I'll be the first to admit this whole situation seems full of things that look oddly coincidental. But we can't draw any hard lines between these events or really explain any of this stuff, certainly not well enough to write a good article."

"We're not writing an article, John. We may be trying to save your life. If somebody tried to have you killed once, they're probably going to try again."

John threw his hands up in the air. "But *why?* There has to be a reason beyond something that happened three hundred years ago." He pointed to bullet number nine on Amy's list. "You think there's a serial killer running around Salem?"

"You think all this stuff would be happening with Rebecca Nurse if it was just about a modern day serial killer? No, I think it may be a lot worse than a simple serial killer."

John shook his head. He was playing the cynic with her because she was posing questions that had already popped into his own head, and the answers he had come up with made him deeply uncomfortable.

Amy went on, "As long as we're going to be open minded and consider all the possibilities, no matter how strange, let's just say that a group of people in our community have been doing some kind of weird magic or witchcraft or devil worship or whatever, and let's just say for a second that it actually works. Let's assume for a second that it gives them abilities nobody else has. It's like discovering atomic power all by yourself when nobody else knows it exists and wanting to keep it secret."

"How many of them are there?"

"If people have something really, really secret they want to protect, they would only let a small number of people know about it, right?"

John nodded.

"So, there were six people around the table that Rebecca Nurse showed you. Let's say there are still only six."

"Six in total?"

"Six who are in charge. There would have to be others as well, but more junior."

"You think it's hereditary?"

"I think it makes sense."

"So we have to figure out who else was at the table and track their descendants." John shook his head. "There could be hundred and hundreds."

"We'll have to put some practical limits on who we actually look at."

John ran his hands over his face. "If this group still exists, I'm sure I know some of them. They could be people I see at dinner parties. The idea of a secret group of my neighbors causing people to disappear and plotting the death of other people just seems so . . . I don't know, so creepy and unbelievable." He thought for another moment. "And it doesn't explain why they are suddenly interested in killing me when they weren't in the past."

"You didn't see Rebecca Nurse in the past, either. Maybe she's trying to contact you because something terrible is about to happen, or maybe she's here because you're different. Maybe you've changed in some way you're not aware of and that's the reason you can see Rebecca. And maybe these other people are perceptive enough to realize you're now a threat when you weren't before."

"Because I set off some kind of alarm?"

"You have a better idea?"

John shook his head then pointed to bullets three and

four. "If that's the case then these questions don't make any sense."

Amy just looked at him for a long moment. "You know they do. And we have to find the answers."

He didn't want to contemplate the idea Julie hadn't just been killed in a tragic accident on a rainy night but that she might have been murdered. At the very thought of it a blackness gathered deep in his guts. He knew if it was true, he would stop at nothing until he had avenged her.

John looked down the list and tried to calm his thoughts. "We have a huge amount of work to do," he said. "I've got to get the hell out of here so I can help you get started."

"No, you're going to stay right here until the doctors say you can go home. I'll get us started."

He felt immense gratitude that she was treating this like a mystery that needed to be solved and not the product of a diseased mind. He glanced toward Rebecca and saw that she seemed to have turned from her embroidery and was watching him with an intent expression, as if urging them to keep pushing in the present direction.

"What are you going to do first?" he asked Amy

"Genealogy," Amy said. "It has to be part of the key and we need to understand it better. The fact that I can see the letter on your arm must mean I'm related to someone who was part of the same . . . witch trials or whatever."

"But you're not even from here."

Amy shrugged. "I was born in Chicago and lived there my whole life. My parents and grandparents lived in the same area. My family wasn't big on the whole family-reunion-meet-all-your-relatives-and-talk-about-the-past kind of thing. If I'm related to people back here, I've been completely unaware of it all my life. But starting tonight, I'm going to find out."

John reached out and took her hand again. "Please be careful and very subtle. It's possible that whoever is after me doesn't realize you're aware of . . . all these weird things as well. Maybe, as you say, I've tipped these guys off somehow, but you haven't. If these people became aware of you, you might become a target, as well."

"I'll be careful, I promise." She glanced at her watch. "I better go start my genealogy homework." Amy kissed her finger and put it against his lips. She was still holding his hand, but was turning to go when Sarah walked in. John watched his daughter's eyes go straight to where his hand gripped Amy's, and then he saw her lips flatten.

"Why is there a policeman outside your door?" she asked in a clipped voice. "Did that shooting incident . . . was that you?"

John nodded and felt Amy's hand slip from his grasp.

"Well, what happened?" Sarah shot a cold glance at Amy. "Why didn't you call me?"

"Things have been a little crazy around here."

"Not too crazy for you to call somebody else."

"She heard it on the scanner."

"I've got to go," Amy said. "Goodnight, John. Goodnight, Sarah."

"Night," Sarah muttered as Amy slipped past her and headed out the door.

Sarah turned her head to watch Amy disappear and the door close behind her, then turned back toward John. "Dad, what the hell is going on? Why did someone try to kill you?"

"I have no idea. I'd never seen him before and don't know who he was. For all I know he picked my room at random because he wanted to kill somebody, maybe anybody."

Sarah crossed her arms and glowered. "Really?"

"What other reason would there be?"

"What really happened to you in the cemetery?"

John tried for a tone of exasperation. "Come on, Sarah. I fell down some steps. At least I *think* I fell down some steps. I can't remember exactly what happened." He glanced at his arm. The letters were invisible. Whatever made them visible had to be more than mere genealogy, because Sarah shared his bloodline. If blood was all that mattered, then she would be able to see the letters. The fact that she couldn't troubled him.

She looked down at him, almost sneering. He knew her anger came from her hurt at being shut out of his life, but there was nothing he could do about it. Sarah was like her mother, firmly and somewhat judgmentally rational. To her there were questions, and there were answers, but the answers that mattered to her were in the measurable, scientific, physical world. Of course there were the indecipherable gray areas of emotion, belief, loyalty, and intent, but in the end, people's actions were the proof positive of underlying feelings. For Sarah, the answers that mattered would never be found in the metaphysical world. But then he wondered whether, before the happenings of the last few days, if he would have been any different.

VII

AS ABIGAIL PUTNAM SWEPT INTO THE ROOM THE others at the table all stood. She ignored them, sat heavily in her chair, slammed her hands down on the tabletop, and leaned forward. She glared around at each of them in turn.

"So, tell me, gentlemen and lady, how it is that a man armed with both a hypodermic and a handgun rushes into a hospital room where a patient is convalescing from a bad fall and concussion, and rather than successfully killing the patient and escaping, the man ends up dead, and the patient unharmed? Can anyone explain this to me?"

Senator Hallowell cleared his throat. "Abigail, no one is happy about what happened, but using that sardonic tone with us doesn't—"

"Excuse me, Senator, but aren't the majority of our efforts directed at furthering your career?"

The man gave her an offended look. "Yes, but only so that we can advance the goals of our coven."

"Nonetheless, you are offended by my tone when we have twice failed to kill this man?"

Cabby Putnam interjected, "Perhaps we should've tried sooner than we did. I mean, we let four years go by between the accident and now."

Abigail raised her eyebrows at the remark. "Lieutenant, I am surprised to hear you open your mouth to criticize or question anyone else after your performance today." The man's eyes narrowed, and his lips became pinched as he bit back his retort. "However, let me remind all of you that for some time after the death of John Andrew's wife we continued to harbor hopes that he would quit the newspaper and leave Salem. We received a number of credible reports that he was drinking heavily, losing his focus on his job, and was considering retirement. It would have made killing him unnecessary."

The senator picked up the line of questioning. "But we're sure we really have to kill him now?"

Abigail turned to him. "I have told all of you that I can *feel* him again, just as I began to feel him over four years ago. His *awareness* is growing. I haven't sensed it since his wife's death because he has kept himself desensitized with alcohol and sadness. But recently something started to change. I am telling you he is a perceiver. He will see beyond the mists of our physical world to the reality beyond. As all of you know he is a direct descendant of an innocent who is among the most powerful of the spirit forces arrayed against us. A visible aura is beginning to build around John Andrews, and it makes me fear that Rebecca Nurse has already found a way to break through to him. When he walked past my shop the other day, I could see it clearly. If he hasn't already, it is only a matter of time before he reaches out and touches another spirit, and we all know which spirit that will be. Once that happens he'll begin to search and dig in earnest. He is a reporter. That is what he does. I am telling you I can *feel* him beginning to reach out. We ignore this at our peril."

"Well, he can reach anywhere he wants," Cabby Putnam shot back. "I'm not going after him in the hospital again. It's too dangerous."

Reverend Winthrop put a fist to his lips and cleared his throat. "If not now, when pray tell?"

"We'll plan something when he gets home," Cabby said. "But we have to be careful. It already looks suspicious as hell." He shook his head. "Dubrowski was a street punk. He'd been around. It should have been easy for him."

Abigail Putnam balled her hands into fists and shot forward in her chair, her heavy breasts bulging over the corner of the table. "Get this through your heads, all of you. Nothing about this is going to be easy. *Nothing.*"

"But," Reverend Winthrop said, raising his finger in a sermon-like gesture. "Think how our Patron will reward us when that most difficult blood is spilled for Him."

Across the table, Amanda Putnam Pendergast looked icily at the reverend and then at Cabby. "And do we know who will be carrying out this mission?" she asked in a cool, ironic tone. "If the last fellow was insufficient, how do we know the next fellow won't be, as well? I know they say third time is the charm, but if we do it incorrectly again, I'm not sure we will get another chance. We *do* have the calendar to think about."

Cabby's eyes tightened. "Thank you so much for explaining that, Amanda. I'm sure none of the rest of us understood it."

"Let us not forget that our enemy is out there," Abigail Putnam said, pointing upward and out in the general direction of the center of Salem. "Not in here." She rapped her knuckles on the table with a menacing thump. "Let us also remember that our actions and decisions are being judged by those above us. If one of us fails, the penalty will come down upon all of our heads equally. Do *not* forget that."

Reverend Winthrop nodded soberly. "Let us conclude with a prayer." He looked around and waited until the other five had folded their hands and bowed their heads, then he began, "Great Satan, Thou knowest we are your true servants. We carry forth thy mission bravely and steadfastly in a world where we are vastly outnumbered by the legions of the other god. Recognize our diligence and our sacrifices and grant us thy strength. We pray that you steel our purpose, shelter our secret loyalty, and help bring us victory in your name. Amen."

FIVE

October 24

ON FRIDAY, THE MOMENT SAM HUDDLESTON
walked into his room on morning rounds, John threw back
his sheets and climbed out of bed. "Okay, this is one jerk
to another. You kept me in here another full day to see if
my brain would explode from giving that guy a head bump.
Well it hasn't, but *I'm* going to explode if I have to stay in
here one more hour. Are you hearing me, Mr. Neurosurgeon?"

Sam looked at John for several seconds before he spoke.
"Irrationality is a symptom of brain explosion."

"Is that supposed to be a joke?"

Sam put his hand on John's shoulder. "We had no choice
but to observe you for another twenty-four hours, but you're
right. You seem to be fine in spite of the fact you exposed
your brain to more abuse—"

"I should have exposed my organs to abuse by gunshot instead?"

Sam failed to keep a straight face. "I'm not saying that, of course. I'm just stating the obvious."

"Because you don't know what else to say."

"Exactly. Doctors, especially neurosurgeons, are terribly intimidated by newspaper editors."

"Because we're more intelligent."

"Exactly. Take for example that recent bit of brilliance you wrote, about people picking up their dog crap. Utterly scintillating. Really."

"Your condescending tone constitutes patient abuse," John said. "I'm pretty sure there's someway I can sue you."

"No doubt, but first get dressed and go down to discharge. We need your bed for a sick person."

"Now?"

Sam nodded. "I should probably examine you, but I don't want to find any more reasons to keep you here."

II

JOHN WAS SITTING IN A WHEELCHAIR JUST inside the glass doors of the main hospital entrance as he watched Amy pull around the circle in the patient pick-up/drop-off area. As soon as she came to a stop, John nodded to the orderly who had brought him down and they headed out the electric doors into the cold October morning. Hospital policy forbade any discharged patient from getting out of their wheelchair until they stepped into the car that was taking them off hospital property, and even though John had tried to argue he was perfectly capable of standing and waiting for Amy to arrive, he had finally bowed to the orderly's insistence.

Amy shut off the engine, came around, and opened the passenger door of her Honda Civic. "Sorry it's so tiny," she said, as she leaned over and worked the passenger seat farther back to give John more legroom. "My boss doesn't pay me enough to get a bigger one."

"What a dreadful pig he must be," John said.

He stepped out of the wheelchair and folded himself into the cockpit of the car. Amy closed the door and hurried around to the driver's side. She got in, slammed her door then turned to look at him. "I'm glad you're out."

"Me, too," John nodded. He felt strange asking her to come pick him up, even though in one sense it was perfectly normal. After all, Amy worked for him, and it was perfectly logical he would have asked her for a ride. However, if he was honest he had to admit he wanted to be with her and talk with her for reasons that had nothing to do with the *Salem News*.

He felt a twinge of guilt that he hadn't waited until Sarah was finished with her morning broadcast and could come to pick him up, but he was angry and disappointed with her for what he considered her selfish and brittle reaction to his attraction to Amy. He knew, at least in part, that it probably had been due to loneliness on Sarah's part. She was a very beautiful woman, but she unabashedly put her career before all else. Because of that the men who had come into her life hadn't stayed too long.

They drove several blocks in silence. As they got closer to the water and the more popular tourist areas of Salem, John could see sidewalks jammed with people dressed in witch or warlock costumes. Instead of thinking they looked ridiculous, as he had every single Halloween before this, he thought they looked terrifying because he was now convinced that there were people in his city who were practicing some kind of unspeakable dark arts. He didn't know their identity or their objectives, but the feelings of safety and wellbeing he had always enjoyed in Salem were things of the past. Now as he looked at each costumed witch or warlock he wondered which of them was playing a silly role and which was deadly serious.

As if she was reading his mind, Amy broke the silence. "I had a chance to find out who I really am last night."

John tore his eyes from the sidewalks. "That's good because I haven't made a bit of progress on learning the other names on my arm. I tried to call Rich several times last night. I know he had a night class, and he's such a space cadet, I'm assuming he forgot to turn his phone back on afterward. What did you find out?"

"Have you ever heard of Giles and Martha Corey?"

John squinted as he tried to recall whether he had ever heard the name. "Wasn't he one of the people who died during the Salem witch trials?"

"So was she. Do you know the story?"

John shook his head. "I just remember the name."

"Martha Corey was accused of being a witch by the same girls who accused Rebecca Nurse, and she was subsequently tried and hanged. Her husband was also accused, but he refused to enter a plea. According to the law back in the 1600s, if a person didn't plea, either guilty or innocent, they couldn't be tried. Corey was arrested for practicing witchcraft, but when he refused to enter a plea, he was tortured."

John nodded. "Okay, I *do* remember reading about that when I was doing my Rebecca Nurse paper in college. Didn't Corey get 'pressed'?"

"The sheriff, whose name was George Corwin, took him into a field, stripped him naked and put boards on his chest and stomach. Then six men placed heavy stones on the boards and they left him like that. Over the next two days, they kept adding more stones, but Corey never cried out or made a plea. Supposedly just before he died, he cursed Sheriff Corwin and the entire town of Salem."

John turned and studied Amy's profile for several long moments. Finally, she smiled, "What are you staring at?"

"So, it's way more than coincidence you can see these bloody letters on my arm."

"You're just arriving there now?"

"Obviously I'm much slower than you. It's starting to look pretty obvious that we're more powerful together than we are apart. Even more reason to keep our enemies from discovering you're a direct descendant of a witch trial victim."

They came to a red light, and Amy looked over at him. Her eyes seemed to glint with something he had never seen in them before. "What do you suggest we do about that?" she asked with the barest hint of a smile.

John knew she was thinking the same thing he was. "Well, we, um, we have to make it look like it's something else."

"I wonder how we could do that?"

John felt his cheeks coloring. He felt as awkward as a high school kid again. "I think," he began hearing the words come out in a far throatier manner than he intended. "That maybe we should pretend we're having an affair. It would be a reason for us to be close to each other and maybe stay in the same place at night. My house or your house. It doesn't matter, but I think it would be safer."

The light turned green. The car behind them honked as the traffic around them started to move. Amy took her eyes from his and looked back at the road. "Yes," she said. For John there was no missing the smile on her lips.

III

ABIGAIL PUTNAM STOOD IN THE REAR OF WICCA Wonders and looked through the one-way glass at the crowds that packed her aisles. Outside on the street, visible through the front windows of the shop, a line of people waiting to get inside wended its way out of sight. Abigail knew, having checked just a short time earlier, that the line extended all the way to the corner. Satisfied at the pace of Halloween shopping was probably going to match her aggressive expectations, she turned away and walked toward the back of the shop.

She stopped at an ornately carved wooden door with a brass plate that announced, Abigail Putnam, President, Wicca Enterprises. A numbered lock was set into the door, and she punched in her combination, heard the electronic click, and walked inside. The office was large and well-appointed, with dark woodwork, a row of floor to ceiling bookshelves along one wall, a grouping of chairs and a couch surrounding a low coffee table on the other wall, a flat screen TV hanging above the couch, and an imposing mahogany desk at the far end. Judging from the furnishings, the room was unmistakably an office, but while it was corporate in certain respects in others it fully reflected the eccentricities of its owner.

Rather than being a rectangle or oval, the coffee table, made of heavy glass atop a brass frame, was cast in the shape of a five-pointed star. At the back of the room, a small raised platform atop the credenza was surrounded by thick candles and held two tall statues made of polished wood that glowed in the soft light. They were The Great Horned God, and The Mother Goddess. The painted ceiling resembled a clear night sky with the shapes of the zodiac delineated. The heavy velvet draperies over the widows also bore celestial motifs. Small figurines of witches, warlocks, satyrs, and other creatures stood on nearly every table surface.

Abigail closed the office door behind her, listened for the telltale sound of the electric lock clicking back into place. Satisfied, she turned and regarded the fussy, overly ornate décor. Alone and unobserved, she allowed her shoulders to slump. The office, like her flowing gowns, long hair, and astrological jewelry, helped reinforce her Wiccan image. In the town of Salem she was regarded as a bit of an odd duck, but one who had turned her eccentricities into a thriving business that had made her a millionaire many times over.

Abigail's lips curved up in a humorless smile. She knew many people in town envied her money. How shocked they would be if they knew she would give up all her money in a heartbeat, every single cent of it, if she could walk out of her life completely, without any strings attached? She gave her head a small shake. She could only allow herself these thoughts in the privacy of her office or her bedroom, and even then only for a few seconds at a time.

In more than one sense Abigail knew she was an actress. The citizens of Salem thought she was an actress in her pursuit of money, but in reality she was an actress for Him, and she was very, very good at her role. Otherwise she would not be standing where she was, able to draw breath, but then again she knew fear was the most potent of all motivations and that any hesitation or failure on her part would be rewarded with a cruelty so terrible most humans could not even *imagine* it. She could *never* allow the slightest trace of inner doubt or disloyalty to creep into her eyes or tone of voice. Her life was a struggle to maintain the appearance of utter devotion and rigid discipline and to make certain the other judges did the same.

There was, of course, the Inquisitor above her, watching her actions, interpreting her motives, keeping her in line as she kept the others in line, and above them all was the great beast himself, Satan. She knew it was utterly human for others to envy those who stood closest to any seat of absolute power. What peasant had not envied the chamberlains and courtiers of a king? Who didn't think being proximate to that power and being able to reflect its terrible image on the world was a comfortable place? She shook her head. Someone who had never been in her position couldn't possibly understand.

Abigail had visited a thoroughbred farm in Kentucky one time where some of the world's most expensive racehorses were bred, and she remembered the stud barn where mares in heat were brought in for breeding. A stallion had been in one of the nearby stalls, a constantly moving thousand pounds of bone and muscle. Abigail recalled the scene as if it had been yesterday. The beast's eyes had been wild and full of bloodshot white, his nostrils flared, his flanks slicked with sweat as the scent of the mare and his need to copulate drove him wild. One of the grooms had opened the stall door to bring the stallion out, and in the split second the boy was inside, the stallion had slammed him into the side of the stall and then pounded him savagely with its hooves. There had been no purpose behind the attack, just need and hunger and fury and awesome power. When they finally managed to drag the boy out, he was dead, his skull flattened.

That stallion had been the closest thing to Satan of any creature she had ever seen. What had her foolish ancestors been thinking when they created the covenant that linked them to Satan? It had been an act of incalculable danger and stupidity. To her mind failed crops and drought and starvation on the edge of the world would have been the better choice. To think that bonding with a god would in some way improve one's lot was arrogance in the extreme. A god did not have a human brain. Gods were intelligent, but not in the way of intellect. They were cunning and driven solely by need and hunger and possessed of unimaginable power. They had no shred of compassion or empathy or loyalty or love. No human could imagine their baseness. They could create or destroy, and they did so for their own ends without the slightest compunction. To be a human near a god was to be an ant near a boot. A god was as mindless as the crushing leather sole unrelated to any causality the ant could imagine.

The one thing Abigail did not understand and which none of the judges understood was *why* Satan needed them. Whether Satan drew power from their worship or whether it just satisfied some mindless hunger for subservience and blood sacrifice, there was no denying his need. Giving Satan his sacrifices was like selling crack cocaine to an immensely powerful addict. Satan did things for them, in turn, things based on the original covenant her ancestors had signed. In return for blood, Satan protected them by granting them long lives, freedom from hunger, and prosperity beyond their neighbors. *That* minimal reward was what her ancestors had asked for in return for their slavish devotion when they might have asked for kingdoms. What a pitiful bargain, the equivalent of selling Manhattan Island for a handful of beads. To understand Satan's observation of their bargain, one needed only look at the way cancer was rotting the body of the Very Reverend Staunton Winthrop. He was rich, and he was old, and his stomach, whatever remained of it, was well filled, but Satan could have given him so much more had Winthrop's ancestors and her ancestors only asked.

Yet here she was, the sixth head judge since Edward Putnam made his foul bargain. She had been selected at the age of fifteen, as all the judges were selected, based on judgments made by the sitting judges of all the children in the Putnam line. They selected those possessing the intellect, strength of character, and toughness to handle the terrible burden. From the time a judge was selected and then told the meaning of his or her responsibility and inducted into the coven, there was no turning back. To refuse to serve, to break the bonds of secrecy, or to rebel against the demands of the office meant death, but not in the sense of an end to one's earthly burden. For a disobedient judge, the sentence of death was Promethean, an eternity—or as close to eternity as the human mind could grasp—of torment at the hand of an angry god. Jonathan Edwards in his famous sermon, "Sinners in the Hands of an Angry God," had come closer to the truth than he ever dreamed, only he had been talking about the wrong god.

Abigail Putnam cast a quick glance at the pictures displayed on the other end of her credenza, several silver-framed photographs of her daughter, Annabelle, and her granddaughter, Elizabeth, taken at their home in Vail, Colorado. Annabelle had been a happy, athletic girl, but not brilliant intellectually and not especially tough-minded. Abigail had been grateful for Annabelle's average endowments because they had excluded her from being selected as a future judge, however she was not foolish enough to think they put her daughter and granddaughter beyond Satan's reach. Should Abigail ever fail in her devotion or loyalty, they would be tormented as viciously as Abigail herself. Satan would ensure the pain she suffered would be multiplied down through the generations and live well beyond her.

She pulled a shuddering breath into her lungs and banished all thoughts of doubt and disloyalty from her mind.

She had so much to accomplish, and regardless of her disgust at what was to come she could not risk any misstep. No matter what her personal regrets or feelings of revulsion might be, her fear of Satan's punishment overwhelmed any thoughts of mercy.

She went across the room to her bookshelf, pressed a hidden switch just beneath one of the shelves. Two old, well-worn leather bound books at the end of a row of similar books moved outward revealing something shaped like a cup. Abigail dipped her fingers into the cup, careful not to let spill what came out on the tips of her fingers. After another second the bookends automatically retracted into the row of books, then Abigail placed the hand with the wet blood on the fingertips on a nearly invisible outline in the dark wood paneling just beside the bookshelf. She felt the answering softness, as if the wood was drinking the blood, and then the entire bookshelf moved silently outward several feet to reveal an opening and a set of stairs that led downward.

IV

MELISSA BLAKE HUDDLED IN HER BLANKET IN the almost absolute darkness that had been her world ever since the day she skipped school to buy her Halloween costume. As hard as she had tried to do mental exercises to keep a grip on her sanity, she could feel her mind slipping. At times she would fall into a fitful sleep and dream about her home and her two younger brothers and her father and mother. Her very Catholic parents had seemed so overly strict and sheltering, so determined to keep her in the stultifying Holy Mercy Catholic School for Girls. Her brothers had seemed so incredibly stupid and obnoxious. Yet now in her half-dreams she saw her parents and brothers for what they were, the most wonderful and loving family anyone could imagine.

She would wake up sobbing as the images of her home faded from her brain. She said prayer after prayer, asking God to hear her sincere atonement for her arrogance and sinfulness. If He would just help her get out of this place she would go back to Holy Mercy and be the best student imaginable. She would attend confession every week and say her novenas and do every single thing good Catholic girls should do.

When she would wake fully, she had moments of clarity, and it was at those times she realized her mind was becoming increasingly sluggish and dysfunctional. She had become so accustomed to silence and darkness because the other prisoners, the boy and later a girl she had heard a few days earlier, assuming they were still even nearby, had fallen into the same defeated silence as herself. Therefore it was a shock when she heard someone lifting the locking bar outside her cell, and then instead of just sliding a bucket into the small room and taking the old one, the person opened the door wide and stood there looking at her.

Melissa turned her head away as soon as it happened because the light that came into the cell was so painful it seemed to sear her optic nerves. The person stood in the doorway for several long moments almost as if they had done this before and knew it would take several moments for her to turn in their direction and try to see them.

When she felt her eyes beginning to accept the light, Melissa turned her head partway back toward the doorway. She recognized the silhouette from the only other time anyone had stood in the light long enough for her to actually see them.

"Why am I here?" Melissa asked, her voice hoarse and unused and barely more than a rough whisper.

"Because you have been chosen," a woman's voice came back to her. The woman sounded fairly normal, not angry, not like some character out of a monster movie. In one part of her mind Melissa knew she was grasping for straws, but even so she felt a blast of hope.

"For what?"

"You will see."

Now that her eyes were becoming accustomed to the light, Melissa wanted to keep the woman talking. She looked again at the woman's silhouette, studying it, trying to calculate the odds. The woman wore a long gown or robe, but Melissa could tell from her voice, as well as from the thickness of her body and the way she stood that she was not a young woman. Melissa was young. She was fifteen, and she ran on the track team at school. Still, she hadn't used her legs in . . . how long?

She put her back to the wall and worked her way to her feet. She felt the deadness in her legs, the sluggishness of her muscles. Could she make a break for it and get past the woman? If she did, which way should she turn? How could she get out? Was there more than one doorway to choose from? What if the one she needed was locked? What could she use as a weapon if she needed one?

"Have you come to get me out?" Melissa asked as she flexed and un-flexed her leg muscles.

"Yes," the woman said, matter of fact. "It is time for the Second Sacrament."

"The Second Sacrament is Confirmation. I'm already confirmed."

"This one is different, dear."

"Different how?" Melissa asked, inching her way off the wall and in the direction of the woman.

"Different church."

"I'm Catholic."

"Yes, I know."

Melissa moved another step forward. "How did you know that?"

"Who else would mutter 'Mother Mary full of grace' so many times in her sleep?"

"I was praying to ask for rescue."

"I know that, too. You all pray to be rescued. It's part of the plan."

Melissa heard so much confidence in the woman's tone, as if she had done this a hundred times before. "Part of *what* plan?"

"You worship your god, we worship ours. These are our Sacraments. This is our way of worship."

Melissa wasn't really listening to the woman because her focus was on inching toward the door. She kept testing her legs, hoping to feel some spring return to her muscles. When she was about three or four feet from the woman, she stopped, summoned her courage and darted forward, aiming for the open space between the woman and the door-frame. Even though her legs felt spongy, she made it to the opening before the woman moved to block her. She stepped into the hallway, looked left, then looked right.

Instantly her breath caught in her throat because there were two people on her left and two more on her right, blocking her path in either direction. She froze and then a voice came from behind her. "Excellent, my dear. You are proving yourself to be a worthy sacrifice."

A second later Melissa felt a staggering shock, so power-ful it was almost like being hit with a club. It cut her legs out from under her, and she fell onto her side and then rolled onto her back. Even though she could not move her muscles, she was still awake, and she looked up at a woman who was in her late fifties or early sixties. She was medium height with long hair shot through with gray, and she appeared heavyset beneath a black gown decorated with celestial sym-bols.

"I know you," Melissa managed, although her lips and tongue felt thick and unresponsive. "You're Mrs. Putnam. You own the store."

"Yes, my dear. I'm sure you have seen me," the woman said. She was holding a small device in one hand that had what looked like two electrodes protruding from the end.

Melissa rolled her eyes so she could see the others. One was a tall, distinguished-looking man who looked strangely familiar, and she thought she must have seen his face in the paper or on TV. He wore a navy blue suit and looked like a grandfather, or the kind of man who ran things, the kind of man people could depend upon. What was he doing here? Another man moved up beside the first and looked down at her. When she got a better look at him her breath froze in her throat because she saw that he wore a priest's collar. Seeing it brought a fresh burst of confusion. She didn't know whether to be more afraid or more hopeful.

"Who are you people?" she managed after a few seconds.

"We are the judges," the first man answered.

"What do you judge?"

The priest stepped forward. He leaned on a cane and appeared to be frail. "The lambs of Christ," he said in a clear voice.

"Please, I don't understand. Can't you just let me go?"

"I'm afraid not, my child," the priest said.

"What have I done to you?"

"Nothing to us, but you have sinned nonetheless."

Melissa was starting to get back the use of her limbs. She moved her head and looked at all these old people staring down at her. "How have I sinned?"

"You have worshipped the wrong god."

"That's not true! I go to church every Sunday. I go to confession once a month. I go to Catholic school for heaven's sake."

"Exactly," said the woman who had opened her prison door. "Now be a good girl. You need to take a shower and get all ready for your Second Sacrament. If you're not a good girl, I'll have to shoot you again with this." She held up the Taser and hit the trigger, causing blue bolts of electricity to spark loudly between the electrodes.

Melissa struggled to her feet and looked around at her captors, the tall man in the navy blue suit and the sickly priest on one side and on the other a huge man with buzz cut hair and small, cruel eyes and just behind him a blond woman with cold blue eyes. She wondered what it was about all of them that struck her as odd, and after another second she realized what it was. They were all looking at her with a sense of barely suppressed hunger, as if her presence here constituted some sort of much heralded event or achievement.

"But I've already been through my Confirmation."

"You need to do it again, dear."

Melissa shook her head, trying to understand their twisted logic. After days of privation and fear and darkness and inactivity, she was having a hard time putting together clear thoughts. Fresh panic bubbled at the edges of her awareness, but she reminded herself she was at least out of her dark prison. She could stay out longer and maybe learn something useful if she kept them talking. "If I need to prepare for my Second Sacrament, what was my first?"

"Baptism," the priest said. "Just like in the Catholic Church."

"Hardly," Melissa shot back.

The priest nodded. "Baptism by Separation," the priest went on.

"My Sacrament was being in that cell, living in the dark and going to the bathroom in a bucket?"

The priest smiled, and with the yellow tint of his skin and his concave cheeks, it gave him a cadaverous appearance. "Yes."

Melissa looked at these people. There was no joke written in their eyes. They were deadly serious. "Baptism is the joining of person to the community of Christ," she insisted.

The priest seemed to be enjoying her confusion and

discomfort. "Yes, and ours is the opposite. It is the separation of a person from the community of Christ."

"That's crazy."

"No, not at all. It is vital for our purposes."

"But you're a priest. How can separating a person from God be your purpose?"

"All is not as it seems, my child."

5.

JOHN ARRIVED BACK AT THE *SALEM NEWS* TO FIND his desk buried by a sea of letters, messages, memos, and back issues of the paper, as well as editorials from other papers that Amy had cut out for him to read. It took him all the way through a lunch eaten at his desk and numerous interruptions from staff writers and others before he was able to get through the piles. When he finished, he buzzed Amy and asked her to step back to his office.

She walked in, eyed his newly cleared desktop, and raised her eyebrows. "You work fast."

He held up her list of fourteen questions and issues. "I have more important things to do right now than running this paper. I want you to have final approval on all articles and layout for today's edition."

"You don't even want to see it?"

He held up the last four days of the *Salem News*. "You don't need me looking over your shoulder. You've done a splendid job in my absence."

"You don't have to say that."

"I know, but I mean it."

"Thank you. What are you going to do?"

"Remember what you said about genealogy?"

She nodded.

"Well, I'm going to try and figure out who 'they' are, meaning the people who tried to kill me two days ago."

"How will you do that?"

"We know one of the men Rebecca Nurse took me back to see was Edward Putnam. I'm going to start with him and try to understand if some of his present day relatives might be involved in this."

"There were five other people in that meeting, right?"

"Yes, a total of six."

"How many judges were there in the Salem witch trials?"

John snapped his fingers and nodded. "Great minds work in the same direction. I looked it up earlier this morning, and there were eleven judges, plus two attorney-generals, plus the sheriff." He turned and looked through the glass walls of his office at the people working at their desks in the newsroom. No one seemed to be paying any particular attention to Amy or him. He unbuttoned his cuff and rolled up his left sleeve. "Putnam's name is easy to read, but he wasn't one of the Salem judges. Another name I'm pretty sure I can make out is that of the sheriff, George Corwin. I think I can also make out the name Hathorne. That would be John Hathorne, one of the judges and interestingly an ancestor of Nathaniel Hawthorne, who changed the spelling of his name because he was ashamed of the connection. There is also a Sewell. That would be Samuel Sewell, also one of the judges and another resident of Salem. The last two names are harder to read, but

I'm pretty sure one is Bartholomew Gedney. He was one of the judges and also a citizen of Salem. And I think the final name is Jonathan Corwin, brother of George and also one of the judges. That would make four of the men around the table judges in the trial, plus the sheriff, plus Edward Putnam, who I'm petty sure was the ringleader."

"Well, I know who my first choice would be."

"For what?"

"For which descendants of those six people who might be involved today. Have you thought about Abigail Putnam, owner of Wicca Wonders?"

John raised his eyebrows. "Our local witch entrepreneur—that would be an interesting way for her to cover her tracks, wouldn't it?"

"My thoughts exactly."

"How do we proceed?"

John thought about it for a moment. "Do you think this time of year involves something special or important for them?"

Amy shook her head. "Duuuh! It's a couple days to Halloween, and they're witches or devil worshippers or both. What do you think?"

John made a face. "Yeah, I guess that was kind of a stupid question."

Amy's face became serious. "Let me just try something on you, and I promise I'm not doing it to dredge up bad memories. Okay?"

John nodded.

"Julie's accident was just a few days before Halloween, and she was driving your car."

He started to shake his head.

"You need to consider it."

He nodded. "I actually have, but if they were trying to kill me back then, why? And why wait four more years? It doesn't make sense."

"But it might make sense to them. Maybe we just don't understand the reasons. Can't you see all the strange coincidences?"

John gazed at her for a long moment, then he nodded. "I don't believe in coincidences."

"Thank you!"

He glanced at the chair in the corner of his office where Rebecca Nurse was working on her embroidery, and he felt a surprising blast of hope and a surge of energy the likes of which he hadn't felt since before Julie's death. In a bizarre way he felt more like his old self than he had in over four years, and as he looked back and forth between Rebecca and Amy, he had a sense of purpose and a feeling as if the three of them had become a team of some sort, a bizarre team to be sure, but a team nonetheless.

He grabbed his computer keyboard and typed in the name of a genealogy search engine he had seen advertised. "While you put today's edition to bed, I'm going to start out doing three things," he told Amy. "I'm going to discover the family trees of the six people I think were around that table and find out which ones live in the Salem area, and I'm going to figure out where Richard Putnam fits into the puzzle. And I'm getting my friend Rich to take me over to the Peabody Essex Institute."

Amy's eyebrows went up at the mention of Rich's name. "Stay sober."

"We're not going out to have drinks. I called him earlier with a bunch of questions about the early Salem witch trials and he told me that The Phillips Library had recently been given a large collection of old papers from The House of the Seven Gables. Rich knows the archivist, and he can get me in to look at them." He shrugged. "I'm going back to the beginning. I know it's not exactly one of our fourteen points, but maybe there's something there that can help us. I'll come back here afterward and tell you what I was able to dig up."

Amy glanced at her watch. "I've got one more thing on my schedule that I haven't told you about yet. Melissa Blake's parents called back, and they're willing to let me interview them at six o'clock this evening. I'm driving up to Beverly to talk to them."

"Melissa Blake?" John asked, wracking his brain to place the familiar name.

"The most recent disappearance. It may be a dead end, but I want to pursue it because of the time of year. Most of the kids who disappear have been runaways or kids from tough backgrounds, but Melissa was an honor student and pretty much a perfect kid."

VI

AT THREE O'CLOCK THAT AFTERNOON RICHARD Harvey came walking through the newsroom and stopped outside John's glass walled office. John had kept the door closed all day, which was contrary to his usual habit of leaving it open so staffers could breeze in with questions whenever necessary, however he had the white board set up facing his desk and didn't want to start people speculating about what he was doing.

"Do I have to knock, O Great One?" Rich said, pushing the door open.

"No, you wouldn't anyway, so come in."

"You've got this board all shoved up against your desk so nobody outside can see it. Are you working on some great piece of investigative journalism, by chance?" Rich walked toward John's desk until he could get a good peek at the white board and the names John had written there. "Interesting," he muttered, as he read. Then he turned to John. "Does Sam Huddleston know you're doing this?"

"Why?"

"I think if he did he might determine he'd let you out of the hospital a bit too early. Maybe your brain is swelling, but not in a way that makes you more intelligent . . . like me."

"Funny."

"Maybe I was wrong, but I was under the impression that the *Salem News* reported on . . . news?"

"This is news."

"Right." Rich turned back to the board. "Hmmm, let's see, Edward Putnam, Bartholomew Gedney, George Corwin, John Hathorne, Samuel Sewell, and Jonathan Corwin. Are we a little late doing their obituaries? They only died three hundred years ago. Haven't the Salem witch trials been done? A few million times?"

"If you weren't such an egregious jerk, I might have told you why those names are on the board."

"Well, let's see. You have Abigail Putnam under Edward Putnam and Senator Hallowell under Bartholomew Gedney, so I'm guessing this has something to do with living descendants. That's news! What is this a Halloween story?"

"It's a secret story. If I told you what it was I'd have to kill you."

"It might kill me to read it. Is that what this trip to the Peabody is all about?"

"You said there were some new papers that might pertain to devil worship or witchcraft?"

"I said some papers were recently discovered in the House of Seven Gables and they were written in mid-to-late nineteenth century. You're the one who assumed they must relate to witchcraft, but if you look out at the sidewalks of Salem, you'd also note that at this time of year, everybody thinks that everything in this city relates to witchcraft." He shook his head. "Why did I open my big mouth?" He took his car keys from his coat pocket and jingled them. "Ready to go?"

John fell silent as they drove across the city to the three-building complex of the Peabody Essex Museum, while Rich concentrated on working his way through the late afternoon traffic. Only a few days before Halloween Salem was totally jammed with tourists who added to the general confusion. As they drove past Wicca Wonders, John looked out and saw that the line waiting to get into the store ran all the way to the end of the block and around the corner. With the car windows up, he could barely hear the screams emanating from the store. Even so he heard them, and they reminded him of why they were going to the Peabody. He squeezed his eyes shut at the sound, but he couldn't help wondering if there could really be anything in a bunch of old documents that might establish a link to some kind of present day occult plot.

Rich parked in a garage near the library and led John up the front steps into Plummer Hall where he asked to see Joe D'Angelo, the head archivist. They had to wait only a minute or two before a tall man with glasses and a half moon of dark hair that surrounded a shiny pink skull came through a door and strode quickly toward them. Instead of a sports coat he wore a navy blue cardigan sweater that had leather elbow patches and looked stretched out from long use.

"Back again so soon?" the man asked.

"Of course," Rich replied, "when you have such a

wonderful new trove of papers from The House of the Seven Gables, how could I stay away?"

"I wondered how long it would take you to get your nose into them," he said, holding his hand out to Rich.

"I appreciate you meeting with us on short notice," Rich said as they shook hands.

Rich introduced John, and D'Angelo gave a little bow. "We exist only to serve the great professors of the world."

"Of course you do," Rich said dryly. "But my friend is a newspaper editor."

"Let me rephrase," D'Angelo said. "We exist to serve anyone who makes a nice annual donation."

D'Angelo took them through the same door he had come through a moment earlier and then down a flight of steps to another door marked, "Rare Books and Manuscripts Section. Restricted Access." He took a magnetic card that hung on a ribbon around his neck, ran it through an electric lock then opened the door when the lock clicked open.

Rich and John followed the archivist into a small room where there were coat hangers for extraneous clothing, cubbyholes for personal effects, an umbrella stand, and a rubber mat that John supposed was for galoshes in the winter. There were also five or six navy blue cardigan sweaters hanging together at one end of the coat rack with, "Property of Phillips Library," stenciled in white letters along the back. On the far wall stood another door that said:

NO FLASH PHOTOGRAPHY

WEAR GLOVES AT ALL TIMES

NO FOOD OR DRINK ALLOWED

Beside the door a clear plastic box hung from the wall, filled with white cloth gloves. D'Angelo reached into the pocket of his cardigan and pulled out his own pair of gloves.

Rich took off his overcoat, hung it up, donned one of the cardigan sweaters, and took a pair of white gloves from the box on the wall. John took off his own overcoat and pulled on a sweater, feeling the bruises in his arms and shoulders as he stretched. He stuffed his briefcase into one of the cubbyholes, put on a pair of gloves then went over to stand beside Rich.

"Ready?" D'Angelo asked.

Without waiting for a reply, he opened the next door and led them into the collection. Right away, John felt the temperature and humidity change. The room was considerably cooler than the rest of the library, and when he looked at several instruments on the wall he saw that the temperature in the room was 65° and the humidity was 45 percent.

"You're interested solely in our new acquisitions?" D'Angelo asked.

Rich looked a question at John, who nodded. "I think the new stuff is all we'll have time for," he told D'Angelo.

The archivist sat them at a research table and then went into the stacks and brought out three boxes that he placed on the table and opened. Inside each box were stacks of letters and other writings all carefully stacked and separated. He showed them how to carefully separate the pages to avoid any possibility of damage.

"These were found recently when they were renovating the house. Apparently they were sealed away many years ago, but we don't know why or under whose orders. You gentlemen have the distinction of being among the first scholars to have seen them.

"I'll be upstairs in the main library. If you need me for anything just hit the buzzer by the door in the outer room and I'll come down. Enjoy."

Rich took the lead in handling the fragile papers, making a small stack by his own chair of some church documents written by pastors of the nineteenth century Salem congregations. He read them and made notes while John busied himself scanning various other papers, looking for anything that might relate to his ancestors, especially Rebecca Nurse or Anne Putnam.

"You know," Rich said as they each went through papers. "Tell me if you already know this, but by all accounts the witchcraft hysteria started in the home of a Reverend Samuel Parris. Parris's family owned a slave from Barbados whose name was Tituba, and Samuel Parris's teenage daughters began to go off into the woods to recite spells they'd learned from Tituba. It was probably thrilling stuff for a bunch of bored girls being raised by unimaginably boring and severe Puritan parents. Apparently their spells became kind of a teenage fad, and while they were probably a lark at first, things got out of hand and something like group hysteria began to spread among the teenage girls of Salem Village. One by one the girls started to have screaming fits, convulsions, twitching, unexplained babbling, and twisting of limbs. Apparently these fits often seemed to be in reaction to prayers or the mention of holy words.

"The local doctor couldn't figure out what the cause was or how to cure it, so Reverend Parris gathered a bunch of ministers from the area. They decided immediately that witches were the cause of the young girl's torment, and they began to put pressure on the girls to name names. Tituba, of course, was one of the first to be accused, but amazingly she was never tried or executed for being a witch."

"What happened to her?" John asked as he continued to scan through the parchments.

"She went to jail but was later released. There's no record of her after that."

"And you mock me for having an interest in this stuff. You're filled with useless facts."

"My PhD thesis at Duke was on the Church's role in validating the belief in witchcraft in Colonial America. I am an absolute fount of useless information, but then I'm a college professor. My knowledge is not required or expected to be relevant. Yours, on the other hand, is, Mr. Newspaper Editor."

"Okay, so tell me this Professor of Useless Knowledge, were there ever any credible rumors that some of the good citizens of Salem were involved in devil worship? I'm not talking about Rebecca Nurse or Sarah Goode or Sarah Osborne, but about the theoretically upstanding citizens who never got accused of anything."

Rich turned from the document he had been reading. "What you have to understand is that the Puritans were, essentially, nuts. They were paranoid, humorless, and fanatical, and they tended to become hysterical over any mention of sorcery, witchcraft, or devil worship. So, of course, there were rumors of lots and lots of things. As far as I know they were all absolute baloney." He stopped and raised his eyebrows playfully. "Why, do you know something I don't?"

"No," John said, a bit too quickly.

"You're working on some story but you won't tell me what it is."

John shrugged. "If I told everyone my stories before we publish them, nobody would buy the paper, right?"

"I suppose, but—"

"Wait," John said. He had been working his way to the bottom of one of the boxes as he listened to Rich. Now, as he reached the last documents in the box his eyes locked on a name that made his breath catch in his throat.

VIII

HE WAS LOOKING AT A BOUND STACK OF PAPERS titled, *The Truth about the Witch Trials of Salem* and below the title the unmistakable signature of Nathaniel Hawthorne. John's heart started to beat faster.

"What have you got there?" Rich demanded.

"Something apparently written by Nathaniel Hawthorne. Says it's the truth about the witch trials."

"Can I see it?"

"Sure, when I'm done."

"If you find something, it would be nice to keep your mouth shut and let your friend, the professor, take the credit for discovering it."

"I don't know why you give a crap. You already have tenure."

"We fight viciously for the smallest morsels of reputation."

"I don't care about credit. You can be the one who gets his name in the paper."

"Thank you."

Ignoring Rich's jealous stare, John started to separate the pages just the way D'Angelo had showed him. Although he was no scholar of historic documents, he noted right away

that Hawthorne's writing appeared halting and disjointed, as
if he had written these words toward the end of his life.

*All of my life I have felt tremendous shame of my
relation to John Hathorne, who oversaw the forma-
tion of the witch trial tribunals and the subsequent
torture and hanging of innocent victims in a madness
that has come to be known as the Salem witchcraft trials. Changing the spelling of my surname was indeed a
weak attempt to conceal my ties to this man. Some may
consider it a selfish gesture, but it was the only thing I
could do to distance myself from the 'Hathorne' name
and curse of evil deeds done...*

John stopped and rubbed his eyes because the old writing
was faded and hard to decipher and because the adrenaline
he had felt when he first saw the title and Hawthorne's name
was quickly fading. After another second he stifled a yawn
and reminded himself that Sam Huddleston's orders had been
to work not more than six hours for the first couple days
back. He probably ought to quit, but if he did he might not
get another crack at these rare manuscripts. He kept reading.

*Like most other residents of Salem, I was taught that
these infamous and shameless witch trials were overseen
by the elders and magistrates of the Colony and were
based on the accusations of a few girls. This had always
seemed believable because Salem Village in the 1690s was
a place inhabited by a few hundred tired and desperate
Puritans who were suffering from hunger, famine, disease, drought, and the continual threat of Indian attacks.*

These settlers, having come to these inhospitable shores believing God would provide them succor only to find themselves nearly at death's door, were easily persuaded that the evils of their existence had been brought about not by God, but by witches.

In spite of the coolness of the air in the room, John felt his eyelids growing heavy. He was about to hand the parchment over to Rich, when he glanced farther down the page and saw something that made his sleepiness drop away.

. . . might have gone unchallenged but for the astounding tale told to me recently by my old and noble friend and Bowdoin classmate, Captain John Bancroft Andrews, who claims to have discovered the true story of the Salem witchcraft trials. Had any other person told me this story, I would have deemed it the raving of a lunatic, however, I have known Captain Andrews to be a man of sound mind as well as great intelligence, sagacity, and courage.

Yet, even as I record what I now believe to be the truth about these witchcraft trials and the evil cult that instigated them, I do so only in the knowledge that I am approaching the end of my own life through which death will put me beyond reach of the cult's vengeance. It is also my intent to secret this document away so that later generations might discover the vital truth, but only after my children and grandchildren are also beyond the cult's reach. Such is my fear of their evil. May God forgive me for my cowardice.

John's heart was pounding as he read these astounding revelations about Hawthorne and his great, great grandfather. Captain Andrews's portrait still hung in the upstairs of his Pickering Wharf house, and finding this ancestral link to his current situation hit him like a shot of adrenaline. He quickly passed over Hawthorne's long digression about his early friendship with Captain Andrews and his relating of how the captain had come to own some sixteen clipper ships and amassed a significant fortune in the "Eastern Trade," as he scanned for more information about the "cult."

Finally, the last part of Hawthorne's work detailed the captain's revelation to him about his terrifying discovery. It occurred in 1860, after Andrews returned from a trip to the Far East on his clipper, *Formosa*. Immediately upon docking in Salem, Andrews sent an urgent note to Hawthorne saying they needed to meet.

When Hawthorne went to see him first thing the next morning, he was expecting to see his old friend, who he described as "always remarkably strong and hearty, bursting with energy and confidence." However, he found that after a little over four months at sea Andrews had deteriorated markedly, and Hawthorne was shocked to see his friend's "pale skin, gaunt face, and yellowing eyes."

What alarmed Hawthorne even more was the story Andrews told him.

The honest and brave Captain told me of the old man he had met in Sumatra who claimed to be a direct descendant of Bartholomew Gedney, one of the judges in the Salem witchcraft trials. According to Andrews, that man, Joseph Gedney by name, swore to him that an evil cult was at work in Salem doing the work of Satan. According to the man's tale, this coven is currently over a hundred and fifty years old, having started its dark work during the Salem witch trials in 1692.

Gedney told Andrews that he learned of this when their grandfather told his brother that he had been cho-sen to be part of this coven. He was to have no choice in the matter, and the reward for disobedience or for reveal-ing the coven's existence would be death. When their grandfather realized that the younger boy had overheard, he ordered the older brother to kill him. Running for his life, Gedney stowed away on a clipper that left Salem on the next tide. He had never returned.

Andrews said Gedney's tale had not convinced him, but the fact that there had been two attempts on his life on the return voyage, including one in which poison was slipped into his tea had made him a reluctant believer. Andrews had burned his lip as he started to take a sip of the hot tea and put it down to cool. A moment later, mistaking the captain's cup for his own, one of the other officers had taken a sip of the now cooled tea and died instantly. The poison had been so powerful that the small drop on Andrews lip had rendered him in his current condition.

Furthermore, Andrews had become convinced that the spirit of his ancestor, Rebecca Nurse an innocent

woman who was hanged as a witch, was trying to commu-
nicate with him. He made me swear to tell no one else of
this claim.

John's breath caught, and he stopped reading, thinking about the implications. Until this moment, some snide,
journalistic corner of his brain had remained skeptical of
everything, of Rebecca Nurse, of the voices, of his memories of the afternoon he fell down the steps. That part of his
brain had remained immune even to Amy's acceptance and
had stubbornly refused to consider any alternative but his
encroaching insanity. Now that final skepticism crumbled
before what he was reading.

"What?" Rich asked.

John shook his head. "It says my great-great-grandfather
thought there was a cult of devil worshippers in Salem."

"Did Hawthorne buy it, or did he think your grandfather
was crazy? I hope it was the latter."

John glanced at his friend. "Hawthorne believed it," he
said, at the same time reminding himself that Rich's skepticism
was the rational reaction. After all, what did Hawthorne's
writing prove other than that Captain Andrews may have
been susceptible to crazy stories?

Still, it was yet another link in an invisible chain that
seemed to bind John Andrews more and more tightly to
Rebecca Nurse and made "rational" explanations increasingly hard to swallow.

Rich laughed. "One thing about sailors, they were incredibly superstitious. Even though everyone from Salem was

purportedly Christian, a lot of the ships that sailed out of here had unusual rituals intended to placate the sea gods or ward off storms and pirate attacks. Other crews, when they discovered their owners had loaded cargoes of Guinea pepper or black cumin, decided those weren't spices but were ingredients for witchcraft potions. In several cases they even mutinied and threw the cargo overboard."

"It's amazing the crap people believe," John said, feeling a sharp twinge of guilt for trying to deliberately mislead his friend.

"Amen to that."

IX

MELISSA BLAKE HAD BEEN LOCKED IN A SMALL room with tile walls and a concrete floor with a drain in the middle. A wooden bench was built into the wall on one side of the room with a floor-to-ceiling mirror bolted into the wall beside it. On the bench lay a clean white bath towel, a fresh bar of soap, shampoo, a comb, and hair dryer. Beside it was a neatly folded white gown.

When she looked at herself in the mirror she saw a person she didn't recognize. Her face was pale and drawn, her cheeks hollow. The clothes she had picked out to wear the day she cut school and went to Wicca Wonder had been clean but intended to make her look like something a punk high school kid might wear. Now they were the real thing, shiny with grease and caked-on filth, matted and wrinkled and impossibly disgusting. There were bags beneath her eyes she had never seen before. Her hair, which she had always kept cut short and clean, looked like the tangle of a bird's nest. *I look like a thirty-year-old bag lady*, she thought to herself as she started to strip.

She threw the clothes on the floor, then went over and turned on the shower. To her delight, hot water steamed out of the showerhead in a high-pressure cascade. Bringing the soap and shampoo from the bench she stepped under the flow and felt the wonderful sensation as the hot water coursed over her body and she started to lather herself clean. She scrubbed and rinsed four times, and then shampooed three times. Only when she was absolutely certain she was finally really and truly clean did she turn off the water and grab the towel to dry off.

When she finished she held up the white robe or gown or whatever it was and saw a pair of panties had been laid beneath it, but no bra. She slipped on the panties then put on the gown, which tied in three places on the side. With everything snugly fastened, she finished by drying and combing her hair, and when she had done that she went over and banged on the door.

Abigail Putnam opened the door after only a few seconds. In the time that Melissa had been showering, Abigail had also changed clothes and now wore an expensive looking royal blue gown with richly embroidered astral symbols. When she saw Melissa she smiled in a way that reminded the girl of how a mother might look at her daughter on prom night.

"My dear, you look absolutely lovely," Abigail said.

Taken by surprise, Melissa said, "Thank you."

She looked past Abigail Putnam, wondering if this might be a chance for escape. Not seeing the other four people, she glanced down at Abigail's hands, and her heart sank as she spotted the Taser.

Abigail Putnam must have followed Melissa's eyes,

because she said, "Please don't be foolish, my dear. It would be a shame to spoil your lovely appearance."

She stood back from the doorway to let Melissa out, and by blocking the way left, she forced Melissa to turn right. They went down a narrow passage carved from native rock like all the others Melissa had seen, until they came to a carved wooden door. The head of some horned demon or devil was carved into it, and it was realistic enough to make all Melissa's fear bubble to the surface. Until that moment she had felt a growing sense of hope. After all she was clean and no longer imprisoned in darkness.

She turned back toward Abigail Putnam. "What's this?"

"Just a door, my dear."

"To what?"

"To a very nice meal that will begin your Second Sacrament."

Melissa wanted to argue, insist she had already performed the Second Sacrament by attending her Confirmation, but she knew it would do no good. She shrugged, and accepting that she had no choice, she turned and went through the door. The moment she passed through she stopped, and her breath caught in her throat.

This room was completely different from every other part of her prison. She had long ago concluded that wherever she was, it was deep underground. Not only were the walls rough-hewn rock, but there was also the absolute, tomb-like silence and the coolness of the dank air. This room, however, seemed very different. The walls were paneled in dark wood, mahogany perhaps. An antique oriental rug covered a floor of random width wooden planks. The ceiling was low, consisting of rough plaster between dark beams. A large fireplace stood against one wall, and a lovely blaze threw warm light into the room. It also dried and warmed the air, so that the room felt cozy.

A comfortable looking couch and several overstuffed chairs spread out in front of the fireplace. Four other judges were seated there, as if they had been awaiting her entrance. They turned their heads as she walked into the room, and then one by one they stood and nodded in greeting.

On the other side of the room Melissa saw a round dining table covered with a tablecloth. A large candelabra held several candles that threw flickering shadows across the table, and the candlelight glittered on silver place settings and china and crystal wine glasses. In addition to the plates and glasses, she saw several large silver serving dishes on the table, and she smelled the unmistakable aroma of roasted meat. Immediately, her stomach began to growl and she realized how hungry she was. She counted six chairs around the table, and hoped she was going to be a dinner guest.

Abigail Putnam followed Melissa into the room, and with a gentle hand on the small of Melissa's back, ushered her toward the table. "I hope you will join us in a celebratory meal," she said.

Realizing she had no more choice in this than she'd had in anything else since she became their captive, Melissa nodded. "Okay."

The four people came from the fireplace and gathered around the table, directing Melissa to take a seat that faced the fire so she would be able to enjoy its beauty. She did as they instructed then waited.

"Allow me to make introductions," Abigail Putnam said. Nodding toward the sickly looking man with the priest's collar, she said, "This is the Very Reverend Staunton Winthrop. And this," she indicated the other woman, who so far had not said a word, "is Amanda Putnam Pendergast." She pointed to the distinguished man with the gray hair, "This is Senator Austin Hallowell, and this," she said indicating the very large man with the eyes that made Melissa uncomfortable, "is Lieutenant Cabot Corwin. And as you properly surmised earlier, I am Abigail Putnam, the owner of Wicca Wonders."

Melissa looked around at all the faces. She was certain she had seen Senator Hallowell's picture in the paper, probably on numerous occasions. She didn't know the others, but they were clearly important people. "You are also a bunch of kidnappers," she said.

Senator Hallowell nodded as he pulled back his chair. "We appear to act with a rashness unbecoming of our station, however, you will soon understand our greater purpose. I assure you there is nothing irrational about our actions or our motives."

When all of them had taken their seats, Reverend Winthrop cleared his throat and bowed his head. Everyone else followed suit.

"To Him who giveth us life, health, and wealth, we offer our thanks," he intoned.

Melissa thought the prayer was pretty strange, but then decided it was no more or less strange than anything else about these people. They had imprisoned her for days, but they hadn't beaten her or raped her or killed her, and now here they were inviting her to a very proper meal. She glanced around at their faces. Other than the very large man with the small, mean eyes and buzz cut hair they looked like the kind of people who didn't usually do stupid or sick things. They sat down at the table with quiet dignity, not like cruel people, not like criminals. As she tried to figure out what was going on, Abigail Putnam reached for the largest of the serving dishes and removed the dome-shaped cover to reveal a roast beef still steaming from the oven. She stood and removed the covers from several other serving dishes where Melissa could see mashed potatoes, green beans, candied carrots, and Yorkshire pudding.

For the next several minutes, Melissa forgot about being a prisoner and also about the mystery of the Second Sacrament, and she filled her stomach with hot delicious food. The other five people all ate as well, but there was almost no conversation. The meal was eaten with a sense of formality as if some kind of rite was being observed, even though Melissa had no idea what it might be. There was a carafe of wine on the table, and her five captors poured some into their glasses and then offered it to Melissa. She refused. She ate until she was quite full, thinking that she didn't know what was coming next but that she shouldn't waste the opportunity. When she finished, Abigail Putnam left the room and returned a moment later with a pumpkin pie and ice cream. Melissa found some room and ate a helping of dessert, as well.

When everyone finished, Melissa felt an air of expectancy in the room, as if her five captors were feeling a sense of excitement or nervous anticipation about what was to come next. Feeling emboldened by her newly clean hair and flesh and her full stomach, Melissa folded her hands on the table.

"May I ask when you are going to let me go home?"

There were several shared glances around the table, but no one spoke up to answer her.

Trying again, Melissa asked, "What exactly is this Second Sacrament?"

"That, my dear, is an excellent question," Reverend Winthrop responded. He sat forward, seeming comfortable acting as the spokesman for the table in spiritual matters. "Your Second Sacrament here tonight will be the undoing of your first Second Sacrament."

Melissa shook her head. "I don't understand."

"We will require you to disavow your membership in the Catholic faith."

Melissa closed her eyes and shook her head. She felt quite certain of her answer. "I will never do that." As she said it she felt the eyes of the large man, the one Abigail had introduced as Lieutenant Corwin, as if they were burning into her. When she glanced at him the intent look he was giving her sent chills down her spine, and she tore her gaze away.

Abigail Putnam cleared her throat. "Let me be perfectly clear on this, my dear, you *will* renounce your membership in the Catholic faith, and you *will* renounce your belief in the Father, the Son and the Holy Ghost. You *will* do exactly as we instruct."

Melissa was shaking her head, but Abigail kept on speaking. "You *may* do these things voluntarily, in the very pleasant setting of this table and in the company of my associates. If you choose not to make your renunciation here, you will be taken into the next room where our methods will be of a cruder nature."

"This is crazy," Melissa insisted. "Why are you doing this?"

"Because the master we serve demands it, my dear."

Melissa thought back to the cryptic statements Abigail had made earlier when she said something about their "other" god and something about sacrifice. "What master are you talking about?" she asked, her voice shrinking to a near whisper.

"The great God Satan," Reverend Winthrop said, as if instructing her in some undeniable truth. "He demands that you perform His Second Sacrament."

Melissa closed her eyes and tried to keep her head from spinning. She felt as if she had been drugged, but she knew that wasn't the case. Instead, because everything she was hearing sounded like it came from the script of some cheesy horror movie, she felt like she had lost her bearings.

"I'm not going to do anything for the Devil," she said

when she opened her eyes and looked across the table at Reverend Winthrop.

Lieutenant Corwin turned his head toward Abigail Putnam and raised his eyebrows in question. When Abigail nodded, he rose from the table, went to the wall, dipped his fingers in a small bowl mounted in a bracket, then placed his hand on one of the flat wooden panels in the mahogany paneled wall.

Melissa heard a click and watched the wall swing back a few inches, like a door coming unlatched. The large man held the section of wall in one hand, but did not swing it open any farther. Instead he turned and looked at Abigail.

"My dear, I'm sure you heard the other two young people who were down the hallway from yourself," Abigail said to Melissa.

"You mean the other two prisoners? A guy and a girl?"

Abigail nodded. "Yes. The boy was a runaway. The girl was a prostitute."

Melissa waited. Already, her stomach had started to churn when Abigail referred to both young people in the past tense.

"We had to decide which one of you would be offered the honor of a dedicatory meal and the opportunity to willingly and peacefully accept the Second Sacrament. Neither of the others possessed anything even remotely close to your moral strength, so our selection was quite simple. You were the only real candidate. The others were not even given consideration."

Melissa was shaking her head. "What did you do to them?"

"We instructed them the same way we have with you. We told each of them it was time to perform their Second Sacrament. To our surprise both of them struggled a great deal harder than any of us would have suspected. They showed surprising moral toughness."

With that the big man swung the hinged section of wall all the way back so Melissa could look into the next room. The room was pitch dark, but even before she could see inside the first thing that hit her was a coppery smell and then the stink of human feces and urine. The stench struck her as even more shocking because she was sitting at a table loaded with expensive linen, china, and silver, but nothing at all could have prepared her for what she saw when the man turned the lights on in the room.

At first Melissa's brain rejected what she was seeing. It had to be some kind of Halloween prank. *Nothing* like this could be real. However, after a second the unspeakable reality of what she was viewing punched through her attempts to deny. She put her hands to her face and screamed, unable to summon any other response.

The room into which she was looking had white tile on the walls and floor. Against the far wall a boy and girl she had never seen before had been shackled to the wall. They were naked, and they were clearly dead, but what made it even worse was what had been done to them. Their bodies were masses of terrible cuts, and their blood was splattered on the white tile walls and pooled on the floor beneath their feet. Even worse their intestines spilled from huge cuts in their abdomens, and hung to the floor like stuffing busted out from grotesque toys. Their faces were frozen in rictuses of unimaginable pain, as if they had been literally dissected while they were still alive.

When Melissa finally ran out of energy to keep screaming and fell into a paroxysm of nearly silent sobs, Abigail spoke once more.

"Last chance, my dear," she said.

X

AT SEVEN-THIRTY THAT EVENING MOST OF THE *Salem News* staff had gone home for the day, leaving just a few reporters who had habitual late-night writing habits still busy at their desks. John had returned to the paper after his trip to the Peabody Essex Museum with Rich, and in spite of his growing exhaustion he was still in his office. After reading what Nathaniel Hawthorne had written about his great-great-grandfather, he felt compelled to keep working. In the hours since he had returned from the Peabody he had used genealogy websites to finish assembling what looked like a pretty complete list of the living descendants of Edward Putnam and the other judges he had seen on his journey with Rebecca Nurse.

Initially the list had been vast, but then he had restricted the names to only those descendants who lived within a fifty-mile radius of Salem and who were between the ages of twenty-two and seventy-five. For each of those people, he had gone into the paper's files and into the Internet services the paper subscribed to and assembled as much biographical data as possible on each one.

Now, having worked well beyond what Sam told him was

allowable on his first day out of the hospital, he sat slumped at his desk staring at the names, fighting the exhaustion that made his eyelids heavy. He might have thrown in the towel several hours ago, except that Rebecca Nurse sat in her chair in office corner, but she was no longer bent over her embroidery. Instead, she was staring hard at John as she had been for the past hour or two.

She was as mute as always, but her gaze had a new intensity. Seeing how her eyes were burning into him John felt a rising tide of anxiety because it seemed Rebecca was telling him that something terrible was getting ready to happen. He had no idea what the thing was, but deep inside he, too, could sense its approach.

He knuckled his eyes, trying to wipe away the need for sleep. It did absolutely no good, but it didn't matter. He needed to keep going. So far he had thirty-seven names in a fifty-mile radius. Of those he had eliminated six because they were over eighty and twelve because they were under twenty. Now he stared at the remaining nineteen names on his board and tried to winnow the list further.

Fortunately Bartholomew Gedney and John Hathorne had no living relatives in the area, making his job easier. Abigail Putnam stood at the top of his list because she owned Wicca Wonders and he agreed with Amy's observation that the store would provide an outstanding cover for real-life occult activities. Also, he now knew Abigail was a direct descendant of Edward Putnam, the ringleader of the group that had framed Rebecca Nurse. Of the remaining names he had discovered, there were two teachers, one college professor, three house-wives, two clergymen, a policeman, an insurance agent, a veterinarian, an ophthalmologist, a sanitation worker, a shoe store owner, three retired businessmen, and a gas station owner. He rubbed his eyes and tried to come up with some way to rank them. He couldn't.

He looked at the extra name he had put up on the board, Kenny Dubrowski, who sat by himself in the upper right hand corner. There were no lines drawn from any of the original judges to Kenny because from everything John had been able to determine, Dubrowski hadn't been related in any way. So, why the hell had he come into John's room and tried to kill him?

He was still sitting there staring at the names without the beginning of a decent thought when Amy came bustling through the newsroom and into his office. "Sorry, we had mechanical problems at the printing plant, and one of the supervisors was sick. I had to straighten some things out before I came back."

"You get it taken care of?"

She nodded absentmindedly as she turned to look at what John had put on the board.

"Nineteen names," he said. "Living descendants who live within fifty miles and who are old enough to have a role in a . . ." he shrugged, "a group of crazy devil worshippers."

Amy nodded as she read the names and the brief bio-graphical details. "Other than Abigail, nobody really stands out, do they?"

"No. That's why I also put Kenny Dubrowski up there. I hoped he might help point us in the right direction, but he's not related to anybody."

"So why did he try to kill you?"

"Isn't that the sixty-four thousand dollar question?"

Amy turned again and studied the board. "Do you think Dubrowski could have been blackmailed?"

"He was out of prison on parole. If he got busted doing something that could have gotten him tossed back inside, he might have been blackmailed. It's also possible he was a guy who would do anything for money, and somebody simply hired him to kill me."

Amy nodded, but she went to the board, erased Cabot Corwin's name from the big list and rewrote it underneath Abigail Putnam.

"You really think so? The guy's a lieutenant on the Salem police force."

"Wouldn't be the first dirty cop in this state. Besides we can always move him back to the general pile if nothing else turns up on him."

John nodded. He felt relief at having Amy in his office, taking a fresh look at what he'd been able to pull together. "I feel something, and so does Rebecca," he said.

Amy turned from the board. "What?"

He shook his head. "I don't know, it's like . . . a premonition. I can see it in Rebecca's face, too. She feels the same thing. Something bad is happening, but I don't know what it is."

"Happening now or about to happen?"

John shook his head. "I wish I knew, but I haven't got a clue."

As John spoke his eye caught a flash of movement beyond his office, out in the newsroom and then a second later the glint of something bright reflecting the overhead light. He turned his head in that direction and was surprised to see Jessica Lodge, the paper's owner making her way through the newsroom toward his office. She was dressed in a long gown as if she was heading out to some formal function. She had a tall, erect carriage that belied her aristocratic heritage and a thin face framed by short white hair and strengthened by prominent cheekbones, a resolute chin and a rather oversized nose that lent an aspect of focus and fierceness to her gaze.

She knocked on the door of his office, but he was already out of his chair heading in her direction. "John," she said as she pushed opened the door. "I am so terribly sorry I was unable to get to the hospital to check on you. I just got back from England this very afternoon, and I'm headed out to some dreadful charity event this evening that I agreed to months ago. How are you?"

"I'm fine, Mrs. Lodge."

"I'm *Jessica*! I'm much too young to be Mrs. Anything."

"I'm fine, Jessica. Thank you for asking."

"What the devil happened? I know you fell or something and were in the hospital with a concussion, but then some fellow broke in and tried to kill you? That's terrible! And bless you, you killed the fellow. Good for you!"

Mrs. Lodge looked around the office, saw Amy standing by the white board and smiled. "And Amy, I certainly didn't mean to ignore you. How are you, my dear?"

"I'm fine, Mrs.—, er, Jessica."

"Good!" She looked over at the white board. "And what's this?"

John hesitated, trying to come up with some way to describe what he was doing without sounding totally insane. "The basic truth is, I'm trying to follow a hunch. It's so unformed, I can't even begin to describe it yet. But if I'm right, there may be the bones of a good story."

Mrs. Lodge turned away from the board and gave him a nod and smile. "You keep it up. I'm just so pleased to see you healthy and back at work. The paper needs you, John."

"Thank you, Jessica."

"Don't stay here all night. Go home and get some rest." She gave them both a wave as she went to the door and headed out through the newsroom.

Amy watched her go and smiled. "It was nice of her to come in. At her age she must be exhausted after all that flying, although it's probably a lot less stressful in a private jet than a commercial airline."

"I wouldn't know," John said with a laugh.

"Me neither, but that's what I've read."

John looked back at his white board and then at Rebecca Nurse. "That's all I can do for now, I'm afraid," he said, realizing he was becoming more and more accustomed to speaking to a ghost. "I know something is happening. I can feel it, but I need to step away before I can think this through any better. I hope you understand. We living humans need our sleep."

Rebecca nodded and gave him what seemed to be a sad smile.

John turned to Amy. "As long as we're going to stoke the rumor mill, let me take you someplace for dinner. I have a lot to tell you about my trip to the Peabody Essex Museum today."

XI

JOHN GOT THEM A QUIET CORNER TABLE AT The Lyceum where they could speak without being overheard. In spite of the flickering candlelight, the romantic setting and a good bottle of chardonnay, their evening began as all business, with each of them filling the other in on what they had done that afternoon. Amy talked about her interview with Melissa Blake's parents, and John told her about the documents he had discovered at The Phillips Library and what Nathaniel Hawthorne had written about his great-great grandfather.

"Okay, one question," Amy said when they had both finished. "How did your great-great grandfather die?"

"He died at sea."

"When?"

"A month or so after he met with Hawthorne."

"How?"

"He got washed overboard in a bad storm, and his body was never found."

"According to whom?"

"The mates on his ship."

"You don't see anything strange in that?"

John gave a reluctant nod. "I didn't used to, but as of today I certainly do. I know I also can't say my parent's death in an avalanche on a ski vacation wasn't just a tragic bit of bad luck. I didn't tell you last night, but I was thinking about it today—there have been other strange deaths in my family over the years. I had a great uncle who had drowned crossing a river while he was fly fishing for trout, a great grandfather who died of an accidental shotgun blast in the hunting field, and the aunt who left me my house was killed by a hit-and-run driver while she was walking along the side of a country road."

Amy looked at him, her eyes wide in amazement. "Holy crap, John, you never stopped to think this is pretty weird?"

"I still can't prove that any of those deaths were related to the coven. I was brought up to think my family just had more than its share of bad luck."

"Did you ever study statistics? You know the odds of those kinds of deaths happening in one family over a few generations?"

"Yeah, I know." He shrugged. "But until now, there was never any actual reason to explain them as something other than statistical anomalies."

"Well, now there is."

"So now the question becomes whether it's possible that others in my family have also had the same mystical revelations? Has Rebecca Nurse been trying to contact my ancestors for generations? That means the question isn't *why now*? Maybe it should be *how does the coven know when it's happened to one of us?* Because they seem to, don't they? Shouldn't we assume that was the reason for the attempt on my life? The timing is a little too coincident to Rebecca's appearance."

"Remember that you said you'd also seen Rebecca four years ago just before Julie's accident? Maybe Rebecca was trying to communicate with you then, and maybe they sensed it."

"But *how?*"

"Maybe you put out a vibe."

John snapped his fingers. "When I walked past Wicca Wonders the other day, just before my fall in the cemetery, I remember I felt somebody staring at me from the store. I couldn't see them with all the reflection, but I remember how the hairs on the back of my neck went up. It was weird because I felt . . . conspicuous like I stood out for some reason."

John shook his head, frustrated that the questions seemed to pile up endlessly, but not the answers. "What about your interview? You said you're pretty sure Melissa Blake wasn't a runaway. How does she relate to all our local disappearances, and does that relate to the coven?"

"Melissa was an honor student, an athlete, and president of her class. She was a happy, popular girl. No way she ran away. She just doesn't fit that profile. Her parents said the only things missing from her room were some of her scruffiest clothes and her purse, and some of her friends said they thought she might have cut school and gone into Salem to get stuff for an upcoming Halloween party."

"Wicca Wonder?"

Amy nodded. "Probably, although the police say they checked it out and there don't seem to be any leads that point in that direction."

"Who checked it out on the police force?"

Amy smiled. "Great minds. I think it was Lieutenant Corwin."

"Wow," John said, his mind starting to race. "So you say she wore crummy clothes, so she might have looked like a runaway. Did she have access to a family car?"

"No. She took the bus to school."

"So if she disguised herself in her worst clothes and took the train to Salem, she might have been mistaken for a runaway. And if the coven has people looking for runaways, they might have picked her up on the assumption she was one."

"When Rebecca took you back to see the witch trial people, didn't one of them say something about sacrificing blood to the Devil? Do you think—?"

John nodded. "Yes. I think we have to assume a significant percentage of the disappearances in the area over as many years as we can trace them may be people who were taken to be sacrificed to Satan."

Amy's face had gone pale. "John, what are we going to do about this?" she whispered. "We can't go to the police because some of them may be involved. If we go to the FBI . . ."

"They'll think we're insane," he said, finishing her thought. "The claims we would make are outrageous, and we can't prove a single one. If we took what we know to another paper, other than the *National Enquirer*, they would never print the story. So far, we can't substantiate a single fact. I've been trying to come up with a plan, but so far," he shook his head. "Right now it's us against them."

"And they know who you are, but we don't know who they are, at least not for sure."

"I think we know who a couple of them are, but who are the rest?" John sipped his wine and looked at her. Even though he could see the fear in her eyes, she was beautiful. She was way too good looking for the likes of him, he told himself, but here she was. She knew the outrageous story, and yet instead of running as far away from him as possible, she was hanging in there. Even more she was offering to stay with him to keep him safe.

Without being aware of what he was about to do until he had actually done it, he reached across the table for her hand. "Well, I know one thing," he said, smiling to try and ease her fear. "We can't fight witches on an empty stomach. It's not allowed."

Rather than pull away, which wouldn't have surprised him, she grasped his hand in both of hers and gave him an answering squeeze. He felt power and passion and purpose in her fingers, and as he looked through the fear in her blue eyes he saw the same things there.

"Enough talk about the unpleasant realities," he said. "Tell me a story about where you grew up in the Midwest."

Over the next hour, as they ordered dinner and had a

bottle of red wine to follow the white, John actually found himself able to forget about everything that was happening around them and enjoy Amy's company. When the check came and he slipped his credit card into the leather folder, he found himself nearly trembling with a nervous anticipation he had not felt in a long, long time.

XII

A SHORT TIME LATER JOHN AND AMY WALKED UP
the front steps of his townhouse. For the past two blocks
he had experienced a rising tide of anxiety, and now as
he paused and fumbled for his keys he felt as nervous and
uncertain as a fourteen year old on a first date. He reminded
himself there was a perfectly cogent explanation for Amy
being here. After all, they had agreed that given the risks,
they were safer together than apart, and nothing had happened that would have changed their minds. If anything,
John believed the danger had increased, even though he had
no proof.

Also, hadn't they both agreed they were going to pretend
they were starting an affair? Yes, he reminded himself. But
then in a fit of near panic, he wondered if everything back in
the restaurant had been role-playing for Amy. Maybe she was
a better actress than he would have guessed and was holding
his hand and looking into his eyes not because of her actual
feeling, but so the other diners would speculate on their possible romance.

Now, as John pulled his keys from his pocket, it occurred
to him that Amy might feel just as awkward as he did. Neither

of them had spoken in the past few minutes, but as much as he wanted to say something to cut the tension, his tongue seemed to be tied to the roof of his mouth. Until this moment things had seemed natural and even reasonably uncomplicated. Amy had brought a small suitcase to work, and they had stashed it inside John's front door before they walked to the restaurant. At the time, he had told himself she would sleep in one of the guest bedrooms, but now he realized how badly he wanted something very different.

He finally managed to get the door unlocked, pushed it open, and then stood back to let her walk in ahead of him. For some reason the sight of her crossing the threshold made him short of breath, as if he realized it was some sort of important barrier, and there would be no going back. Other than his daughter or the wives of friends, she was the first woman who had come into this house since Julie died, and he felt a combination of sadness that he was finally closing one chapter of his life and excitement at what might lie ahead.

He followed her inside and closed the door. "Can I offer you a drink?" he asked.

She turned and regarded him and then shook her head. "Thanks, but I've had plenty."

He smiled, feeling impossibly awkward. "Well, I can carry your suitcase upstairs and show you your room if you're tired, or we can talk for a few minutes."

Amy gave a little shrug, and he realized she felt as uncertain as he did. Unable to stand the silence, he grabbed her suitcase and started toward the stairs. "Let me at least show you the guestroom," he said, rushing the words. He started up the stairs and heard her footsteps coming behind.

He turned on the second floor lights and led her to a corner bedroom at the end of the hall. He realized he hadn't even had time to check to make sure there were sheets on the bed, but he supposed there were. Flipping on the lights he walked ahead of her into the room, relieved to see that everything seemed to be ready for an overnight guest. He went into the bathroom and made sure there were towels on the racks, soap in the dishes, and toilet paper on the roll.

When he turned around Amy was standing very close to him. His heart caught in his throat as he looked into her eyes and then without thinking he reached for her. She came toward him as if this was what she had been waiting for, as well. She tipped her head up to meet his, and as they kissed he felt the dam of passion and desire he had been holding inside for a very long time suddenly give way. He pulled her into a hard embrace and felt her arms come around his back, her fingernails digging into his shirt.

Swept up by a tide of hunger for her, he forgot everything else. For that moment there was no Rebecca Nurse, no witchcraft, or devil worshippers to worry about. There was nothing but a beautiful and passionate woman and himself. He was responding to his need and to her answering heat, and not worrying about anything else, and he was starting to edge her back toward the bed when the pain hit. It was like a sledgehammer between his ears. Immediately his knees started to buckle from the suddenness and intensity, and he sank against her.

"John?" he heard her say, a sharp note of worry in her voice, but it sounded like she was speaking to him from a long way away.

The pain came again, and this time he heard a sound as well. It was a woman, and she was screaming, her agony so utterly blood curdling that he had never heard anything like it. He knew she was being tortured to within an inch of her life.

"John?" Amy said again. "What's the matter?"

She staggered under his weight, and he realized she was the only thing keeping him from hitting floor. He felt like someone was pounding a stake down through the top of his skull. His stomach rebelled with nausea, and his equilibrium fell away completely as if he'd just had a fresh blow to the head that had brought his concussion roaring back. "Someone's being killed," he managed to say. "A girl. Can't you hear it?"

"No," Amy said. "I can't hear anything."

The screaming was going on and on. The girl was suffering in ways he could not begin to imagine. Through the occasional lapses in her gut wrenching cries he heard another voice shouting, "Recant! Reject Christianity! Reject the Catholic Church! Say it! Say it and the pain will stop."

"Oh, God," he said, "it's horrible. They're killing her."

"Who is killing her?"

"The judges. I can hear them shouting at her. They want

her to reject Christianity, and they say the pain will stop. But her screams . . . they're so horrible . . . whatever they're doing to her."

The pain and the screaming seemed to tear John right out of his body. He was unaware of time or place, and he had no idea how long it lasted. When the screaming finally faded to silence, and the pain in his head lifted, he found himself on the floor of the guestroom. He was curled into a ball, and he realized he had been weeping and that Amy was lying on top of him, almost like she was protecting him from the pain and the terrible screams.

When she felt him stir, Amy lifted herself away. John pressed himself up to a sitting position and stayed like that with his head between his knees.

"How do you feel? Are you okay?" Amy asked in a gentle voice.

John nodded his head. "I'm okay, but I'm sure I just heard somebody being tortured and maybe murdered."

Amy rubbed his back and massaged his neck. "Can you stand?"

"I think so." He rolled onto his knees and made his way shakily to his feet. As he straightened up he looked at the chair beside the dresser and saw Rebecca Nurse sitting there. Just as earlier, she was looking at him, and he could see the tracks of tears on her ghostly cheeks.

"You heard it, too, didn't you?" he said to her.

Rebecca nodded, her face a mask of sorrow and anger.

"Do you know this woman? Do *I* know her? Why am I

hearing her screams as if I'm standing in the same room?"

Rebecca only looked at him.

He turned to Amy. "I know it seems like I'm totally insane, but you have to believe me. I really heard that. It wasn't just in my head."

Amy nodded slowly. "I can't hear it, John, but I know something terrible is happening. All these signs are pointing to it. Even if I didn't believe you can see and hear things I can't, there are two other things that prove I'm right. First, I can see the letters on your arm, and second a man tried to kill you in the hospital for *no apparent reason*. Only, the two of us know there is a reason, and it relates to the coven."

"Yeah, the coven that we can't tell anyone else about without them thinking we're absolutely crazy."

Even though she couldn't see her, Amy nodded her head toward the chair where Rebecca Nurse sat. "You're forgetting that we do have one other important ally."

John stumbled over to the bed and sat. Whatever was going on, whatever it was they were fighting against felt overwhelmingly evil but also well hidden and powerful. "How are we ever going to figure this out?" he asked, letting his shoulders slump. "And even if we do, how are we going to stop it?"

Amy came over and put her hands on his shoulders and looked into his eyes. "I don't think we would have been dragged into this if we didn't have some chance of success."

"Oh yeah, well I'm starting to wonder if a whole bunch of my ancestors haven't also been dragged into this, and if that's the case *they* didn't seem to have had much success. I don't know why I'm any different."

Amy gripped his shoulders tighter. "Even though we don't understand what it is we need to know or what weapons we might have at our disposal, we have to believe the information is out there to be found and the weapons are, too. We just need to find the strength and the courage to keep digging."

He put his arms around her waist and pulled her tight. They held each other like that for several moments and then Amy pulled his head down toward the pillow. When he lay down, she pulled off his shoes and then went around to the other side of the bed where she kicked off her own shoes and lay down beside him, spooning tightly against him. She reached down and pulled the comforter over them and then turned off the light.

SIX

October 25

JOHN TOSSED IN HIS SLEEP, DREAMING FITFULLY
of being trapped underground in a maze of dark passages.
The sound of terrible screaming carried faintly down the
rocky passageways. It frightened him, but at the same time he
felt compelled to try and help the person who was suffering.
He went through door after door, utterly lost and directionless, but he never seemed to get any closer to the source.

When he woke up, it was totally dark outside. For a few
seconds he didn't know where he was, and then the previous night came back to him. He remembered coming up here
with Amy and then kissing her, and then he remembered the
screams that had sounded in his head. Their effect had been
so powerful and terrible that his knees had buckled as they
seemed to drag him toward some black dungeon of uncon-
sciousness.

In spite of that, he had been aware of Amy climbing into bed beside him and holding him tightly as he surrendered to sleep and his terrible dreams. Now, he rolled over, wanting to reach for Amy again, but to his surprise the other side of the bed was empty.

He sat up, rubbed his eyes, and looked over at the bed-side clock radio that showed a few minutes after four a.m. "Amy?" he said.

No answer.

He climbed out of bed, slipped on his shoes, and went to the bedroom door. He saw the glow of dim lights coming from the downstairs, and he heard the soft rustle of a footstep. He froze and listened, but he heard no more movement. The house was silent except for the ping of his steam radiators keeping the cold Massachusetts night at bay. He had a sudden terrifying thought that members of the coven had somehow snuck into his house and taken Amy.

A mixture of fear and anger rose up in him, and he wished he had a pistol or another weapon in the house. He thought for a second and then tiptoed down the hall to his upstairs den where he reached above the mantle and took down Captain Andrews' cutlass, a souvenir from his days as an ensign in the fledgling United States Navy during the War of 1812. He started down the stairs, putting his feet close to the wall to keep the old steps from squeaking.

Pausing on the bottom step, he heard the sounds of tearing paper coming from the living room. The soft glow of light he had seen from upstairs emanated from the same place, as if a single lamp was burning. He moved silently across the entry hall and peered around the corner.

"Amy," he said when he saw her bending over what looked like a picture frame. "What are you doing?"

She looked up in surprise. She held a paring knife in one hand and seemed to be working the paper backing loose on one of his paintings. A glance at the wall revealed it was the portrait of Rebecca Nurse.

"I had a bad dream," she said. "It woke me up, and I couldn't get back to sleep. I lay there beside you and started thinking about Rebecca Nurse and how you said your aunt made you promise you'd always keep this portrait in your house."

John nodded. "You started to wonder why."

"Yes. I thought there might be a hidden message or something." She pointed down at where she had been cutting away the paper backing. "I hope you don't mind."

"Have at it," he said. Then after a second or two he asked, "What kind of dream did you have? Do you remember?"

"A very claustrophobic one. I dreamed I was lost in some sort of underground place with all these different passages. I heard screaming, and I kept trying to get to the person who was screaming in order to help them. I ran and ran, but I never could find them."

John looked at her and felt a tremor of fear run up his back. "I had the same exact dream."

She looked up from her cutting. "What do you think it means?"

He shrugged. "I think it means you should follow your instincts. Keep cutting."

He turned on several more lights then looked over her shoulder as she finished removing the paper from the wooden frame. Afterward he helped her hold the painting up so they could inspect it. After a few moments of looking and feeling the inside of the frame for some hidden message, she sat back and shook her head.

"Nothing," she said. "I was so sure there would be something."

"Let's try and get some better light," John said, taking the portrait out of her hands and starting toward the kitchen.

When he got there, he turned on the full battery of overhead and countertop lights he had installed. Putting the portrait atop a section of granite counter, he pulled up two stools.

"Have a seat," he said, then went to the kitchen utility drawer and rummaged around until he found a magnifying glass. Using the glass under the much brighter light he started inspecting the back of the canvas. After a few minutes, he straightened up and shook his head. "Nothing on the canvas that I can see." He bent back over and started in with the magnifying glass again.

"I'm afraid I was wrong," Amy said.

"I just want to check the stretcher frame before we make that call."

He examined the wood across the top, then down one side, across the bottom, and started up the final side. He was three-quarters of the way to the top when he saw it, a place on the inside of the stretcher where wood was a slightly different color. Digging a fingernail into the different colored spot, he felt the material give way.

"This isn't wood right here. I think it's wax," he said. Amy handed him the paring knife, and he carefully began to dig out the old wax while taking care not to damage whatever was behind it. The task was time consuming because over the years the wax had grown nearly as hard as the wood itself, but gradually he exposed what seemed to be a shallow indentation someone had dug into the stretcher, and what looked like a piece of paper that had been rolled up very tightly and hidden away there.

With her thinner fingers Amy was able to reach inside the opening and pry the rolled paper loose. It had been tied with a ribbon to keep it rolled up, and now as they both looked at it, Amy asked, "Well?"

"Be my guest," John said.

II

AMY CAREFULLY SLID THE ANCIENT RIBBON OFF the paper then put the paper on the counter and began to unroll it very gently. The paper made cracking sound as it came open, but it did not fall apart. She held the edge down to keep it from rolling back up again, and they both read what was written there.

To Whomever May Find This,

Know that I, Captain John Bancroft Andrews of Salem, Massachusetts, am of sound mind at the time of this writing. Though what you will read below may lead you to question my sanity, know that every word is true to the best of my ability to ascertain it. Know also that if you are reading this and the claims herein have been previously unknown to you that I have met with an unnatural death which prevented me from making these facts public. Until now I have only shared this tale with one other person, my good friend, Nathaniel Hawthorne.

What I have to say concerns what have come to be known as the Salem witch trials. This series of shameful events, which occurred in 1692-3, are generally assumed to be a product of the religious hysteria and superstition of the time. However, I have learned that this is a carefully constructed lie and the witch trials were orchestrated by a secret coven of devil worshippers. This coven, led by a group of six persons who called themselves judges, had lost faith in the Christian God during a time of failed crops, Indian attacks, and rampant disease in the early days of the settlement of Salem.

This truth was not brought to light until the year 1860, when on a voyage to Sumatra in my clipper, Formosa, I encountered a man by the name of Joseph Gedney, whose ancestor, Bartholomew Gedney was one of the original judges in 1692.

The Joseph Gedney I met was a dissolute man, financially ruined and given to excessive drink. However, my years at sea, in which I have captained many different ships and led countless men, have led me to believe I am a good judge of character and that I can tell when a man is lying or telling the truth. I would stake my life that the tale Joseph Gedney told me one evening in Sumatra was the whole truth.

According to Gedney, when he was a young man he had been jealous of his brother who was three years older and the family favorite. One summer afternoon on his brother's fifteenth birthday, young Gedney had crawled beneath an open window and eavesdropped on a conversation between his brother and their grandfather, and he had overheard the grandfather tell the brother he had been selected to become one of the six judges of the coven.

Afraid to be caught eavesdropping, but consumed by curiosity and jealousy that his brother was being chosen for something special, Joseph Gedney crept closer to the window. He overheard his grandfather say that member-ship in the coven was offered selectively within families to sons and daughters who seemed to have the inner toughness to carry a dangerous secret, the great secret of which god they worshipped. The grandfather explained that back in the early days of Salem, when the colony had suffered from failed crops and the threat of starva-tion, Indian attacks, and rampant disease, a small group of colonists had decided to turn from the Christian God and ask for Satan's protection. In return for their wor-ship, they had asked for long lives, freedom from hunger and prosperity beyond their neighbors. They had also promised human blood sacrifices.

The young Joseph Gedney had been so horrified at the words coming out of his grandfather's mouth that he stumbled away and climbed into the branches of a huge chestnut tree. He spent hours as the day grew long and the temperature started to drop, trying to decide what he should do. Should he go to the church or the police? How could he turn in his grandfather and his brother, his own flesh and blood? And who would believe him? He barely even believed it himself. After all, a small voice tried to tell him, it could have all been a story his grandfather *made up. It could all have been pretend. Only he knew it wasn't. He knew his grandfather's voice, and he knew what the old man sounded like when he was being serious. His grandfather had been deadly serious.*

Finally, feeling terribly torn but deciding he had no other choice, young Joseph decided to go to his local minister. Its had been well after dark when he walked up to the back door of the minister's house and knocked. The minister came to the door and looked down at Joseph with surprise, asking why the boy was out so late at night and why he was shivering.

Joseph had cautioned himself to tell his story in a calm and methodical manner, so that the reverend might believe at least a portion of what he would hear. However, when he came face to face with the man of God, his story came rushing out in a torrent he was powerless to control.

The reverend hushed him and brought him into the kitchen. He told Joseph to remain right there, warming himself by the stove, and saying he had to get something he left the room. A moment later, Joseph heard footsteps and looked up to see the minster walk back into the kitchen followed by his grandfather and brother.

"We have been expecting you," his grandfather said.

As he looked into his grandfather's eyes, into the familiar, loving face, he saw a coldness there he had never experienced. The old man was looking at him as if he was some complete stranger, someone for whom he had no emotional feeling whatsoever. Joseph's eyes went to the reverend and saw the same thing, a terrible coldness. Only Joseph's brother seemed horrified and full of fear.

"You spied on us, didn't you, boy?" his grandfather demanded.

Knowing there was no use in lying, Joseph nodded.

"You heard about the coven, didn't you?"

The boy nodded again.

The grandfather put his hand on Joseph's brother's shoulder and pulled the boy to him. "I have told you of the importance of our secret pact, haven't I, son?"

Joseph's brother looked down at the floor, but he nodded.

"I have told you of the importance of blood sacrifice to Him who hath saved us, haven't I?"

At first Joseph's brother seemed frozen, but then his grandfather gave him a gentle shake. "Haven't I?"

This time Joseph's brother gave a small nod.

"It would normally never be necessary to sacrifice one of our own, but in this case one of our own has pried into secrets he should never have learned about."

The grandfather turned to Joseph again. "Boy, we cannot trust you to keep our secrets, can we?"

"I . . . I won't say anything," Joseph said in a trembling voice. "I promise."

"He lies," the reverend said immediately. "He came to me unable to hold back the words."

The grandfather nodded and looked down at Joseph's brother. "Get him."

"What are we going to do to him?" Joseph's brother asked, even though the answer was obvious.

"Take him into the woods and sacrifice him," his grandfather said, speaking with little emotion as if he was talking about killing one of the family sheep.

Joseph looked toward the back door but saw the reverend had already moved to block his exit. "Don't fight us, son," he said. "There is no escape."

Joseph's grandfather pushed his brother forward. "Get him," he said again.

Joseph glanced at the wood-burning stove next to where he was standing. A pot of water had been heating on the stove when he got there. A knife lay beside it on the brick shelf. Without thinking, he grabbed the pot, feeling the handle sear his hand but not stopping. He threw the boiling water into his reverend's face and heard the man scream.

"Get him," his grandfather shouted at his brother.

Joseph grabbed the knife and brandished it toward his brother and grandfather while the reverend milled around the room screaming and holding his hands over his face. "Don't make me hurt you," Joseph said to his brother and then he ran out the back door.

According to Joseph's story, the boy ran down to the wharf and found a ship still being loaded in the night and due to sail on the next tide. He slipped into the warehouse, grabbed a sack of corn, threw it over his shoulder, and followed the line of sweating men up the gangplank and into the hold of the ship. When he dumped his corn, he found a place where he could squeeze himself between several rows of bags and stay out of sight.

The loading took only another thirty minutes or so, and then the ship was closed up and the crew went ashore to have their last chance to get drunk in a tavern before they set sail. During the dark night as Joseph huddled amid the sacks of corn, barley, oats, and other produce, he listened to the scurry of rats, but he also heard the unmistakable sounds of a late night search being conducted along the docks. No one was calling his name, no one saying he was a runaway. It was a search conducted by a small group of people who shared a terrible secret and who needed to find him and kill him so their secret would never be leaked.

Joseph's heart pounded with fear throughout the dark night lest the searchers sneak aboard the ship and discover him, but even before the first rays of light made their way through the cracks in the decking, he heard the scurry of feet overhead and felt the ship subtly shift as it drifted away from the dock and began to move toward the open ocean.

Joseph remained hidden for nearly two more days, when thirst finally forced him to make himself known to the captain. By that time they were well out of sight of land, and he was put to work as a crewman for the rest *of the voyage. He eventually jumped ship in Sumatra and there he worked for The Dutch East India Company for many years until illness and a propensity for drink had rendered him unemployable.*

The night I met Joseph Gedney in a Dutch tavern on the Sumatran waterfront, he came to my table and introduced himself in a quiet and humble manner. He said he knew I sailed out of Salem, and that he knew he was quite ill and had but a short time to live, and that before he died he had a story he needed to tell someone from Salem. He said he had kept the story secret for these many years because he still feared the long arm of the coven might find him even on the other side of the world. He also said he had asked a number of others about me and that all of those he asked attested to my honesty and good Christian character. He said he had trusted in those same traits in others early in his life and been sorely disappointed, and hoped he would not be disappointed now. He entrusted me with his story, and I have brought the burden of Joseph Gedney's truth back to Salem.

I might have returned with a great deal of skepticism about this outlandish story if not for two other things. First, on the return voyage, there were two attempts on my life. One occurred late at night during a storm. Someone crept up behind me when I was at the wheel and hit me over the head. Apparently they were dragging me toward the rail, preparing to throw me over when they were interrupted by several other sailors who were just coming on deck. The second attempt involved poison in my tea.

While those attempts on my life might have been almost impossible to link to Joseph Gedney's revelations, the sudden appearance of the ghost of Rebecca Nurse, my great grandmother who was hanged in the witch trials, can be linked to nothing else. This astounding and inexplicable phenomenon can only be explained by the fact that I have gone mad or that through my interest in the coven I have excited certain spirits. At this point I do not believe I am going mad. My rationality in all other respects remains intact. To the contrary, I believe Rebecca Nurse is trying to help me find some way to defeat this coven of devil worshippers.

I should add that I believe with all my heart that the coven continues its evil work. I say this based on the number of unexplained disappearances each year in the area around Salem and Boston. Certainly blood sacrifice by a coven of witches could be the reason. Unfortunately, I have as of yet been unable to determine the names of the six judges, but my meeting with Joseph Gedney must have been overheard by one of my crew who is also a member of the coven. This has led them to know of me.

The poison from my last voyage has left me in a weakened physical state. Even though I need rest and recuperation, I am going to sea when the next of my clippers sails. Even though my doctor has tried to forbid this voyage, my life expectancy will be far shorter if I remain here within reach of the coven. Of course I have not told him that.

I am writing this document so that, should I be killed before I can complete my mission, someone in my family who comes after me and who might also be approached by the spirits of the dead, might know this is not the stuff of insanity. Know instead that the salvation of your community, your state, your country, and perhaps of the world is at stake.

I am,

Your Humble Servant,

Captain John Bancroft Andrews

John read the contents of the letter twice, and when he finished the second time he took a deep breath and blew it out slowly. "I think at every single turn, part of my brain has tried to deny the possibility that this is anything but craziness, but this . . ." He shook his head.

"We have to accept there are things we can't understand, or that seem to be beyond the reach of science."

John nodded. "There is one thing I do understand, however." He looked out the window at the darkness, tried to stuff down the voices of fear that were telling him not to do it, and he came to a conclusion. "I need to find a way to get back inside that mausoleum, and I think I need to do it right now. Whatever was happening to that girl was happening down there somewhere. I can feel it, and I just have to hope I'm not too late. There has to be a reason why Rebecca Nurse took me in there in the first place. She wants me to go back."

He looked away from the window and saw Rebecca sitting across the room in a chair by the kitchen fireplace. She was looking at him with a somber expression, as if acknowledging the unfairness of the task she had set before him.

"If you're going down there, I'm coming with you."

"No," he said. Even though he desperately wanted company, he glanced again at Rebecca. "I think she means for me to do this alone."

"John, you can't. You just got out of the hospital. Please let me come."

He took her hands in his and turned to face her. They were standing very close and he could see small flecks of darker color in her arctic blue eyes. "You are the first good thing that's happened to me in a very long time. Please believe I fully intend to get back here safely so I can find out whatever it is we're supposed to have together. But please also understand that if I don't go after them, they will *definitely* come after me again. I have to believe next time or the time after that, they're going to succeed. I'm certainly no hero, but I'm not going to just sit here and let them kill me."

She stepped into his arms and put her head against his chest. "You really won't let me help?"

"I'm not trying to be macho. Neither of us understands this occult stuff, so I just have to go with my instincts here. Rebecca is telling me to do this alone. That's what I think. Help me get ready, and I'll be back soon. I promise."

III

THIRTY MINUTES LATER JOHN WALKED OUT HIS front door alone and climbed in his car for the drive to Harmony Grove Cemetery. He wore his running shoes, a pair of black running tights and a black hoodie over his Patagonia Expedition Weight long underwear. He carried a Maglite with four D-batteries in the handle. Made of metal, it was extremely bright but also heavy enough to use as a weapon. In addition to the light he had Captain John Bancroft Andrews' saber and his cell phone. He had no illusions about being able to call for help, but he knew he might need the camera to record evidence he might find below ground.

He drove through nearly empty streets and parked at the curb outside the cemetery walls. Still pitch black dark, a glance at his watch showed five-thirty-seven. He knew the cemetery gates would be locked tight, but on his other visits he had noticed trees whose branches hung out over the cemetery walls. They ought to allow him to get on top of the wall and drop safely to the ground on the other side.

He climbed out, locked his car, and started walking along the wall, looking for a tree with low branches. It was a few degrees below freezing, he thought, as he watched his breath fog out in front of him and heard the ice-rimmed grass crackle beneath his feet. He went several hundred yards before he found a tree with low enough branches to climb onto and at the same time a branch that drooped low over the wall. A quick look around showed no one around, no early dog walkers or joggers, no prowling police cars.

With a quick jump he locked his hands around the lowest branch and swung his leg around it. Every muscle in his arms and back and each one of his still tender bruises cried out in protest, but he ignored the pain and pulled himself into a sitting position atop the limb. From there it was easy to climb a little higher, move to the opposite side of the trunk and start sliding out the branch that hung over the wall.

When he was about ten feet out from the trunk he felt the limb begin to sag under his weight, but then it stopped when it came to rest on the wall. He shinnied out the last few feet, his balance badly compromised by the skinny limb beneath him. His heart started to pound, and his hands grew slick with sweat. All he needed was to fall from this height and break his neck and the coven would be off the hook. He couldn't let that happen. He went another foot and felt himself starting to tip. With a wild grab he was able to reach one hand out to the wall and steady himself. He scooted another foot, got his other hand on the wall and finally his knees.

He took a second to steady his breathing then looked down. The height was greater than he might have hoped, but the ground looked flat and even. He saw a spot a few feet ahead where he could drop into an open spot with what looked like azaleas on three sides. Thinking the bushes might break his fall if he came down off balance, he crawled over, hung by his hands, and let go.

He hit and tumbled sideways into one of the bushes, grateful that his hoodie was there to absorb the scratches and pokes from the branches. Clawing his way to his feet, he moved from the bushes and hurried up the hill toward the Putnam section of the graveyard. Even in the predawn with the white headstones just barely visible, the pentagram formed by that particular group of Putnam headstones stood out to him. They seemed brighter than everything around them somehow, as if they provided a beacon, fed by the infernal energies produced by the coven's sacrifices.

The sight brought a fresh wave of fear, and he closed his eyes and shook his head to clear the image. When he opened them again the pentagram continued to burn just as bright. After another second he gave up trying to make it go away and started to trudge up the hill toward the Putnam mausoleum.

With each step his fear seemed to grow as he pictured the steps at the back of the mausoleum and the barely visible red mark in the wall. He remembered the way the door had swung back soundlessly, how lights inside the dark passage had seemed to sense his presence and grow brighter as he came closer.

The dark monolith of the mausoleum loomed at the top of the hill, a solid blackness even darker than the night sky. As he drew close he stopped to listen, but other than a distant siren and the faint rumble of a jet engine far overhead, the cemetery was deathly quiet. Even the voices he had heard the other day were silent.

John waited until he was at the back of the mausoleum before he turned on his flashlight. As he aimed the powerful beam down the narrow set of cement steps, the light seemed to peter out in the pooled darkness at the bottom. He took a breath, grasped the rusted iron railing and started down. He could see ancient cobwebs hanging from the walls and waving in the breeze. Dry leaves, blown into the stairwell by the wind, crackled underfoot. He was hyperventilating as he reached the bottom step and shined his beam on the faint red handprint. Pulling off his glove, he placed his hand on the red imprint, feeling the cold lifeless stone beneath.

Nothing happened. Part of him felt grateful, but he also knew he needed to get inside the secret door. He rubbed his palm against his hoodie, blew on it to warm it up, then put his hand back on the print. Still nothing.

He wracked his brain and looked around hoping he might see Rebecca Nurse, that she might show him how to get through the door, but he seemed to be alone. He put his hand on the red mark several times more, moving it slightly, blowing on it again, concentrating, and asking the door to open. The stone remained cold to his touch, and the door did not move.

Frustrated, he finally climbed the steps and stood for a few seconds, looking around at the Putnam graves as he tried to understand what he was doing wrong. He shook his head. He had no idea.

IV

GETTING OUT OF THE CEMETERY PROVED TO BE much easier than getting in. He found a spot where the ground rose up against the wall and made it easy to jump up, grab, swing a leg up, and climb on top. The ground dropped away on the other side, which made the drop a little tricky, but John used his knees as shock absorbers, and he tumbled and rolled when he hit. Pulling himself to his feet, he hobbled to his car and drove home.

When he got to the house, he went up to the front door and let himself in, calling Amy's name as soon as he was inside. Met with silence, he tried again. "Amy?"

Doubting she would have gone back to sleep he went up the stairs, thinking she might be in the shower. He checked each of the upstairs bathrooms, but she wasn't in any of them. Back downstairs he went into the kitchen and saw that Amy's purse and coat were missing. Where would she have gone at six-thirty in the morning? Had she gone for a walk? If so, why would she have taken her purse?

Worried but assuming there had to be a reasonable explanation, he turned his cell phone on and checked for messages. He had four from Rich, but he didn't have any others. He dialed Amy's number, but it rolled right over to the message. He was pacing the downstairs of the house, trying to decide what he should do when the doorbell rang.

Feeling a huge surge of relief, he rushed to the door and pulled it open, then blinked in confusion. "Rich? What are you doing here?"

Rich was giving him a squirrelly look. "What the hell's going on?"

John held up both hands. "Time out. What are you talking about?"

"Why did your assistant editor, Amy, call me and tell me to meet her at Harmony Grove Cemetery?"

"Huh?"

"Yeah! She got me out of bed and said it was some kind of life or death situation. It was weird enough that I got dressed and started to head over there. I called you on your cell but you didn't answer, so I decided I'd just stop by here and make sure it wasn't some kind of weird prank. But then I thought why would a theoretically responsible adult pull a dumb ass prank like that. I'm assuming Amy is a theoretically responsible adult, so what the hell's going on?"

John's brain was racing. Why would Amy have gone to the cemetery? Did she have some reason to think he needed help? Did somebody call or come to the house, and if so, who was it and what did they tell her? And where was Rebecca Nurse? He realized he hadn't seen her since he got back. He turned away from Rich and looked around, but there was no sign of her ghost.

"Hey, John, I'm over here."

"Yeah, I know. Just hang on a second."

John ran his fingers through his hair as if trying to rake his thoughts into some order. It was useless. What the hell was he going to tell Rich?

"Rich," he said, turning back around. "I think Amy may be in trouble. I've got to go to the cemetery and see if I can find her, and I know it's a huge imposition, but I'd like you to come. Will you?"

Rich looked at him and scowled, but then a wry smile crept in. "For my good buddy?" He shrugged. "Why not? Since I can't get any more sleep tonight I might as well go someplace where people sleep all the time." He hooked his thumb over his shoulder. "My car?"

V

THEY WENT TO JOHN'S CAR WHERE HE RETRIEVED his flashlight and saber, then to Rich's car, which was in a no parking zone in front of John's front door. Rich eyed the saber as he clicked the locks on his car.

"Were you expecting pirates?"

"I don't have a gun."

"Will you tell me what the hell's going on?"

"Yeah, once we find Amy."

"But until then we're going to wander around with a sword? This is not what normal people do in Salem."

"This is not a normal situation. Take my word for it."

Rich shook his head but climbed behind the wheel and started the engine. The night was starting to give way to the first gray light of morning, and streets were beginning to stir with the start of the morning commute. Still the roads were mostly deserted, and they reached Harmony Grove in no time. Rich made a slow circle of the cemetery, but John saw no sign of Amy's car.

"That's weird," he muttered as they finished a complete loop. "You're sure she said to meet her here?"

"I don't think I'd forget Harmony Grove."

"No, I guess even you wouldn't forget that."

"What do you want to do?"

John took a breath and let out a long sigh. "I guess we need to go inside and see if she's there. I don't know how she would have gotten here without a car, and I don't know how she would have gotten inside, but Amy's pretty resourceful."

"Maybe she came in a taxi."

John remembered that Amy had left her car at the paper and walked home with him. He nodded. "That makes sense, but if she's not outside the walls, she's inside, and how did she get there?" A dark feeling rose up in his gut even as he spoke, and he tried to shake off the picture that formed in his mind of Amy in danger, perhaps badly injured . . . maybe even dead.

Rich pulled over to the curb and shut off the engine. As the car went dark and quiet, John glanced around, wondering if even now he and Rich were being observed. "You don't have to do this," he said, sounding braver than he felt but believing his friend had involved himself enough already.

Rich looked at him and scowled. "I didn't drive you here to drop your butt off and leave."

"Well, I'm just warning you, we have to climb a tree and shinny out on a limb to get in," John said. "But it's really not that bad. If I can do it, you can do it."

Rich looked at him and screwed up his face. "Didn't you ever bring dates here when you were a kid?"

"To the cemetery?"

"Yeah, best place in town. Deserted, safe, and the girls

got kind of freaked out so they didn't want you to take your hands off of them."

"Why are you bringing that up now?"

"Because if you'd ever done that you'd know about the back gate. Nobody ever used it, and it was always locked but it was easy to pick the lock." Rich climbed out of the car. "Come on."

John shook his head, frustrated that he had just about killed himself going over the wall earlier when he could have just played with the gate lock. He followed his friend around the corner to the back of the cemetery where a wrought iron gate was set into the brick wall.

Rich glanced back and saw that John had brought the flashlight and saber. "The sun's coming up. I don't think we need the flashlight."

"Yes, we do."

"And we need the sword because?"

"Because we do."

They went up to the gate, and Rich fished around in his pocket until he came out with a paperclip. "Each term paper has one." Unfolding it and sticking it into the lock, he said, "Let's hope this works the same as it used to in the old days."

He fiddled with the paperclip for a few seconds, until John heard a faint snap then watched the gate swing open. "Voila," said Rich.

Before they started through the gate, John handed Rich the saber. "Here. You may need this."

"I think you've gone around the bend."

"That would be preferable to me being right."

"About what?"

"Just come on."

John led the way into the cemetery and up the hill toward the Putnam plot at the opposite end. As he strode along one of the paved lanes, he looked around hoping to spot Amy. When he didn't see her his anxiety began to spike. He looked up the hill at the pentagram inscribed by the five white tombstones and the gloomy shape of the mausoleum. He didn't know why or how, but he felt a strange certainty that Amy was up ahead. At the same time he thought of Amy, he also thought about his great-great grandfather, his parents, and Julie, and his suspicion they had all been murdered by the coven. As those thoughts rolled through his mind the fear that had been locked in his gut all night long began to change to white-hot anger.

He found himself striding up the hill, while behind him Rich puffed, "Where are you going?"

"Just follow me," John called back.

When he reached the Putnam plot, he looked around again, but there was still no sign of Amy. He turned and without hesitation went straight for the steps that led down to the secret door beneath the Putnam mausoleum. He pounded down the steps then turned to wait for Rich, who had stopped at the top.

"What are you doing down there?"

"Just come down here. I think this is where Amy went."

Rich came down the steps looking very uncertain. He

pointed to the old metal door set into the wall. "That thing doesn't look like it's been opened in a hundred years."

"It probably hasn't, but this door has." John pointed to the red hand shaped stain in the wall.

"What door?"

"Look, Rich, you have to believe me when I tell you I went through this door the night I fell down these steps."

Rich was looking at him as if he thought John was severely concussed all over again. "Um, there's no door here," he said gently.

"Just listen, okay? I fell down these steps. I was bleeding and banged up, but I put my hand on top of this red print sort of by accident, and when I did the whole wall opened up."

"Uh-huh."

"Goddammit, it really happened!"

"Okay, so do it. Open the door."

"I tried earlier tonight, and it didn't work, but I know it *does* work. You're a religion professor. Help me figure this out."

Rich held up his hands. "Hey, I'm a professor, not a . . . voodoo guy."

"Rich, I'm telling you it *did* work. You gotta believe me. Help me figure it out. *Please!* Amy's life could depend on it."

Rich took a deep breath and shook his head. "Okay, what exactly did you do when you got it to open?"

John looked around. "I was flat on my back. I rolled onto my knees, then I grabbed that shelf right there," he said, pointing to the stone shelf that protruded from the wall beside the old metal door."

"Okay, so grab it."

John grabbed the shelf, then put his hand on the red stain. Nothing.

"Something has to have been different."

"Yeah, but what?" Rich asked.

John threw his hands in the air. He could *feel* Amy's presence on the other side of the wall, and he felt panic starting to rise up inside. If he didn't get the door open soon, he was going to be too late, he *knew* it. "I don't know!" he shouted.

"Okay, calm down. You said you were bleeding."

"Yeah."

"Did you have blood on your hand?"

John looked at him, suddenly remembering the way the wall had felt when he put his bloodied hand against the stone. It had been almost as if the wall was drinking the blood. "Yes!"

John dug into his pocket and felt for something sharp. When he felt nothing he grabbed the saber and tried its blade on his hand, however it was far too dull. "Gimme your paperclip," he demanded.

Rich handed him the clip and John stabbed it into the tips of three fingers in turn, ignoring the pain as he punched the skin deep enough for each fingertip to bleed. "Here goes nothing."

He squeezed the cuts until blood ran down each finger, then he put his hand on the red stain. Immediately the stone seemed to soften, and John's eyes went wide as once again it felt as if the wall was suckling the blood from his fingertips. As soon as that happened, the wall began to open.

"Holy hell," Rich said from close behind him.

"Yeah," said John. He felt a sense of shock it had actually worked, also a burst of fear, but along with it a thrill of victory because he had found his way into the coven's secret lair. As he stepped through the opening, his exultation vanished as the screams began to sound in his head. They were shrill and violent and seemed to go right through him, and the screams weren't just one person or two or three. There were so many of them, as if fifty or even a hundred people were all being boiled alive at the same time. He clutched his hands to his head, and his knees started to buckle.

He felt Rich's arm come around his chest. "You okay?"

John nodded, and Rich let go of him, but several seconds went by before he could speak. "Can't you hear that?"

"Hear what?"

"The screaming?"

"I can't hear a thing."

John managed to get his feet back beneath him. He tried to drive out the sound, and even though he managed to some extent, it was there in his head, an almost physical presence with the sharpness of a migraine. The pain made him feel puny and weak, and in the next instant he thought about how ridiculous he and Rich looked, two men with a flashlight and ancient saber between them, facing how many enemies? Were they going to find six people down here or fifty-six? Would their enemies be armed, or was it possible they had powers

John had never guessed at? What did any of that matter when he knew Amy was down here? It didn't. He felt her presence like a magnetic force pulling him forward.

He put his hand against the wall to steady himself, and after a few seconds he started forward but turned when he heard Rich's footsteps behind him. "Last chance," he said. "There's no need for you to go any farther."

Rich was looking around in amazement at the door and the rough stone steps that descended into darkness and looked like they had been cut from the earth many years earlier. "And let you have all the fun?" He shook his head. "No way."

"Suit yourself," John said, starting down the steps. Just as the first time he came here the lights in the walls seemed to sense his presence and glowed brighter and brighter as he and Rich got close and then began to fade as soon as they went past, eventually going completely dark.

"What is this place?" Rich whispered.

In spite of the brain-splitting screams that filled his head, John could hear his friend's whispers. That meant the screams were coming to him through some kind of perception beyond his five usual senses, but tonight, unlike the first time, he hadn't heard them until he went through the door. He had no answers, just questions, but nothing surprised him any more. They continued to descend, going down until John guessed they were forty or fifty feet underground, and the stairs finally stopped and the passage became a long tunnel.

"There's a coven in Salem," John whispered back.

"What kind of coven?"

"Witchcraft and devil worship. I didn't say anything before because I didn't think you would have believed me."

"I wouldn't have."

The passage was perhaps ten feet wide and seven or eight feet high, with rough rock walls and a stone floor. The lights continued to brighten and fade as they moved as silently as possible, their occasional whispers low, their feet scuffing softly. The passage seemed endless, but then John saw that up ahead that it ended in a T, and they would have to choose between going left or right. John tried to sense where the screams were coming from, but they seemed to be filling his head from all directions at once.

"Which way?" Rich whispered.

John shook his head, but then Rich pointed to something on the stone floor. John saw something dark going to the left, and he flicked on his flashlight and squatted down. In the light the mark Rich had seen glistened wetly, and when John touched it with his finger it felt sticky.

"It's blood," he whispered. He knew it had to be Amy's, and he felt a blade of fear run down his back. "This way."

He started left, moving quickly, but then slowed when he saw several doors up ahead. The nearest one, on the right, was constructed of thick oak with heavy wrought iron hinges and a stout crossbar that acted as a lock. As silently as possible, John removed the crossbar and opened the door onto a small room that looked and smelled as if it had recently been used as a prison cell. A filthy blanket lay crumpled in the far corner, and a bucket a foot or two from the door reeked of feces.

When he turned away he saw three other doors with similar bars, two on the left and one more on the right. He opened each one and looked inside, but all were empty. Farther down the passage they came to another door on the right, but this one was not barred. John opened it and peered inside at what looked like an institutional bathroom with white tile on the walls and floor. There was what looked like a central dressing area, a shower and toilet. It, too, was empty.

As John moved down the passage and more lights began to glow up ahead, he could see the passage dead-ended in another door. This door was different from the others, which were plain, and was made of richly polished wood with ornate carvings, in the center of which a demon's head stood out in bas relief.

"What the hell is this?" Rich whispered as he came up behind.

"I guess we go through it," John said. He put his hand on the knob, twisted, and swung the door inward a few inches, revealing a room that looked like it belonged in an old house. John's eye took in paneled wooden walls, a beamed ceiling, a pegged wooden floor with old oriental carpets. A round table stood on the left side of the room covered with a linen tablecloth. There were four people sitting at the table, two women and two men, but they had their backs to him. Even so, he could tell neither of the women was Amy.

The screaming that had been in his head the whole way

through the narrow passageways but which he had managed to wall off and contain at a manageable level now rose again. It became a physical assault, filling him until there didn't seem to be room for anything else and he felt like his scull might burst from the pressure. He fought the blinding pain, but at the same time he felt a white hot rage take hold of him as he looked at four of the people who made up the coven.

He didn't yet see their faces, but he didn't care. He hadn't articulated his intentions until now, but he realized he wasn't here to report them to the police. Anything he would accuse them of certainly wasn't provable, and even worse the police would question his sanity. In the end the members of the coven would almost certainly go free. No, he realized as he stepped through the door, he wasn't here to report them. Even though it turned his stomach and went against every single thing he had always believed, he needed to find the conviction and strength to kill them all, in order to make certain they would never again murder innocent people.

He wasn't shocked when the first person turned around and he recognized Abigail Putnam. However, when the Very Reverend Staunton Winthrop turned to look at him, and also Senator Austin Hallowell and Amanda Pendergast, he was unable to hide his shock. These were people of tremendous respectability in Salem, people with money and power and prestige, people no one would ever believe could have done the terrible things they had supposedly done in the name of Satan. Even as he saw them and recognized them, he felt his resolve weaken.

Seeing these familiar faces made the horrible things he had been so certain of only moments before seem much more unbelievable: the Satan worship, the blood sacrifice, the systematic murder of members of his own family. These people weren't his best friends, but who was he kidding? He couldn't bring himself to start killing them. What was he going to do, start bashing their brains in with his flashlight while they sat around a table? And where was Amy? There had to be some explanation that made more sense than all of this confusion. He felt the furious energy that had driven him here begin to dissipate, almost as if it was running out the bottoms of his feet.

Reverend Winthrop smiled and waved John forward. He coughed wetly into his fist then said, "Please do come in. We've been expecting you."

The old man's tone of voice, the lack of any hint of conflict or concern gave him further pause. He took a step forward, knowing his face was a mask of total confusion. This was all so utterly unexpected. So was the blow to the back of his head that brought complete blackness.

VI

JOHN'S FIRST AWARENESS WAS PAIN, A TERRIBLE pain like a knife blade at the base of his skull. A second later the pain began to radiate outward, down his neck to his shoulders and out to the ends of his arms. His shoulder sockets and wrists burned as if they were on fire.

Even before he opened his eyes, he felt the dizziness, the nausea, the sense of complete and utter dislocation. He knew he was concussed, and immediately he wondered if he had been hallucinating and whether he had once again fallen down a flight of stairs. His memory was so bizarre: searching for Amy in an underground passageway, prison cells, a carved door opening into an underground dining room where a group of people had been waiting for him. He remembered Rich. Had Rich really been with him? What had happened to him? And what about Amy?

When he opened his eyes, his vision was extremely blurry, but he realized his head was hanging limp and he was staring down at a floor of white tile. An attempt to move his arms brought an electric shock of fresh agony from his shoulders to his wrists. Raising his head and turning it to either side showed him he was spread-eagled against a white tile wall. It looked like there were black metal shackles on his wrists that were anchored to the wall. Putting weight on his legs took some of the pressure off his wrists and shoulders.

Unable to rub his eyes, he opened them wide and blinked again and again, trying to clear away the cobwebs that made it so hard to focus. "Ahh, John, you're coming around," someone said. He recognized Rich's voice. Was he a prisoner, too? Rich didn't sound as if he was in pain, rather he sounded almost pleased. John turned his head in the direction of the sound and kept blinking, trying to see.

At first all he saw was a blurred shape moving in front of him. He squeezed his eyes closed and looked again. It was Rich. He recognized his friend's face, but Rich's smile wasn't full of the usual humor. There was a feral gleam in his friend's eyes.

"What's going on?" John managed after a few seconds.

Rich shrugged. "You were magnificent tonight, or should I say, this morning. You were diligent and courageous, the same way you play hockey, I might add. You always push into the center of the action, and I have to hand it to you, you don't back down. I don't think a lot of people would be stupid enough to open that secret door and then head inside armed with," he laughed, "a flashlight. You even gave me the saber."

John rolled his neck and tried to see beyond Rich, but his eyes wouldn't yet focus. His mind was reeling as he tried to make sense of what he was hearing. He noticed that Rich seemed to be dressed in some sort of white smock, like something a lab scientist might wear. His other senses were also starting to work, and as he started to breathe through his nose, above all he noticed the room was filled with the overwhelming stench of human excrement.

"You're part of them?" he asked, his voice coming out as little more than a whisper.

"Yes," Rich responded. "And very soon I'm going to be one of the judges. I've been chosen to take Reverend Winthrop's place. As you might have noticed, he's quite ill with cancer."

"That's a real shame for him," John managed.

"Well, yes, but he's going to live a lot longer than you will . . . unless you get smart."

"What are you talking about? Where's Amy?"

Before Rich could speak, John heard a moan from someplace nearby. He recognized Amy's voice. "Amy?" he asked. "Are you okay?"

The same sound came back to him and he realized that she must have been gagged in some way. "Let her go, Rich, you have me."

"That's such a brave response."

"Well it smells like somebody else wasn't very brave, Rich old boy. Did you shit your pants?"

"No, no, John, I'm afraid not, but some other people . . . well let's just say they spilled their guts."

John had never heard anything like the coldness in Rich's tone of voice. It was as if his very close friend, the man he had known and partied with and played hockey with, his perpetually horny college professor buddy had an evil twin. The man talking to him now was cold and sardonic and . . . evil.

John was shaking his head and blinking his eyes furiously, trying to shake off the effects of the blow to his head, and as his eyes began to clear the sight that greeted them made him think for few seconds that he *had* to be hallucinating. He looked to either side, and what he saw simply wasn't possible. It wasn't. It *couldn't* be.

"Jesus," he whispered. He felt the bile rise in his gorge and swallowed to try and keep from vomiting, but he had simply never seen anything like this.

Rich laughed. "Probably not gonna find him down here. This place belongs to the other guy."

John looked to either side and felt any hope he might have harbored for a miraculous rescue or an ability to somehow turn things in his favor vanish utterly. He could see three people who had been shackled in the same way as him, but their now lifeless bodies sagged like stored marionettes. Blood pooled at their feet from the unspeakable damage that had been done to them, and what was worse, their intestines hung from their eviscerated abdomens like red and purple rope.

John shook his head, unable to keep his voice from trembling with the edge of hysteria. "Did you do this?" he hissed.

"Cabby did these three. From what I understand, it's been his specialty for many years."

"*Cabby?*" John knew Rich was referring to Lieutenant

Cabot Corwin. "You're supposed to be a liberal college professor, but you're on a first name basis with Corwin?"

"We're closer than you might imagine."

John closed his eyes. Whatever he could have imagined, nothing could ever have prepared him for this. "Who were they?" When he opened his eyes again, he looked at the faces of the two dead girls and the dead boy. "Was one of them Melissa Blake?"

"Yes," Rich said with a tone of regret. "Not our best moment, I'm afraid. She did attract a bit too much attention to our activities."

"You thought she was a runaway?"

"Yes."

"Why do you do . . . this?"

"Well," Rich said, his tone shifting, suddenly sounding like a college professor who wanted to tutor a bright student. "Before the sacrifice we break them down. We put them in a dark cell in total isolation for a few days. We call that the Sacrament of Separation. Sort of the opposite of baptism. Then we lead them through the Sacrament of Renunciation. Sort of the opposite of Confirmation. Then we lead them through the Third Sacrament, the Sacrament of Blood, where they become married to Satan in death. Sort of the opposite of the whole Sacrament of Marriage thing."

"You torture them?"

Rich nodded. "Satan especially values the strong character, the grudging renunciation given only in the last throes of unspeakable pain, and the ability to capture the spirit of one who was such a strong supporter of His hated enemy."

"She was a high school girl."

"Of the three we have sacrificed this month, she was by far the most worthy. She would not deny her religion, not even at the end when she was in unspeakable pain and knew there was absolutely no hope, when all she wanted in the world was for the pain to stop. She held out until death."

"You are sick beyond words." John ripped at his manacles, trying to tear them loose from the wall but only managed to slice them into his wrists.

"Not at all. I recognize that I have made a Faustian bargain. People make bargains all the time with the Christian God, but they get absolutely nothing out of it. I, however, am going to be very wealthy, I will never be hungry, and I will live a long time."

"Doesn't Reverend Winthrop have cancer? Isn't he dying?"

Rich waved a hand, dismissing the question. "Yes, but he's eighty-four. Satan has fulfilled his side of the bargain."

John closed his eyes and opened them again. There was something they had both avoided. He didn't have any idea what Rich's reasons were, but he wasn't sure he could stand to see Amy if she looked anything like the people on either side of him.

"Let me ask you a question," he said, trying to forestall the inevitable. "Did you have anything to do with Julie's death?"

Rich shrugged. "It was supposed to be you, old boy. You were starting to become *aware*."

"Of Rebecca Nurse?"

"That old bag's been trying to stir things up with your bloodline for years, for generations! Fortunately for us, whenever she appears to one of you and you start to realize the coven really exists, your astral signature lights you up like a flare."

"Astral signature?"

"The non-corporeal part of you. The part that can inter-act with the spirit world."

"You *saw* me?"

Rich shook his head. "Abigail did. She is our seer. And another of us saw you, as well. The inquisitor."

"Who is that?"

Rich shook his head. "Sorry. Not allowed to speak the name."

"Even though you're going to kill me?"

He nodded, and then he clapped his hands and let out a laugh. "That's what I love about you, John. Even though you're our prisoner, and you know you haven't got a chance in hell of getting out of here alive, you're planning your next move. I really am going to miss that about you. You don't know how to lose. You don't know how to get knocked down and stay down. It's an amazing characteristic."

Rich looked at him a moment, almost with a sense of fondness. "I gotta tell you that you are, like, an amazing plum for me. I got you in here and brought you all the way. You didn't have a clue. And I gotta also tell you how big your sacrifice is going to be. For Satan to get the blood of someone with the *awareness*, that's big. It's huge. Your blood is, like, a hundred percent pure octane, whereas most people are like five octane. Your Sacrament of Renunciation is going to be *amazing!*"

John closed his eyes and shook his head. Deep inside something strange was happening. He felt like two different people. One person was filled with rage, a white-hot, unquenchable rage that burned like plasma. The other felt only abject terror, but not for himself, only for Amy. If anything was going to break him, it would be when they made him watch her suffer, and he was absolutely certain they intended to do just that.

"Where is Amy?" he demanded, unable to stand the suspense any longer.

"I thought you'd never ask," Rich said. "Cabby, could please bring in our other guest?"

A second later, Cabby Corwin appeared with Amy. She was totally nude except for a gag that kept her from making anything but unintelligible sounds.

"This is quite a lovely woman," Rich said. Then he dropped his voice to a whisper and added, "I hope you've been banging her, but I suspect you haven't. Cabby and I were talking about maybe the two of us ripping off a little piece, but," Rich shook his head, "that would profane our religious ceremony and no doubt offend the others."

As John looked at Amy he felt a huge jolt of sadness. She was heart-achingly beautiful, and it seemed sad beyond words he was never going to consummate the love he now silently acknowledged for her. He looked away as Rich clicked the locks on her ankles and wrists, but then he looked back at her and met her eyes. He saw her fear, and his heart burned with almost unbearable love and pity and fear for what was about to happen.

Cabby Corwin left the room and returned a second later buttoning up a lab coat similar to the one Rich wore. Both men put on goggles and the kind of hair coverings doctors wore in operating rooms, and John knew it was to avoid blood spray from getting on them. Cabby went out of the room again and returned pushing a cart similar to a drinks trolley a butler might use. Only this pushcart was filled with an array of knives, scalpels, hooks, and other torture instruments so hideous John could only imagine their use.

Corwin pulled out a pair of latex gloves, and as he pulled them on, he turned to look at John. "Ready to watch, Mr. Andrews?"

John's heart was beating incredibly hard. Never in his life had he felt the nuclear anger that had been building inside him for the past several minutes. He felt his eyes almost rolling back in his head, but then he heard the other voice, the one he had only heard once or twice before.

It was Rebecca Nurse, speaking as if she was right there beside him. "You believed you had no weapon," she whispered. "But you are wrong. *You* are the weapon, John Andrews. *You* are the weapon."

Cabby was selecting from among his scalpels, taking his time, drawing the process out for the effect it was having on both John and Amy.

I am the weapon, John intoned to himself. *I am the weapon.* He pulled with all his strength against the shackles, but nothing happened. He looked right. He looked left. They had taken off his coat when they knocked him out, and he wore only a long sleeved shirt. The cuff buttons on his left sleeve had come undone, and the letters Rebecca Nurse had burned into his arm were visible. Instead of the reddish brown color of dried blood they were now bright red, and as he stared at them, they began to turn the blistering shade of burning coals.

Cabby finally chose one of his scalpels and turned toward Amy. He went toward her, took her right hand and made a deep, slow incision in her palm. Amy let out a deep groan, and John felt his anger ratchet even higher. Then, in the next second, he felt his own anger joined and strengthened by something outside of himself.

He looked to his right and saw Rebecca Nurse holding his right hand, and immediately he realized she was binding her eternal and unquenchable anger to his own. His left arm was burning now, painlessly, but the flames were licking out from the letters to color the flesh for several inches on each side.

Cabby sliced into Amy's other palm and at the moment he heard Amy's heart-wrenching cry of pain he felt another jolt of anger. When he looked to his left where his entire forearm now seemed to swell as if it was about to explode in a shower of lava, he saw the ghostly form of a young woman holding his left hand. Unlike Rebecca Nurse, this young woman was dressed in modern clothing. Beyond her he could see many, many more forms, men and women, boys and girls, all of them indistinct but in some way very real, all of them standing hand-in-hand as if linked through time and death by their unquenchable rage. As he turned his head and looked at Rebecca Nurse, she nodded, as if telling him to let himself go.

I am the weapon.

John did not understand what happened next. The manacle holding his left arm exploded outward. A piece of the metal flew loose to ping off the tile wall. Cabby and Rich turned to look just as the right manacle also snapped off. John's mind was a blur of voices, but he saw Cabby coming toward him, a bloody scalpel gripped in his right hand. Without knowing why, operating on some level of instinct he'd never realized he possessed, John aimed his left arm at Cabby. As he did something red and hot exploded from his fist. In the next instant it looked as if Corwin had been shot point-blank by a twelve-gauge shotgun, as the center of his chest literally ceased to exist and he flew backwards into the tile wall.

Rich looked at John, his cockiness having vanished and a look of panic now in its place. He turned and raced from the room. John felt the shackles on his ankles give way and he moved away from the wall, his mind a sea of confusing voices but his actions certain. He ran after Rich and saw him going through a door on the far side of the room, away from the door through which they had entered earlier.

Reverend Winthrop was still at the table, as were Senator Hallowell, Amanda Pendergast, and Abigail Putnam. As the senator struggled to his feet John aimed his fist and released a second bolt. It caught Hallowell in the throat and nearly severed his neck. Without stopping he swung his arm and shot Amanda Pendergast, whose chair flew over backward as her ruined body splayed out across the rug. John noted that her hair was still perfectly coiffed and her ice blue eyes stared sightlessly up at the ceiling.

He slowed at that point. Abigail Putnam was already on her feet, backing toward the door through which Rich had run. John didn't trust himself to speak. He felt Rebecca Nurse and Melissa Blake inside his head along with so many others. In his wild anger he felt a surge of joy as Abigail put her hands up and shook her head in mute supplication. He let her take two more steps. He could see she was about to turn and run when a bolt from his hand caught her squarely in the chest and blew her half apart.

The final person was the Very Reverend Staunton Winthrop. He stood up, frail and consumed by cancer but he kept his head erect. "Damn you to hell," he said.

"No, actually damn *you* to hell," John said, and then he fired.

VII

JOHN FELT THE SPIRITS URGING HIM TO CHASE after Rich, but he refused. Whatever had happened a moment earlier, whatever force had been in his body seemed to rush out of him as quickly as it had come. He felt pain again in every single fiber of his being. He was shaking and almost staggering with weakness as he turned and went back into the chamber where Amy was still shackled to the wall. He went to the cart where Cabby had kept his torture instruments and found the key. He unlocked her wrists and ankles, then went outside and tore half of Reverend Winthrop's shirt from his bloody body and used the rags to quickly bind her palms.

"Can you walk?" he asked.

She was terribly pale and drawn, but she nodded and he led her toward the door where he had first come in. John found his flashlight on the dining room table, but he wasn't worried about being attacked. Rich had fled the other way, which probably meant there was another and perhaps closer exit, but he didn't want to risk getting lost. He needed to flag a taxi and get Amy to the hospital, and after that he had one more thing to do before he was finished.

Keeping his arm around her waist for support, they walked through the passages, retracing his earlier route, and finally came to the door that led to the outside world. The door had closed, but John put his hand against the rags he had tied around Amy's palms and came away with enough blood to open it again when he put his hand on the red mark.

The door swung out, and they climbed the steps into the bright morning sunshine, and they walked together to the street where a minute later they were in the back of taxi heading to Salem Hospital. They had barely spoken since he had freed her from the shackles, and even now they looked at each other without speaking, both realizing that they would only talk about what actually happened when they were alone and there was no chance of being overheard.

He walked Amy into the emergency room where she told the nurse at the desk that she had been working in her yard when her stepladder tipped over and she fell onto a picket fence and cut herself badly on the pickets. They went into the waiting area and sat together for several minutes.

"How do you feel?" Amy asked.

"Stronger than I did a little while ago, but I still feel like I just ran a double marathon on an empty stomach."

"Be careful, John."

He looked at her out of the corner of his eye. She knew as well as he that there was one more thing he had to do even though he wasn't sure he had the strength or the stomach for it. He nodded. "Yeah."

"Call me."

He gave her his house key. "I'll meet you back at my house."

"Okay."

He got up, flagged a taxi to take him to his house where he got his own car and drove to Salem State University. He parked his car in a No Parking zone and walked up the front steps of the building that housed the religion department. Knowing Rich's office was on the top floor, he waited for the elevator and when it came, he hit the button for four. When he got off he turned right and went down to Rich's closed office door.

"I don't know if I'd go in there right now, Mr. Andrews," one of the department secretaries said in a soft voice. "I don't think he wants company right now."

"He's upset about something?"

She nodded. "But I didn't tell you."

John forced a smile. "I never heard it from you." He gave his head a jerk in the direction of Rich's office door. "I think he had a big fight with his wife. I'll go in and check on him."

"Don't say I didn't warn you."

He nodded, went over to Rich's door, and finding it locked, he knocked hard.

"Who is it?" Rich demanded. His words were slurred almost as if he had been drinking, but John was pretty sure that wasn't the case. A second later he heard the unmistakable sound of a trashcan banging and then retching, and he knew Rich was throwing up.

John knocked again.

"Go away."

He knocked a third time, and finally he heard Rich shuffle toward the door. The lock clicked and the door opened. Rich looked at him, his eyes so dull and unsurprised that John wondered if Rich had known it was him the whole time. John walked into the office, and smelling the stench of fresh vomit, he shut the door. Rich walked around and dropped into his desk chair, seeming to lack both the muscle and skeletal mass to hold himself upright, and sagged in the chair like a beanbag.

He looked up at John through bloodshot eyes. "Well, I guess you win, old boy. Have you come here to kill me?"

John shook his head. "I hope not, but I will if it comes to that."

"You think I'm going to name names, give up everything and everybody?" He shook his head. "Sorry, not my style."

John already knew that, so he didn't bother trying. "How many are you?"

Rich gave a humorless laugh. "Not that many. Twenty-five or so."

"Less five?"

Rich nodded. "So you're not going to kill me, what happens next?"

"You saw what I did to Cabby. I did the same thing to all the others. I could do it to you, but I don't want your family to see you like that." Even as John said this he doubted it was true. He no longer felt the nearly inhuman rage that had burned so bright and left him so utterly depleted when it departed. He no longer had the spirits of Rebecca Nurse and Melissa Blake and all the others to add to whatever he could summon from within himself. But there was no reason to tell Rich.

Rich looked away from him and out the window. He took a deep breath and let it out slowly. "So," he said.

"Yeah, so."

Rich stood up from his chair. There were tears in his eyes, and they suddenly broke loose and started down his cheeks. He didn't bother to wipe away a line of snot dripping down to his upper lip. "Can you fix it so my name doesn't get lumped in with the others?"

"Maybe. I'll try for Lisa's sake. Does she know?"

Rich closed his eyes and shook his head. "No. She's true blue Episcopalian."

He grabbed the handle on his office window, twisted it, and pulled the window inward. The wind came into the office brisk and cold, clearing the air and helping John to feel a little stronger. Rich looked down at the cement four stories below and let out a shuddering breath.

"Do it," John said. He heard the pitilessness in his voice and felt sparks of white-hot anger begin to grow inside. "Do it now."

Rich grabbed a wooden chair and pulled it over to the window. He climbed on the chair, then stepped onto the sill. He turned once and looked back at John. "You know, it's not an excuse, but when you're doing something to pacify a god, it doesn't seem as bad as it is. At least not at the time."

Before John had a chance to say any more, Rich dropped headfirst toward the cement below. A second later John heard a muted thump and then somewhere a woman started to scream.

VIII

JOHN TORE HIS SHIRT OPEN, MUSSED HIS HAIR, then went out and called out to the secretary, "I tried to stop him, but I was too late."

A stunned silence fell over the hallway. A second later, phones began to ring, and then several students came barreling out of a stairwell having run up. "Professor Harvey just dove out his window!"

John said nothing. He went back into the office, closed the window, sat down in one of the chairs, and waited for the police. A little over an hour later, after taking care of the body and talking to almost everyone else who could serve as a witness, Captain Brad Card came into the office.

"Twice in one week," John said when he saw Card walk through the door. "Isn't this off your normal beat?"

"You tell me," Card said. "You were the last person to see Professor Harvey alive?"

"Yes."

Card looked at him for a long time. "And why were you here?"

"Rich and I were friends. I knew he was deeply troubled about something, and I came up to see if I could help."

"Exactly what happened?"

John told him the story he had been rehearsing in his mind. "I knocked on the door a couple time before Rich came and unlocked it."

"Was it unusual for him to lock his door when he was in the office?"

"You'd have to ask his secretary."

Card nodded. "So when he opened the door, how did he seem?"

"Disturbed, over-adrenalized."

"And what did he do?"

"Closed the door, locked it, and went straight to the window, which was already unlatched. He swung it open, climbed up on the chair and stepped onto the sill."

"What did you do?"

"I tried to grab him, and we started to grapple. He managed to shove me back, and then he said, 'It didn't seem so bad when I did it, but it does now,' and then he just turned and dove headfirst."

Card looked at him without expression. "That's it?"

John nodded.

"What was 'it'?"

"No idea."

Card looked at him a long time. "Right," he said at last. "We'll be in touch."

IX

JOHN WENT BACK TO PICKERING WHARF, PARKED, and used the spare key he hid around the side of the house to let himself in. He found Amy asleep on the couch in the living room beneath the watchful eye of Rebecca Nurse's portrait. Her hands were covered with thick white bandages, and he presumed she was probably knocked out on painkillers. He knew she might have gone up to the bedroom where they had slept the night before, but he also understood why she had chosen to lay down right where she had.

He turned and looked up at the portrait of the woman he had always found so incredibly unpleasant, and he nodded. "Thank you," he whispered, feeling a blast of gratitude and knowing he would never allow that portrait to go out of his possession for the rest of his life.

He went upstairs and found a blanket that he put over Amy, and he watched over her as she continued to sleep for much of the afternoon. When she finally awoke at around four o'clock, he went over, sat beside her, and smoothed her hair away from her face.

"How about some tea?"

She nodded, and by the time he came back into the living

room with two steaming mugs she was sitting up. He put one of the mugs on the butler's table, and she managed to pinch it between her two bandaged hands and take a sip.

"Do you remember what happened?" he asked.

She nodded. "A lot of it. Rich called the house in the middle of the night. He said he was outside in his car and that you had called him and told him to come get me." She closed her eyes and shook her head at the memory. "I was still half asleep, and I believed him. When I went downstairs, I got into his car, and we drove to the cemetery. He kept saying he was afraid you were in trouble, and I was just so worried for you I didn't ask any of the questions I should have. He knew about a gate he was able to unlock, and we went rushing inside trying to find you, and then we went down those stairs, and I saw an open door and people were waiting for us."

John nodded. "I must have triggered some kind of warning when I tried to get in the first time, or maybe they were even watching the house and knew when I left. I wasn't able to get into the secret door at first, so I came back here and found you gone. I was really worried, but then Rich came to the door and said you had called him and told him to meet you in Harmony Grove. I believed him, and we went racing over there to try and find you."

"They were going to torture both of us to death, weren't they?"

He nodded. "They were going to make me watch while they did it to you."

She looked at him and at his left arm. "How did you do that?"

He shook his head. "I don't really know. I remember being scared to death for you and at the same time angrier than I have ever been. I felt so utterly powerless until I heard Rebecca's voice in my head telling me I was the weapon. The next thing I knew, Rebecca was holding my right hand, and then I felt the spirit of that poor young woman take my other hand, and she was linked to the spirits of so many others. All of their terrible anger added to my own, and suddenly the shackles holding my wrists and ankles just blew apart. It was like there were many voices in my head all at the same time, and part of what happened next was because I wanted it, but at the same time I felt like I was also the instrument of all of their rage."

"And so that . . . power came from all of you at once?"

John nodded. "And when it left me, I was more exhausted than I've ever been in my life."

"Did you kill all the others?"

"All but Rich. He got away."

"When you left me you went to find him?"

"What happened?"

"He killed himself. I told him he had to, and that if he refused he had seen what I could do. That was a lie. I don't think I could have summoned that kind of power again, and in any case, I couldn't have done that to him."

"How do you feel?"

"I'll miss him, but it was the right thing to do."

SEVEN

October 26

WHEN JOHN WENT INTO WORK THE NEXT MORNING, he was still exhausted. After making a roast chicken dinner for Amy, he had left her to go pay his respects to Lisa Harvey, Rich's widow. It had been a painful evening because it reminded him of his own loss four years earlier. Also, in spite of how devastated Lisa had been and in spite of his best attempts to give whatever comfort he could, John had been unable to completely still the voices of suspicion that played in his head, asking how much Lisa had known about Rich's Satan worship and whether she might be part of it herself.

When he had come home Amy had been upstairs in bed, and he had undressed and crawled in next to her and gone immediately to sleep. When they had awoken that morning they had cuddled and talked for a time, and when Amy's body language convinced him it would be more than okay with her, they had made slow and very gentle love.

"I could put my arms around you, but I felt like I couldn't really touch you," she had whispered afterward.

"You touched me more deeply than you know. Besides, we'll have lots more opportunities in the future." He had told her this, feeling a joyous bolt of certainty as he said it because he knew that it was true.

II

IN SPITE OF BEING ALMOST TOO TIRED TO WORK,
by noon John had approved several stock photos of the Salem
State University campus, looked at a preliminary mockup of
that afternoon's front page, reviewed Rich's obituary, and
had written an editorial on suicide and the loss to the community of a fine teacher, a wonderful husband, father, and a
good friend. Just as he finished typing the last sentence, he
looked up from his computer and saw Brad Card walk into
the newsroom. Somehow he wasn't surprised.

Card looked in the direction of John's office, saw John's
wave of acknowledgement and started toward him. Card
could see through the glass walls that John was alone, so he
pushed the door open a few inches. "Mind if I come in?"

"Please do. You have more questions about Rich?"

Card shook his head. "Something else. It's kind of a shot
in the dark, but I wondered if you might possibly be able to
help shed some light on several disappearances."

John felt a tremor, but he shrugged to try and cover it up.
"Who?"

"Abigail Putnam for starters. It's four days before Halloween, her store is as busy as it ever gets, and she has vanished.

Also, Reverend Staunton Winthrop, Amanda Pendergast, and Lieutenant Cabot Corwin have all been reported missing."

"And you're coming to see me because?"

"Because my gut tells me you might be able to help."

"How? I know all the people you mentioned, but I don't know any of them well."

"You said that Professor Harvey said something unusual just before he jumped. Do you remember what you said?"

"He said, 'It didn't seem so bad when I did it, but it does now.'"

"What you think he meant?"

John shrugged.

Card looked at him for a long time. "I think you know more than you're telling me. I also know that Amy Johnson, your assistant editor, was brought into the emergency room at Salem Hospital yesterday with two very nasty injuries to her palms. Nurses described the person who brought her in, and it sounded an awful lot like you."

"Really? Well, it was."

"And she fell off a stepladder and got two perfectly symmetrical wounds?"

"Picket fence."

Card nodded. "I drove past her house. She doesn't have a picket fence."

John looked at Card but said nothing.

"I'm not accusing you of anything. I'm asking for your help," Card said after a long silence.

"What do you need?"

"Come with me to Abigail Putnam's office."

III

JOHN TENSED AS CAPTAIN CARD PARKED HIS unmarked state police cruiser in front of a fire hydrant just down the block from Wicca Wonders. They climbed from the car, Card locked it, and then they started working their way past the crowd of shoppers dressed as witches and warlocks who were either waiting in line to get inside or who had just come out of the store and were standing around comparing their purchases with their friends. As he approached the front door, John tried to steel himself against the screams he knew would assault his ears any second, but as he stepped up to the front door nothing happened.

There were several loud objections from people farther back in the line as Card and John went through the front door, but a quick look from Card's no-nonsense cop face seemed to quell the trouble. They moved through the store to the counter at the back where Card showed his badge to a woman who had an assistant manager badge on her witch costume, and then asked her to point the way to Abigail Putnam's office. The woman glanced at the badge then jerked her head and led them through a door at the back of the store and down a short hallway to a closed door.

"She's not in there, but I guess you know that," the woman said.

"Thank you. We do. As you know Ms. Putnam has been reported missing, and we've been given permission to search the premises in hopes it might help us locate her."

"Be my guest," the woman said.

Card tried the door, but it was locked. "Here," the assistant manager offered. She stepped up to the keypad on the door and punched in a code of six numbers. "I'm not actually supposed to know this, but I watched her do it enough times I couldn't help learning it."

With the code punched in, an electric lock clicked, and Card pushed his way inside. "Thank you," he said to the woman, who was already heading back out to the sales counter.

John followed Card into the office and looked around uneasily at the dark and overly ornate surroundings. He was still surprised he could hear no screaming, but then he realized he probably shouldn't be: he supposed what he had done had set the spirits free. As he stood there taking in his surrounding, he realized Card was watching him.

"What?"

"Is there anything in here that might relate to your friend, Professor Harvey?"

"Why do you ask?"

"We dusted for prints this morning and found his, among those of the other missing persons, over by the bookshelf."

John remembered how Rich had run out a different door

than the one he and Amy had used when they escaped from the underground chambers. Was there some kind of hidden entrance here, he wondered?

He went to the bookshelf and began to examine the leather bound spines, pulling out each one until he came to two books together at the end of one shelf that seemed to be fakes. They would not budge when he tried to pull them out, but when he pushed one of the spines, he heard a soft click and felt the books slide outward as if pushed by a spring.

"What the hell is that?" Card asked.

"I have no idea," John said as he gazed at the two "books" that now protruded about twelve inches from the shelf. He tried to pull them out or turn it, but it would budge no farther. A closer look showed him the top was open. He put his hand into the opening, expecting to feel a key or perhaps a button, but was shocked to feel wetness.

He pulled his hand out and saw that his fingertips were covered in something red, and he knew immediately what it had to be.

"What the . . .?" Card exclaimed.

"It's blood," John said.

He folded his fingers and wiped the blood on his palm, and at the same time he looked around for what he knew he had missed so far. It took nearly two minutes of looking, before he found it, a place on the next shelf down, at the end of the row of books, where a bookend created enough space for a hand to slide into the dark opening and find the very faint red handprint. John pressed his bloody palm to the print, felt the corresponding softness as if his palm was being licked clean.

In the next instant, several feet of bookshelf moved outward several inches and then swung on silent hinges to reveal a set of stone steps leading downward. John turned to look at Card whose hand had gone to the gun in the holster at his hip. "I don't think you'll need that, but you can't be too careful."

"What's down there?"

"Just come." John went to the steps and started down, and just as had happened when he went through the secret door beneath the mausoleum, the lights began to grow brighter, lighting the passageway ahead of him. He heard Captain Card's footsteps coming behind as they both descended to where the passageway leveled out. Just as had happened below the mausoleum, they walked what seemed like a very long way before they encountered any other doors.

"Here," Card said, handing him a pair of latex gloves. "Don't touch anything until you're wearing those."

After he donned the gloves, John tried each door they came to, ascertained that the room was not the one he was seeking and kept moving.

"What the hell is this place?" Card asked after they had been walking for perhaps ten minutes.

"I don't know what you call it."

"But you've been down here before." It was not a question.

John hesitated, then nodded. "Yes."

They walked until they came to a T where they had to

turn left or right. John paused, closed his eyes, and tried to picture the passage they had just come through and its orientation to Harmony Grove Cemetery. "I think we have to go left," he said.

"Whatever," Card said.

They continued to walk the long passageway, encountering more doors. John looked inside each one but did not try to explore them. At the end of the passage they came to a door he recognized: polished mahogany with the bas relief carving of a daemon's head.

John turned and faced Card and told him the story he had been rehearsing ever since they first entered the underground passage. "Rich Harvey was involved with these people," he said. "But in the end he couldn't live with what he'd done. I don't know how he did what he did. I don't know what weapon he used. I can't explain any of it, but here it is."

John opened the door and stepped into the room with the paneled wooden walls, beamed ceiling and pegged wooden floor covered with old rugs. He saw the dining table on the far side and the door through which he and Amy had fled, but his mouth dropped open as he looked for the bodies. They were gone. He blinked stupidly, then looked at the walls or the rugs for the telltale stains of the gore that had splattered everywhere when he killed five people a little over twenty-four hours earlier.

"This is impossible," he said in a choked voice as he hurried toward the wall where there had been a door into the white tiled room where the three bodies hung from their shackles. He tried to find some way to open the door, a red mark where he could put his bloody hand, but there was nothing.

"This is impossible!" he said, turning to glare at Captain Card as if this was his fault.

Card said nothing, but simply shook his head. "It's not impossible," he said in a very soft voice. "I was pretty sure we wouldn't find anything down here."

"Well, two days ago this was an abattoir. There were four dead bodies in this room and four in a room on the other side of this wall. I'm telling you! I saw them!" He almost said that he was the one who had killed some of them, or at least that he had helped by becoming the instrument where the focused rage of spirits of the victims found release. "There were three dead kids in that room," he said, pointing to the wall.

Card simply nodded. "I believe you."

John paid no attention, but plunged onward. "They had been tortured, and their intestines were spilling out onto the floor, and . . . you what?"

"I believe you."

John looked at him for a long moment. "Why?"

"You think Salem is the only place where something like this might have happened?"

"It's not?"

Card shook his head. "Not by a long shot. We believe the covens are international in scope."

John considered that. "Who is we?"

"I'm not at liberty to disclose that. Maybe down the road, but not now."

"Why is it a secret?"

"Because we don't know who our enemies are. *You* didn't know if I was one of them when you led me down here."

John nodded. "I wondered about it, but I decided that being totally paranoid serves no purpose."

"It may serve more of a purpose than you think."

"Why is it just the two of us?"

"Why do you think?"

"Because you wanted to be able to decide how to spin this?"

Card nodded. "How would you suggest we report this: State Police report occult activity and devil worship in Salem? Is that what you would recommend? Would that improve the public safety and increase the credibility of the police?"

John shook his head. "I don't know what I'd do, but you had eight people killed down here and one suicide. People aren't going to ignore that number of disappearances."

"Tell me again who the dead people were?"

"Five were members of the," he paused, feeling strange about speaking the word out loud, "coven. Reverend Winthrop, Lieutenant Corwin, Amanda Pendergast, Senator Hallowell, and Abigail Putnam."

"And Richard Harvey was the sixth?"

"No, Richard said he had been selected to take the place of Reverend Winthrop."

"But he hadn't yet?"

"Apparently not."

"Damn," Card said under his breath.

"What?"

"We know very little about these people, but we do know that every coven has six judges. The most senior judge is also known as the inquisitor. Inquisitors are responsible for keeping the others in line."

"Who does the inquisitor report to, Satan?"

"Is that supposed to be a joke? Actually we don't know. We think there is one person who all the inquisitors report to, but we haven't had any success identifying them. Do you have any idea who the sixth person might be, here in Salem?"

John shook his head. "With the exception of Cabby Corwin all the other people were wealthy and high-profile."

"Corwin was also wealthy. He just kept it quiet."

"That means the sixth person is probably the same, right? Wealthy and high-profile?"

Card nodded. "The problem is, that's a large group in a place like Salem. And since one was an Episcopalian priest and another was a senator, we know it could be almost anybody."

"So, what are you going to report?"

"That we found absolutely nothing out of order. You okay with that?"

"You're a cop and you're asking *me*?"

Card smiled. "I would like to make sure you're not planning to write a huge article in the paper accusing me of covering this up."

John thought about that for a moment and then nodded. "Fair enough."

IV

WHEN HE GOT BACK TO THE PAPER, JOHN SAT AT his desk, rested his feet on an open drawer, and tipped his chair back. He regretted telling Card he wouldn't print anything about what happened in the underground chamber, but something else was bothering him. Something big. He closed his eyes and tried to shut out the noise coming from the newsroom. What was bothering him? He was overlooking some important fact, but when he realized what it was part of him absolutely refused to believe it. What he was thinking could not be possible.

He got out of his chair, feeling weakness in his knees, and he started walking toward the formal and ornate office on the far side of the newsroom. He stopped halfway across the newsroom, and while he pretended to look over the shoulder of one of his reporters, he took a minute to study Jessica. She was just about the most perfect boss he could imagine: hands off almost all the time, supportive when she was needed, rich enough from other sources not to care whether the paper made money. He was about to ruin everything if he was wrong.

He resumed walking and strode up to her office door. He

gave the glass a quick knuckle rap and pushed the door open. Jessica was on the phone, and she snatched it away from her ear and covered the mouthpiece with her hand. "What is so important you can't wait to be properly invited to enter?"

"I had an idea I wanted to run past you."

"You need an immediate answer?"

John shrugged. "Kind of."

Jessica rolled her eyes. "Hold on." She put the phone back to her ear. "I'll call you back in just a moment." She hung up, then looked up at John. "Okay, what?"

John thought her voice betrayed more tension than usual. "I have an idea for a series of articles, but it's unusual enough I thought I ought to run it by you."

"Go on."

"As you know my friend Richard Harvey killed himself yesterday, and there are five other people missing in Salem."

John thought he caught a glint of something in Jessica's eye. Anger? He couldn't be sure, but he didn't stop.

"There's a rumor—just a rumor—that these people were all involved in some kind occult group. It's nearly Halloween, and I thought we ought to run with that rumor and do a full investigatory series."

Jessica looked at him, and her eyes narrowed. For just a second her face seemed hard and so empty of its usual warmth that she looked almost like a gargoyle. "The missing people are my friends and some are my relatives," she said in a hoarse voice.

John nodded. He thought about Julie and his great-great

grandfather and how the coven had killed them. "I know that, but we're not supposed to let our personal feeling stand in the way of our reporting."

"So you want to make this paper look like the *National Enquirer*."

"I just want to sell newspapers."

"The answer is no. I'm surprised you even had to ask."

John shrugged. "Okay." He started to turn away then looked back at her. "One more question." He plunged ahead. "How did Rich Harvey know you had gone to Cornwall?"

He let the silence hang. She opened her mouth and closed it but said nothing. When enough time had gone by, he said, "Well, anyway." He turned and walked out of the office.

V

AT HOME THAT NIGHT HE GRILLED SWORDFISH for Amy and topped it with a fresh tomato salsa. He also made a green salad and served everything with a well-chilled premier cru Chablis. He sat beside her, cut her food, and fed her because it was too hard to manipulate a fork with her bandages. After they finished the food, they sipped the wine and talked late into the night.

He told her about his meeting with Captain Card, how they discovered a door in Abigail Putnam's office that took them down into the underground passages and how all the dead bodies had been taken away.

"Did you tell Card the bodies had been there?"

"Yes."

"What did he say?"

"That he believed me, and that Salem isn't the only place the covens exist. It's an international problem, and I think there's some kind of secret law enforcement group that's trying to find them and destroy them. That's what Card implied, but he wouldn't share any details. He said each coven is run by six judges, and that the head judge is the inquisitor."

"We only knew about five, right?"

John nodded.

"That means we didn't get them all. Do you have any idea who the sixth one is?"

"Card says they're always high-profile, wealthy people."

"That could be any of a hundred people in Salem."

"There is one individual who frequently travels internationally, doesn't like to divulge their travel itinerary, and yet Rich Harvey knew exactly where she had gone on her last trip."

Amy's eyes widened. "Jessica Lodge?"

John nodded.

"How sure are you?"

"I'm very sure."

Amy thought for a second. "Do you think she knows?"

"What? That I know?" He nodded. "She absolutely does."

"What are you going to do?"

He let out a humorless laugh. "I could have killed her right there in her office, but I didn't want to go to jail for the rest of my life, and that's exactly what would have happened. And then somebody else would just rise up to take her place. We don't know the names of the others in the coven, so the killings would continue. What's worse, I have a feeling that all Jessica's international travel might mean that she's in touch with other covens in other places."

Amy closed her eyes and shuddered. "I hate all of this." She opened her eyes again and looked at him. "What does it all mean?"

"I think it means that whatever is going on, we're deeply involved, and it's only just beginning."